Beneath Apricot Skies

by

Janice Horton

Published in 2008 by YouWriteOn.com

Copyright © Text Janice Horton

First Edition

The author asserts the moral right under the Copyright, Designs and Patents Act 1988 to be identified as the author of this work.

All Rights reserved. No part of this publication may be reproduced, stored in a retrieval system, or transmitted, in any form or by any means without the prior written consent of the author, nor be otherwise circulated in any form of binding or cover other than that in which it is published and without a similar condition being imposed on the subsequent purchaser.

Published by YouWriteOn.com

For:
My real life romantic hero, Trav.

Chapter One

When the Greyhound bus pulled over in Baytown, Innes Buchanan stepped off. He dropped his heavy tartan backpack and bagpipes onto the boardwalk and inhaled deeply, feasting his eyes on the shimmering white sands and glittering blue waters of the Gulf of Mexico.

Air drenched in spray and oxygen, rather than dust and grit, made him want to chill here for a couple of days, sleep on the beach and swim in the sea. In a shaded spot called Jack's Place, at a driftwood table, he gave serious attention to a chalkboard menu.

'What'll it be, cowboy?' asked an old man whose pencil was poised. 'Steak? I got a sixteen ounce T-bone with your name on it.'

Innes glanced again at the chalkboard and his stomach growled with hunger. It was twelve dollars for the steak.

'Nah, I'll go for the burger, the fries, and a cold beer, thanks.' Innes decided as he settled into a seat made comfortable by so many before him and stretched out his long legs. From behind dark sunshades he watched as small boats silently moved in and out of the harbour.

Life seemed so easy here.

'You any good at playin' those?' Jack gestured towards Innes's feet where his backpack and bagpipes lay.

'Aye, I can play,' he replied.

'I'll pay you a hundred bucks to play at my sister's beach wedding tonight. She's marryin' Bobby MacKenna, a Scotsman, like yourself.'

Innes considered the offer for a moment. With a hundred dollars, he could sleep in a bed rather than on the beach. The latter had lost its appeal once he noticed how many gulls were nesting there. 'Do you rent rooms here?'

'Yeah, we got rooms. All overlookin' the bay and with air-con too.'

'And a shower?'

'Sure.'

'Okay, although as you can see, I'm not exactly dressed for a wedding.'

In his worn clothes, scuffed boots and dusty Stetson, he looked more Texas cowboy than Scottish piper.

'Don't worry 'bout that,' Jack told him. 'It won't be a problem to find you the right clothes for the job. How long are you plannin' to stay here in Baytown?

'Just a couple of days.'

'Then back to Scotland, eh?'

'Aye. I'm on my way home.' Innes let slip a troubled frown and presumed this was when Jack expected his transient customers to spill their lives and their troubles. It had to be good for business. A few beers and an ear from someone who had nothing else to do but to listen whilst he made his living.

A while later, when he returned to clear the empty plate and hand over a room key, Jack tried again, hoping for a loosened tongue and some conversation. 'Another beer..?' he suggested.

'No thanks, I'll save it until after the wedding, seeing as you're paying me a hundred bucks....'

'Don't have much conversation in ya' for a Scotch guy,' Jack grumbled as he pointed up the stairs. 'First room on the left.'

Innes was glad of the clean room above the bar. He immediately turned up the air-conditioning to maximum chill and took a shower. After which, he found a bottle of cold water in the small fridge. Then, with his body clean and cool, his thirst quenched and his hunger satisfied, the last thing he was aware of as he lay exhausted across the bed, was the huge expanse of glassy calm sea that sparkled just beyond his balcony.

Soon he was dreaming vividly. Of pink, apricot, and emerald light reflecting through a gold and crimson horizon. He was home, flanked by fertile Scottish countryside and undulating scenery. To his right lay the valley where the River Nith flowed through farmland, past old stone bothies, simple cottages and magnificent castles, until it eventually surged into the Solway Firth. To his left the land soared upward to soft grassy mosslands and rough shooting grounds, all sheltering pheasant, grouse, and partridge, in verdant feathery bracken and purple flowering heather. As he slept on, he soared like an eagle over Clan Buchanan lands.

Two hours later, a loud bang on the door woke him. He rubbed his eyes and tried to make sense of the strange surroundings and long shadows around him.

'Who is it?'

'I've got you some clothes for the wedding,' said Jack's voice, 'and it's time you got down to the beach.'

Innes scrambled from the bed. 'Okay,' he said, 'I'm coming.'

'Dearly beloved, we are gathered here today....'

Orley MacKenna stood on the sand in an ivory silk bridesmaid gown. Amongst her long tumbling copper-red curls she wore Hibiscus and Ginger Thomas flowers, which mixed with the salt-tainted air, filled her senses and caused her eyes to water. It had to be the combination of pollen and sea air. It couldn't be anything to do with her father getting married even though she could hardly believe it. Or, that after all these years, he had another woman in his life besides her.

Her father must have sensed her turmoil, because he suddenly hesitated and turned from his bride to search for his daughter's approval once more: *Is this really okay with you, Orley?*

Orley smiled encouragingly. It had been a lifetime ago that her father had migrated from Scotland to America with twenty pounds in his pocket and a heavily pregnant wife on his arm. In Texas, Mac became a respected and hardworking cowhand and when Orley's mother, his dear wife Maggie, had died when Orley was just six years old, he had brought up his daughter alone.

Orley and Mac were never parted. He took her with him wherever he found work. He would have given her his last cent and he often had. In the early days, he had put food in her mouth and gone without himself.

Never once had he given up on her. 'Leave little Orley with us' the rancher's wives had begged of him. 'The girl needs a roof over her head and proper schooling.'

But her father, a big burly hard-as-iron man with a heart as soft as a marshmallow, would crouch down on his knee and look his daughter straight in the eyes and ask: *Is this really okay with you, Orley?*

And with a shake of the red hair she had inherited from her mother, she would always reply, 'I have a roof over my head - a roof of stars.' And to prove she was educated she would quote Rabbie Burns.

'Do you, Robert MacKenna, take this woman for your beloved wife...?'

Orley held her breath. Knowing her father's vow would commit him to his beloved new wife and that in the very same moment - at twenty-one years old - she would be free whether she wanted that freedom or not.

'Fly away Orley and go see the world. Go to Scotland and stand on the ancient battlements of Edinburgh castle. See where I proposed to your mother all those years ago….'

Maybe she would. It would be good to get out of Texas.

She'd had good times and bad – more recently they had been very bad – and in the ruins of her broken heart she needed to find herself again. Would she find herself in Scotland she wondered?

Her father repeated his vows.

Orley watched his face; it was etched with a lifetime of honesty and love. She had grown up believing that a man's word once spoken actually meant something. It had been a hard lesson to learn the truth and Billy Mitchell had taught her a couple of things her father couldn't.

The first was that other men lie and cheat and cannot be trusted. The second thing was much worse because it taught her something about herself: she had a temper that she couldn't control.

So what would she do with her new found freedom? She couldn't go back to being a cowgirl. Those days were over. She had gone from being one half of a nomadic ranching duo to a single beach-house spinster in the blink of an eye.

Perhaps she should ask herself what she wanted from life? Although, it would be easier to ask what she didn't. There was a whole list of those.

'I never thought I'd fall in love again,' her father had said when explaining how he felt about Martha. 'Which shows that love can still come knocking when you'd pretty much given up on it.'

Orley had agreed this was some comfort.

'And if it's okay with you, Orley, I'm gonna ask her to marry me.'

Okay with me?

On the beach, her father was wearing an expression she didn't recognise on him. He looked like a man who had just won the state lottery or something. Martha was smiling sweetly up at him. Tears in her eyes. Her chin tilted upward and wobbling with emotion. She was no great beauty but from the way her father was gazing back at her anyone would think he was marrying Miss Texas.

Was she a little jealous?

No. Not jealous. Sad.

She and Billy were to have been married this year until she found him rolling in the hay with Anna Rae Williams. She had discovered them herself. Seen everything with her own two eyes. The whole lying cheating scene was branded on her memory like a hot-iron on a cowhide.

'You're gonna have to learn to control that temper of yours, Orley,' her father had always warned her. 'It'll get you into a whole heap of trouble one day my girl.'

One day it had and she'd ended up in the jail.

'Better you found out his true nature before you married him,' was the only comment her father made after he posted her bail.

Billy hadn't know about her temper or he would have thought twice about doing what he did. She hadn't known he was a liar or that the gun was loaded. Perhaps it was a relationship doomed from the start.

But it didn't always have to be like that, she could see that now. Her father and Martha had given her reason to believe that love still existed and that everyone had somebody for them.

Martha was lovely and the best thing that could have happened to her father upon his retirement. Just when he needed his rough edges smoothed and his wanderlust tamed.

'I now pronounce you husband and wife.'

As Mac kissed his bride and the wedding party began to move towards their reception marquee, a distinctive sound rose up through the twilight and everyone stopped to listen to it. It was a sound like no other. Raw and rousing. Sweet yet unrefined. Orley's heart began to race.

It was the sound of bagpipes.

A piper appeared, handsome in his full highland dress, walking towards them to the tune of *Scotland the Brave*.

The scene took her breath away. The haunting sound touched her soul. Behind him the sun was ablaze as it began setting on the sparkling waters of the bay and as the sound of wailing and honing filled the air, she realised she was openly crying.

Bagpipes always did that to her.

She wiped the tears away with the back of her hand, only to see that her father was crying too.

'Ah, the pipes! The sound of the bonny homeland.'

Orley had never seen this bonny homeland her father spoke of. To her, Scotland was a place of childhood stories, a magical place too far away to be real: like Narnia or Neverland.

Her father came to stand by her side and to embrace her with one sturdy arm. 'One day, Orley,' he said intent on comforting her, 'the pipes will play for you on your own special day.'

When the piper's rendition ended, everyone applauded, and her father was still heartily singing *land of the shining river, land of my heart forever*, as the sun dipped below the horizon and guests made their way to the beach marquee.

Orley took her glass of Champagne to the shoreline, and as pink tipped clouds tumbled over silver-crested waves and small boats scurried towards a darkening harbour, she contemplated the end of her rag-tag lifestyle.

'I was tired of being a cowgirl anyhow,' she told herself.

Yet, if she was honest, cattle and horses were all she knew. She gazed across the empty beach and imagined how it would feel to ride a horse over those golden sands and through the foaming surf. She loved to ride and one day, she decided, she would keep a stable full of horses. Horses were more dependable than men anyhow.

She was sipping champagne with her eyes fixed on the shimmering liquid gold horizon, allowing herself sad lonely thoughts and to make more promises about being brave and independent, about leading a life of her own, when a voice startled her.

'I see you enjoyed the pipes. Would you like me to play again, just for you?'

Orley spun round to see the handsome piper standing before her. His bagpipes poised. She dragged her eyes over the bare knees beneath the heavy kilt and the sporran that he wore so low, and blushed. Not only did he look like a native Scot, he actually sounded like one too.

'You're really Scottish?' she said, thinking aloud.

'Aye, the last time I looked I was!' He laughed.

It was a deep friendly laugh. He sat down beside her with his bagpipes across his knees. His black eyes sparkled from behind dark lashes.

Orley's face grew hotter. 'That would be lovely but let me get you a cold drink.' She rose as elegantly as the tight silk dress would allow. 'Champagne or beer?'

'Oh, beer, thanks.' he said, removing his heavy wool jacket.

Orley found herself staring for far too long at the well-muscled body that seemed encased in a cotton shirt at least two sizes too small for it.

'It's so hot, don't you think?' he said.

'It's the humidity,' Orley muttered. 'I'll get you that beer....' She swished towards the marquee feeling light-headed and, blaming the Champagne entirely, she lifted a couple of beers from an ice bucket and returned to the beach. 'Where in Scotland are you from?' she asked.

'Nithshire.' he replied.

'Oh,' she said vaguely. 'Only, my folks came from Edinburgh.'

'Nithshire's aboot fifty miles from Edinburgh,' he said.

'Oh,' she said again, listening intently to his accent.

After finishing his beer, he leapt to his feet and with his left arm gripping the tartan bag, he brought the pipes back to life once more. In response to his lips and his long capable fingers on the chanter, they released a long low moan.

Staring at the piper's arms as they bulged and flexed through his tight shirt, Orley almost let out a moan of her own. Playing the bagpipes, it seemed, was something of a workout.

'You have'ny told me your name,' he said between puffs. 'I canny really play if I dinny' ken your name...'

'It's Orlene,' she said, 'but everyone calls me Orley.'

'I'm Innes Buchanan, and it's my pleasure ta' play for you on this fine evening.'

As he began to play, he closed his eyes and slowly tapped one foot to introduce the pace of the tune. His face was full of concentration. His dark lashes flickered on his sun-baked cheekbones, and his hair, damp and tousled, hung forward over his forehead like a gypsy's.

Orley recognised the tune immediately. It was The Skye Boat Song. *Speed bonny boat, like a bird on the wing, onward the sailor's cry.*

Her father had sung it to her when she was very young. All those years ago, yet she could still recall the lyrics.

Carry the lad that's born to be king, over the sea to Skye....

Swept up, Orley closed her eyes in an effort to stop those ominous tears.

Immediately, Innes changed tempo and now tapped his foot so hard that he stamped the sand. This time, the tune took her to earlier and happier times, when her parents would play their recordings from Scotland and dance the *Moniave Jig* in the kitchen. She clapped her hands and called out for Innes to play on. Then, as he settled down beside her to play the exquisite *Mairi's Wedding*, she quietly gazed at him like a moon-struck hare.

'One of my favourites that one...' he told her breathlessly.

'Thank you Innes, you play so well...'

He grinned. A wide grin that caused a ripple of ridiculous excitement to pitch in her breast and surge through her whole body.

'But why the sadness?' he asked. 'If I am not being too personal'.

That was it. All it took. The wedding, the music, and the champagne, caused her to crumble in front of him and it seemed that nothing would stop the stream of hot tears flowing through her fingers.

Innes offered her a cotton handkerchief from his pocket.

It smelt of heather and damp moorland, or at least, Orley thought it did.

'It's okay, I'm used to it.' he said to her kindly.

'You are?'

'Yes, whenever I play my pipes, people weep.'

She giggled and tried to explain herself. 'My life is moving on and that's no bad thing. Now I have my freedom.'

'And what will you do with that freedom, Orley?'

He looked into her eyes. He was sitting so close that his arm was pressed hard against hers.

'I'm gonna' travel,' she said determinedly, drawling in an accent that revealed she had never been out of Texas in her whole life. 'I'm gonna pack up my two-bit Baytown job and see the world.'

'Sounds like a good plan. They say travel expands horizons and broadens the mind,' he said sincerely.

They were almost touching noses.

Innes continued to chat and she found herself leaning towards him, enjoying his company and wanting more of his heat, more of his conversation. She observed the moisture on his upper lip and actually found herself wondering what it might be like to kiss him. 'And what brings you here from Scotland?' she asked, keen to change both the subject and her errant thoughts.

'The cattle business. I've been touring the Lone Star State looking into different cattle breeding programmes.'

This remark took all other thoughts out of Orley's head. 'And what differences did you find?'

Innes laughed. 'Oh, they lay mostly in profitability. What about you?'

'Until a few weeks ago I was a cowgirl.'

Innes raised his dark eyebrows in astonishment. He must have pegged her as a Southern-Belle rather than a Red-Neck Woman. 'You're kidding me, right?'

'No, I'm not kidding, but don't worry you're not the first to think that a girl couldn't ride a horse, holler like a coyote, rope mustang and brand steer....'

Innes roared with laughter and mimicked her Texan twang. 'Heck, I found me a real-live Daisy Duke!'

Orley almost looked offended.

'I'm sorry,' he said. 'Please do tell me what a cowgirl is doing down here in a place where people only sail and fish?'

But before she could answer, her father called her from the marquee. 'Would you care to join us?' she asked.

He hesitated for a second.

'I'm sorry. I suppose you want to change out of the kilt?'

'Aye. Thanks again for the beer.'

'It was nice to meet you, Innes.'

'You too,' he answered.

'You know,' she said as she started to walk away from him, 'one day, I hope to see Scotland.'

'One day,' he replied, 'I hope to be the one to show it to you.'

But his voice had become an inaudible whisper amongst the breaking waves and shrieking gulls.

Chapter Two

Martha's daughter Tanya was travelling through Italy and Switzerland and had been unable, at such short notice, to make it back for the wedding.

'Just go ahead without me' is what Tanya had evidently said, albeit long distance, to the matrimonial news and Martha didn't seem to mind too much. 'Can't expect her to rush back from Europe. It would cost too much for a start.'

Orley considered that as her father had offered Tanya a paid-up airplane ticket back to Texas in the time for the wedding, and that it had been politely declined on a postcard sent from Bern, that Tanya might be having too much fun to come home.

She couldn't help but to be impressed. Not just with her stepsister's glamorous travel arrangements, but also the sense of independence she so obviously possessed.

Switzerland, Orley fantasised, sounded so very exciting. Alpine resorts, snowy mountains and real log fires. Then her thoughts would drift over to Scotland and to heather-filled glens, old castles, and crackling fires.

As she helped Martha to pack up her things for the move next door she asked more about Tanya and the places she had visited.

'Oh Rome, Venice,' Martha sighed pensively. 'All those exciting places you see on the Travel Channel. You see, Tanya left Texas to follow her dream.'

'To expand horizons and broaden her mind?' Orley suggested, her voice quivering as she quoted the romantic words of Innes Buchanan, whom she suspected might be on his way back across the Atlantic Ocean by now.

'No, to meet Mr Right.' Martha replied quite categorically as a photograph fluttered from an old yearbook. 'Oh look, that's Tanya on her graduation day.'

Orley picked up the photograph and was a little disappointed to see an overweight, fuzzy haired and buck-toothed girl, in a dress that resembled a pumpkin.

'What a great dress,' was all she could think to say, as Tanya, trawling the world in search of her foreign beau, wasn't exactly the Lara Croft she had somehow expected her to be.

Martha's cottage, it had been decided, was to be sold. But it was badly in need of some renovation before it would attract buyers, and so, as Orley didn't want to be around the newlyweds too much, she suggested that she moved into it for the time being. 'And while I'm there, I'll give the place a lick of paint. My treat.'

'Let her do it,' Mac had advised. 'After my accident, when I was no use to man or beast, Orley learned to fix up all manner of things all by herself.'

The accident he was referring to was the catalyst to his retirement and had involved a fully-grown bull and a metal gatepost. There were no prizes for guessing who'd come off worst.

When Martha looked over the MacKenna home, it was clear she recognised Orley's creative flair. 'I would be very happy for you to work your magic on my tired old cottage,' she said to her appreciatively.

Later that afternoon and throughout her shift at the downtown steak diner The Golden Coral, Orley's thoughts were preoccupied. They ricocheted from her stepsister's worldwide manhunt to Innes Buchanan's untimely departure. Innes, she decided, had unsettled her with his good looks, his Scottish accent, and his bagpipes, at a time when she was feeling emotionally detached. So it was a good thing she wasn't likely to see him again.

She tried to focus on her own travel plans but it wasn't easy with all the noise and distraction around her. She flitted from table to table clearing away plates and distributing drinks whilst scribbling on her notepad and trying to accommodate the demands of her customers.

'Hey, waitress. More coffee!'

She meandered over to the big guy in dirty overalls with a pot of hot fresh coffee while he was hollering like a bull with a sore head.

She fantasised about a summer spent in Scotland, where she might visit Edinburgh Castle only to find Innes Buchanan on the battlements with his bagpipes, saying to her: *'Would you like me to play again, just for you?'*

Stop it, she told herself. Stop thinking about him.

Winter in the Alps, spring in Paris, she contemplated determinedly. Her new confidence all down to her father's encouragement and her sister Tanya's adventurous example.

So, with her thoughts a million miles away, she somehow managed to pour hot coffee straight down her customer's leg. His screams yanked her right out of her daydream.

'Oh my gosh. I'm so sorry!'

She began mopping up immediately but her apology went unheard.

'Look what ya' doin'. Ya' stupid bitch!' the customer yelled.

'*What* did you just call me?'

The guy had a face like an incensed bull.

'An 'effing stupid bitch!'

Orley wanted to rope him, bring him to his knees, and spank him with a molten branding iron. How dare he speak to her like that. She wasn't stupid. Until a few weeks ago, she wasn't even a waitress.

She slapped her notepad onto the table. The clatter in the diner stopped. Everyone seemed to hold their breath as the angry man stood up and towered over the slim flame-haired waitress.

Orley stood her ground and with one hand on her hip, the other hand poured what was left of the boiling contents over the guys half-eaten meal.

'I may be a bitch, Mister,' she said defiantly, 'but I sure ain't 'effing stupid!'

There was a collective shriek as his clenched fist rose into the air and then, from nowhere or so it seemed, the Scottish piper appeared.

Orley did not recognise him at first, without his kilt or his bagpipes, but a second glance and she knew for sure it was him. She would have recognised those strong arms anywhere.

Innes floored the guy. And in one swift movement, he had whipped off Orley's apron and with one powerful knee in the guy's spine, had him trussed up like a steer.

The diner erupted into thunderous applause.

Orley, in the meantime, found herself being unceremoniously bundled out of the double swing doors.

'Hey! It's that rude customer you should be throwing out!' she protested. 'I promise it won't happen again!'

Loosing her job, she realised, would put her travel plans on hold until she could find another and, in Baytown, at the end of the tourist season that was going to be impossible.

'No way. Hit the highway. You're the worst waitress we ever had.'

She stood outside the diner for a moment. The heat from the midday sun bouncing off the pavement in front of her. It was too hot to stand still so she began to walk. She wasn't sure where she was going but all roads led to the harbour.

She was in despair about loosing her job and feeling elated all at the same time – because Innes Buchanan was still in Baytown.

Suddenly he was behind her.

'Hey Orley, where are you going so fast?'

She turned, blinking and shading her eyes from the intense white-light of the midday sun, so she could see him. He was dressed in baggy-style khaki shorts and a t-shirt. He looked so very different. He was panting, either from the exertion of his fist-fight, or from running to catch up with her. 'Heck, I needed that job!' she told him.

'Well in my opinion, you're better off without it. And it's lucky I was just passing, or you'd be on your way to the hospital right now, or worse - the morgue.'

'Hey, I don't think so. You floored him with a simple cowboy move. Nothing clever about that.'

Innes grinned. 'Oh, I see. So next time, I should just mind my own business?'

'What next time? You said you were heading back to Scotland?'

His eyes were shining with what she suspected might be irony. 'I had to see you again, Orley, before I left,' he said.

The way he said her name caused her stomach to flutter.

'And where has your Scottish accent gone?' she demanded. He still had a Celtic lilt, but certainly wasn't talking broad Glaswegian anymore.

'Oops, you caught me out!' he said without embarrassment. 'See, I canny play the pipes if a dinny talk like this....'

She laughed. Her anger melting away in the heat of the day. 'Come on,' she said, 'I think I owe you lunch. There's a little place down the street.'

And he replied, 'well, it's probably the least you can do after I saved your bacon.'

At The Crab Shack, they ordered crab's legs and Orley explained that she did not eat bacon or any other animal meat. 'It's from working on every ranch in Texas. Meeting the meat - if you know what I mean. I don't eat cows, sheep, birds or pigs.' She cracking a huge crab's leg at its knuckle and effortlessly extracted the soft pink meat with a two-pronged fork. 'Here have some..?'

'No, it's okay, I'd like to have a go at this myself. It looks fun.' But holding the foot-long leg in his grasp, snapping and pulling it, the shell fractured and the meat eluded him. 'A canny git ma' meat!' he exclaimed in embarrassment.

Orley wiped her hands on a napkin and quoted The Selkirk Grace.

'Some have meat and canny eat, some have meat that want it. But we have meat and we can eat, sae let the lord be thank it...'

'I'm impressed! The words of the Baird.'

'Yes. Yet somehow I too lack the accent.'

He looked sheepish. 'Aye, you got me. I did put it on a wee bit. All of course for the benefit of my American audience.'

She smiled forgivingly. 'I was surprised to see you today, Innes.'

'Well like I said, I really wanted to see you again before I left for home.'

'And when are you leaving?'

'In a couple of days.'

'Oh.' At the sound of her own disappointment, her face turned the colour of her hair.

He looked bemused and gave her one of his dazzling smiles. 'Tell me more about your ranching days, Orley.'

She was more than glad to tell him. It gave her an anchor. Something interesting to say. 'Well, I grew up on the biggest and best. I tagging along with my father and then, as time went by, we teamed up. It's the only life I've ever known and why I'm such a lousy waitress.'

'And you said your parents were both from Scotland?'

She was amazed at how much of their first conversation he could recall. All she could remember of that emotional, champagne charged meeting was the liquid black eyes, the moist full lips, the powerful arms, and the lightness of his fingers on the chanter.

'Oh yeah. In Scotland, my Dad was a cattle farmer but without cattle or a farm. So, he and my mum left for Texas, where in those days there was plenty of both. Soon after that, well, they got me and, sadly, mum died when I was only six....'

As she told him about her life, Innes stared at her from across the Formica table. She suddenly felt unnerved and wondered if she had actually managed to bore him rigid.

Then he leaned forward across the tabletop as if he had something quite intimate to say.

There was that champagne feeling again.

'I'd like to take you out tonight, if that's okay...?'

She always refused dates. Always and without exception. But, as Innes was leaving in two days time, and she would certainly never see him again, she explored the possibilities....

'Where would you like to go?'

His British arrogance assumed she had accepted.

Deciding his manners weren't as crude as American egotism, she told him that the Pirate's Cove was popular.

'It's on the boardwalk and they have a live band every night.'

'Sounds good. Let's meet up at seven, in Jack's Bar?'

'Okay. At seven. Jack is my new uncle, if you didn't know.'

'Aye, I know. That's how I found out that you worked at the diner.'

'Hey! I thought you said you had just been passing?'

Chapter Three

The Pirate's Cove had a live band. Only tonight, it was a one-man band. A buccaneer-like character with a guitar, a gold tooth and a parrot on his shoulder, strummed soulful songs like Margaretville, Brown Eyed Girl and American Pie, as Orley and Innes sat at a small table overlooking the bay eating Cajun food and drinking wine.

Orley ordered fish and Innes chose chicken which he described as hot and spicy. 'A bit like yourself,' he told her.

A comment that had her blushing furiously and wondering if she had overdone her perfume.

'You look really lovely tonight,' he also said, making reference to her long flowing skirt and fine gauze blouse with tiny coloured beads on it.

She smiled and couldn't help but to be charmed even though she told herself it was a shame he didn't mean a word of it. That he was just playing lip service.

Dragging her eyes away from him, she looked out of the open window at the blue-green colours of the Gulf of Mexico and tried to look comfortable. She was feeling far from it. Innes was a bad influence on her. He made her feel weak instead of strong, vulnerable rather than resolute.

He reached across the table as if to bring her back to him.

A painful static-charge cracked between them. They both yelled and began to laugh as Orley pulled her hand away and a silver charm bracelet shook at her wrist.

'That's really pretty,' he noted.

She shook it again to show it off.

'My whole life is on here,' she told him. 'Everything that ever happened to me is symbolized by a charm on this bracelet. See that one?' She pointed out a tiny silver star and Innes leaned forward to inspect it. 'That was the first one. My mom bought it after she had seen a falling star when she was pregnant and wished for a girl.'

'What a coincidence,' Innes told her. 'Because the night we met, I too saw a falling star.'

Orley's eyes were open wide. 'Really, and what did you wish for?'

'Oh, the same thing - a girl.'

She giggled.

'And who gave you that one?'

He pointed to a silver cowboy on a horse and she quickly snatched both hand and bracelet away. But it was too late: she knew he had glimpsed her pain. 'I don't want to talk about it. Shall we order some more wine?'

'Oh dear,' he remarked. 'I picked the unlucky charm there.'

'They drank another bottle of wine and then danced slowly to the pirate crooner's *Georgia On My Mind.* As the music played on, the lights of the harbour danced with them, reflecting off the small boats that headed towards the shore. Above, in a clear black sky, stars twinkled. Yet, they all paled in comparison to the twinkle that Orley saw that night in the eyes of Innes Buchanan.

She was quite drunk when she decided that this was the most romantic night of her life. When, swaying in Innes strong arms, she told herself that Innes Buchanan was the cure to the sickness in her heart, and that with him, she might forget about Billy Mitchell and her broken heart. One night in Innes's arms and she would have a new face in her dreams: a new affair to remember when she closed her eyes at night.

Orley was a little unsteady on her feet. Innes guided her back to their table cupping her elbow lightly with his hand. He offered her some water.

'Let's get some air,' she said, 'let's walk along the beach.'

Innes picked up the tab and they left the Pirate's Cove. They walked out into the moonlight. It was only a short walk along the beach to Jack's place. Orley took off her shoes and paddled along the waters edge. Innes watched her carefully. She walked towards him from the languorous surf, her long hair blowing against her neck and shoulders, moulding to the roundness of her breasts.

'You look just like a mermaid,' he said with a look in his eye that she immediately recognised as lust. She gave him a long look and linked his arm.

They walked together onward and upward, until eventually climbing the stairs to the small room above Jack's bar, where the shadows were longer and the air cooler than of late.

Innes opened up the balcony doors and allowed the fiery colours of the sky to flood the room. To Orley, it was as if these past two days had led only to this moment. How easily she had dropped her defences with him. Yet how far was she prepared to go; all the way perhaps?

Standing in the half-light, Innes drew her hands to his lips.

She recalled their first meeting. She had wanted to kiss him then. She focussed on his tentative lips as they nuzzled each of her trembling fingertips and wondered where this night might lead.

In one fluid movement he had pulled her so close that their bodies were moulded together. His mouth was pressed against hers. His breath was quick and hot. His body hard. His arms slid down her body. His hands followed and a deep groan escaped from his throat.

A mind-blowing ache tugged at a place deep inside her.

Her heart leapt against her chest like a wild mustang against a fence. His kisses deepened. His tongue flicked over hers. A moan escaped from deep within her own throat. It took all of her presence of mind to open her eyes and ask herself what on earth she was doing?

As Innes's hands sent lightning bolt shudders down her spine and his hot mouth slid across her neck, as his heady male scent energized every nerve in her body, she heard herself cry out 'I can't do this!' The sound was high and shrill as if coming from somewhere else in the room. Not from the lips that wanted to be kissed or the body that desired his touch. But as her words struck the air, the breathless anticipation became silent unease, and the moment was lost.

'It's okay, it's okay, we don't have to do anything. It was presumptuous of me....' His voice was low and apologetic.

He had already moved away.

She already missed his warmth.

Needing to distance herself from the bed before she changed her mind, Orley walked out onto the balcony. This was all too much. His sensual lips, his deep Celtic voice, his warm breath upon her skin. The liquid depths of his black eyes. The raw intensity of emotion that he aroused in her....

He followed her outside. 'We have incredible sunsets in Scotland, just as beautiful as these,' he told her as he wrapped his strong arms round her like a warm shawl.

They gazed outward towards the golden light that had all but fallen away from the edge of the world and Orley felt confused about everything except the way that Innes Buchanan made her feel.

The following morning, Innes was at breakfast when she walked into Jack's bar. She was wearing sawn off denim shorts and flip-flops. She sat down opposite him, crossing her long golden legs. She looked at him purposefully from behind dark sunshades.

Innes seemed hardly able to drag his eyes from the t-shirt that defined the fullness of her breasts and the taut slimness of her body. 'You're looking surprisingly good this morning,' he said as she took off her sunshades and grimaced at him.

'Well in that case, I must look better than I feel.'

'Coffee?' asked Jack, with a fresh pot in his hand.

'And two aspirin, please,' pleaded Orley.

'What on earth were you two drinking last night?'

'Wine,' they both said together.

'Ouch' said Jack, 'I'll be back in a moment....'

In that moment they didn't speak. Orley felt awkward. She was embarrassed about her behaviour the night before and still feeling a little unsteady. 'I want to thank you,' she eventually stammered, 'for last night. I had a lovely time.'

Jack came over with two glasses filled with a soupy concoction that had jalapeno peppers and ice floating about in it. Orley groaned. 'Oh Jack, please tell me that this does not have any alcohol in it?'

'All you need to know is that it works. Isn't that right, Innes?'

'Aye, so it does. Bottoms up.'

Innes and Orley spent the rest of the day sunbathing and surfing at the beach. They laughed together like old friends.

Then as the sun was setting, and they became aware of the carefree mood of the day slipping away from them, they dwelled upon the following morning when Innes was to meet with his flight out of Galveston.

They ended up having their final meal together at the Crab Shack, as Innes said it would always hold a special place in his heart.

Orley hoped he felt the same about her and doubted that, after tonight and saying goodbye to him, she could ever step inside its crustacean encrusted walls again.

'Can I look you up when I eventually get over to Scotland, Innes?' she asked him.

'Aye, I'd really like that.'

She was just contemplating the unfairness of life, of finding someone that might have been able to restore her faith in love, only for him to go away too soon, when Innes said something so surprising that it caused the crab claw in her grasp to suddenly escape and shoot across the table.

'I have a job for you, if you want it?' he said.

'A job?'

'Yes. On my farm in Scotland....'

He seemed not to notice her absolute astonishment.

'You know all about Highland Cattle. You told me so.'

'Did I?' She took a deep breath and a slug of wine whilst trying to recall what she did or didn't say. 'Erm, did I say that Highland's are lean and hardy. They live out all year. They calve easily and have thick shaggy coats and sweeping horns, and are also very, erm, cute....'

'Cute...?'

She nodded but her head was spinning.

'Yeah, that's exactly what you said. You also said you wanted to see Scotland. Although, I have to tell you that Scottish farming is on its knees and when European subsidies are finally withdrawn, things are not going to be easy....'

'And how is Scottish farming different from Texan ranching?'

'In lots of ways but I am going to mix the two and establish a new herd. You could help me with that.'

There was a pause between them. A great big silence.
'And where would I stay?'
'With me.'
Her imagination brought to mind a bothy exactly like that in Braveheart.
'With you...?'
'Aye, and my mother and my brother. We have plenty of room at Glencorrie.'
Glencorrie.
He was grinning at her. His eyes sparkling and willing her to accept his offer.

She was just about to say a resounding 'yes' when a voice she hardly recognised as her own calmly said, 'but I don't even own a passport.'

'Is that an excuse, Orley? Are you saying no?'
'No. I'm not saying no....'
'Then you are saying yes. That's fantastic. When you get your passport, I'll send you a plane ticket. I'll offer you a decent salary and throw in your accommodation. Do we have a deal?'

He moved in closer. The only thing between them on the shiny plastic upholstered bench seat other than stray splatters of crabmeat was Innes's outstretched hand.

Orley wanted to take it but her own hand was proving to be unpredictably clammy and wavering. She tried to say something but couldn't find the words. Was she perhaps more interested in the man than the job? Yet, she needed a job more than she needed a man, didn't she?

Wincing, she looked up to find he was still waiting with his hand outstretched. 'I'm s-s-sorry...' she stuttered.

Innes stood up, left a fold of dollars on the table and without another word, he walked away.

Orley fled to the ladies room.

Away from his presence, she tried to make sense of her situation. She splashed cool water on her hot face and tried to rationalise her response.

She was afraid. That was it. The last time she let her heart rule her head she got it broken into a million pieces. In the mirror opposite, a terrified girl stared back at her.

'So much for being brave and independent,' she told her reflection.

When she eventually ventured outside, the sun was sitting low in the sky and it took a moment to see that he was still waiting for her.

Without a word, they walked towards the beach.

Anguish played heavily on Orley's mind.

'Come and sit with me...' he said, as they strolled towards the sand dunes. The beach was quiet, almost deserted, except for the usual restless populace of nesting gulls. They sat together and stared out at the darkening horizon. A breeze blew across the coarse sand grasses making whispering sounds that Orley found strangely comforting.

'I'm in need of a cattle manager and you have all the right experience.'

She nodded her head.

'The night we met, you offered to help me, do you remember?'

She was still nodding.

'You also said you wanted to travel.'

Yes, yes.

'In particular, you mentioned that you would like to see Scotland.'

'Yes. It's something I have dreamed of my whole life!'

'So this,' he said, waving his finger, 'you and me. This is fate. Do you believe in fate, Orley?'

She thought hard. Yes, she believed.

'I need to think and I need to talk to my father. I'll let you know my decision in the morning, Innes.'

He studied her through half-lowered lids.

'Okay,' he said. 'That'll do.'

He seemed satisfied that she had at least agreed to sleep on it. Although, she suspected that perhaps neither of them would get much sleep that night.

Orley knew that her father would advise her well and put some real perspective on the matter. To her surprise, he was remarkably positive. 'I see this as a working holiday opportunity,' he told her, 'a job combined with a chance to travel, and with your lifetime of ranching experience, it's no wonder he wants you.'

Orley agreed, even though she was doing more wanting than she was telling. She faked a glum face. 'And it's not likely I'll find another job here in Baytown at the end of the summer season. So I suppose I've no choice.'

They both knew this was an outright lie. She had a job if she wanted it at Uncle Jack's Place. Did she want it? Did she really want to serve beer and bar food all her life in Baytown: or did she want to farm cattle in Scotland with the gorgeous Innes Buchanan?

Oh, thank the Lord I didn't sleep with him.

'And if -' her father explained, 'this job in Scotland doesn't work out, then you simply join up with Tanya and travel with her in Europe.'

There was suddenly every sense in going and Orley was feeling so euphoric, that if Innes Buchanan had then said he was going to the ends of the earth to farm elephants, she might have just agreed to that too.

The next morning, Orley stopped off at the post office to pick up an application form for a passport, which she was determined to have filed that very day, if of course, her father still happened to have her birth certificate somewhere amongst their possessions.

For the second morning in a row, she found Innes sitting alone in Jack's bar eating breakfast.

'Pancakes…' she told him, sliding into the seat opposite, 'are unhealthy and full of fats and sugars.'

He gave her a tense smile. 'Good job I ate yours then.'

They stared at each other. Eyes narrowed. Mouths fixed.

Innes eventually broke the tension. 'Well, what's it to be?'

She waited until the last piece of maple syrup laced pancake had passed his lips before she spoke.

'You have to know that I am a deeply suspicious and untrusting person. I never ever forgive people that do me wrong and I have a terrible temper. Do you think you can handle all of that?'

Innes thought seriously about what she had said for a moment and replied, 'I think we can get on. You see, I suspect nothing and no one until it is far too late. I trust too easily for my own good. I am forgiving to a fault and, consequentially, people think they can walk all over me. I think we could be good for each other. What do you think?'

'You mean were are like opposites attracting?'

'That's exactly it.'

'Okay. Then I will come to Scotland and be your cattle manager.'

The grin returned to his face. 'Good. I mean where else am I going to find a real cowgirl other than here in Texas, right?'

'Yeah right. And what do you think your folks will think of you bringing home a real live souvenir?'

Innes's eyes narrowed over the rim of his coffee cup. 'I think they'll have time to get used to the idea while you are sorting out your passport.'

They headed out towards Galveston airport in Orley's father's new Buick, but despite that they still had much to say to each other, the words weren't easy to find.

Orley found herself gibbering on about traffic jams and how the Interstate they were travelling on was the oldest in Texas, as if he really needed to know that sort of thing.

Innes hardly spoke either and she wasn't sure if that was down to her fascinating knowledge of the area, her doubtful driving skills, or any regrets he might be having about asking her over to Scotland.

As they left the Interstate and joined the causeway that led onto Galveston Island, The Scholes International airport came into view and, before they both knew it, they were pulling up at the departures terminal and Innes was out of the car, gathering up his backpack and bagpipes.

'I'm so glad this is not goodbye,' he said.

They were already announcing his flight.

'Yeah me too. I'll see you soon,' she told him stoically.

He pulled her into his arms and kissed her. It was a long slow kiss.

She clung to him for the time it lasted and bravely said. 'Go on, you'd better go.'

'Here, I got you something. A present. Open it when I've gone.'

He pressed something into her hand as he walked away.

Orley felt a distraught sob rising in her throat.

'You get that passport sorted out quickly, you hear me?'

'I will.' She looked down at the small velvet box in her hand and quickly looked up again to thank him, but he was already out of sight.

Chapter Four

At Glencorrie, in the Southern Highlands of Scotland, August sunshine filtered through the pine trees surrounding the old house, encouraging ivy and wisteria to climb the ancient walls, securing unstable chimney stacks, and binding together dangerously loose stonework.

Fergus, Innes's younger brother and hardworking stalwart of the Buchanan estate, was busy hauling a moth-eaten standard of St Andrew up the flag pole and hanging a 'welcome home' banner over the entrance porch. Fergus was looking forward to Innes's return, mostly because he longed to meet up with his fellow Young Farmers in the village pub again and to get drunk. A luxury that with Innes away he could neither fund, as he had just paid the electricity bill at the threat of being disconnected, nor participate in, because he had no choice but to get up at five o'clock every single morning to tend to all the sheep.

Running the farm almost single-handedly had aged him beyond his twenty-two years.

Inside the great house, a flame burned in the vast open fireplace of the drawing room and stone gargoyles at either side of the hearth stooped purposefully in order to warm themselves, at a fire that exuded no heat whatsoever.

Similarly, Lady Buchanan, seated in her favourite fireside chair, displayed no warmth either while she waited for her eldest son and the heir to all that surrounded her to arrive home. She drummed her fingers on a chair more aged than herself and considered how after four long months in the United States, Innes should be more than ready to settle down with his bride-in-waiting, Miss Davina McKenzie, who had the patience of a saint and was a woman entirely worthy of marrying her eldest son.

Four months ago, however, Innes had expressed a strong reluctance to this mutually beneficial union. 'I cannot possibly marry my neighbour for her lands and money!' he had protested but his mother had only laughed without amusement. 'There are animals to feed, workers to pay, and tenants to house, Innes.'

Then she had dealt him a terrible blow.

She disclosed the death duty tax bill she had been hiding under her pillow for the past six months.

'Oh. I see,' he had said quietly. 'This changes things somewhat. In fact, it looks like we're facing bankruptcy.'

Davina McKenzie, was the only daughter of the neighbouring wealthy McKenzie clan. She had both nobility and affluence and had once been linked with Prince William from when they where at St Andrew's together. It had been all over the papers. Although, nothing had become of it, except to advertise Davina's preference for a man with a grand title.

Lately, her family and indeed Davina herself, had set their sights on Innes, the newly appointed Laird of Buchanan.

Sickeningly, Innes had once overheard himself being described as 'virile husband material' by Davina's father Gregor McKenzie, who had qualified this statement by adding, 'in the absence of abundant choice.' Innes had felt like a prize tup and wondered if they would insist on him providing a sperm count.

'Father will be turning in his grave.' Fergus had groaned.

'Nonsense,' Lady Buchanan had insisted. 'For hundreds of years marriages have preserved peace, retained lands and secured titles. I have taken council with a lawyer and paved the way with Gregor and Daphne McKenzie. It's the only way out of our situation.'

'And where was your council before father died?' Innes snapped. 'Or, when our grandfather was too damn stubborn to hand everything over before we had to pay all this tax - and end up in this situation?'

He had walked over to the window. His eyes fixed on the winter-ravaged landscape outside, while his knuckles, like his teeth, were set white and clenched in the pockets of his moleskin trousers.

Would it matter if he did marry Davina? It's not like he was saving himself for anyone. He didn't believe in love or

Santa Claus or the tooth fairy. His mother might be right. It might be the only way.

His mother had her lips pursed. She was damned if she would see Innes inherit only to loose everything. 'The best you can do for us, Innes, is to unite us with the McKenzies.'

'But he can't!' Fergus yelled.

Up to this point, Fergus had only been listening. Taking in the situation. 'It's not right. It's morally wrong!' he suddenly objected.

'Wrong..?' his mother snapped. 'How can it be wrong? We are all aware of Davina's fondness for your brother.'

Fergus had looked to his brother. 'But he doesn't love her. Do you Innes?'

'What does that matter?' his mother had hissed. 'When it will save us from the poor house?'

Fergus glared at Innes.

Their mother wouldn't let up. She had the grit and tenacity of a terrier when she wanted her own way.

'What more could you possibly want in a wife than beauty, popularity, and personal wealth? Innes, you do like Davina, don't you?'

'I course I like her. Everyone does. She's quite pretty. She's certainly very rich. I suppose I could do much worse….'

Fergus raked his unruly hair with his big hardworking hands until it stood upright and when he could bear the conversation no more he erupted. 'For God's sake, Innes, this marriage has been arranged for you by our mother, her accountant, Davina's parents, and a bottle of single malt whisky. Surely you can see that?'

Innes shrugged. He couldn't see it. All he could see was bankruptsy and ruin. 'Can't Fergus marry her instead?' he remarked to his mother glibly. 'Is the deal exchangeable?'

'*You* are the Laird, Innes, *not* your younger brother.'

His mother was inexorable.

Fergus could only bite down on his lip and wait until his mother left the room, and she did so hastily, no doubt to telephone the McKenzie's with the good news.

Innes, who had failed to notice his brother's face contorted with anger, began to pour large celebratory drinks.

'Fergus, will you do me the honour of being my best man as it seems that I am soon to be married?'

Unable to contain himself, Fergus ran at his brother screaming.

Innes turned round with a tumbler of whisky in each hand. His eyes shot up under his dark brows in surprise as he had not seen Fergus in such a foul temper since he had trounced him on the last shoot.

Fergus threw a fast punch.

Innes lay unconscious for the best part of ten minutes.

When he awoke, his clothes reeked of whisky and his head was thumping. He leapt up ready to defend himself against more blows but found Fergus sitting quietly, sobbing with his head in his hands. 'Bloody Hell, Fergus, what's got into you?'

'It's just not right. Your marriage to Davina. It's like rape and pillage.'

Innes checked his jaw for dislocation and scoffed at the remark. 'Hardly. I believe she actually wants to marry me.'

'Her parents want her to marry you and all they want is lineage. How can you even think of going through with this when you don't even love her?'

'Love, unlike commitment, is over-rated.' Innes retorted. 'Women marry for love. Men should marry for logical reasons.'

Fergus lifted his grief stricken face. 'You mean lucrative reasons?'

Innes suddenly realized his mistake. It was a very big mistake indeed. He had never seen his brother cry. Well, not since he had accidentally shot him in the leg once when they were boys. 'My God, Fergus, *you* are in love with Davina....'

Fergus nodded his dishevelled head.

'How long have you felt this way. Why didn't you say?'

Fergus's chin was wobbling too much to reply.

Innes didn't know what to do. Especially as Davina was probably being told the happy news of their engagement right at that very moment. Yet here was Fergus, his own brother, his own flesh and blood, mortally-wounded with a broken heart. 'Erm, this changes things somewhat again,' he said. 'Don't worry. I'll make it known I've changed my mind. It's a fiancé's prerogative after all.'

'But what about her dowry?' Fergus groaned. 'What will we do?'

Innes rubbed his bruised chin and checked his teeth for breakages. Yes, there was still the 'not-so-small' matter of her dowry. Not that it was called such a thing anymore, but it amounted to the same, several million in both pounds and acreage. 'You'll have to get it instead. Mother's right, Fergus, amalgamating the clans would save our Estate and secure theirs but she's wrong saying it has to be me. You will marry her instead.'

'But I can't!' Fergus wailed. 'Davina has never shown any interest in me. It's always been you: the tall dark and handsome one.'

Innes looked at his brother. 'How can that be true? You are exactly the same height and colouring as me – and we are often mistaken for each other.'

There was a difference of course. They both knew it. Fergus was stockier and stronger when it came to hauling sheep and tossing cabers and Innes was the one with the honours degree in business management. Not that it had done him much good, as he had returned from university to find the family estate in ruins, literally. Not that any of that was Fergus's fault.

'Besides,' added Fergus. 'I don't have a title.'

'Then we'll just have to get you one. I'll tell her the truth. I'll tell her she's got the wrong Buchanan and point her in your direction.'

Fergus looked horrified. 'You can't. I want her to fancy me not feel sorry for me and how will you get me a title? I think she'll need more reason than that to prefer me over you. You'll have to make her *not* like you anymore, Innes.'

Innes looked to be unsure of this tactic. 'Is that your plan. You want me to be nasty and horrible to her so that she goes off me and onto you?'

'Yes. Make her think you don't care. Tell her you don't find her attractive or something, then she'll go right off you and love me instead.'

They both sat in silence, drinking whisky and thinking hard.

'It just might work,' said Innes. 'I'll mortgage the house. That'll pay off the taxman and take the pressure of us all until you marry Davina.'

'Mortgage the house? You can't do that. Father would turn in his grave and mother wouldn't allow it. Never a lender or a borrower be was their motto!'

'And probably the reason behind our demise. Using OPM or Other People's Money is sometimes sound business management. Anyway, we won't tell her. We'll get all the creditors off our back first and tell her afterwards.'

Innes's plan was harder to instigate than he expected. When he approached the bank he was refused, not because of the rundown condition of the ancestral pile, which it was agreed was still worth an absolute mint, but because he had no way of making any monthly repayments. The income from sheep, it was revealed, only went back into producing more sheep and hadn't produced a profit in over ten years.

On his second attempt, he presented a business plan projecting an income derived from breeding cashmere goats as well as the sheep. 'Cashmere and wool fibre is selling like gold in London,' he told the bank. But they were still not impressed enough to release any funds.

Determined to find a way, Innes went to ask the advice of the newly formed Agricultural Enterprise Committee, and it seemed from their favourable response, that he had come to the right place and asked the right question at exactly the right time.

'Funding,' they told him, 'has just been allocated from the European Union to prevent future outbreaks of Foot and Mouth disease and BSE. The UK government want to do everything in their power to help Scottish cattle farmers.'

From that moment on, Innes was determined that Glencorrie would produce cattle.

'The future of Scottish farming lies in quality beef production,' he was told. 'Come back to us with a business plan based on producing top quality Scottish beef and you are in business. We offer sponsorships to those willing to research innovative new ways to produce beef.'

Innes left the Enterprise Committee offices with his business brain buzzing.

He knew nothing about raising cattle but the more he considered this opportunity the more it made sense to him.

Why had he presumed that in the recent wake of scares and outbreaks that beef would be off the menu?

Consumers still wanted meat but gone were the days of cheap and plentiful. Quality and traceability was the way forward. With enthusiasm, Innes did his homework and at the internet café in Thornfield, he paid two pounds to use the World Wide Web for half an hour. From typing the word 'Beef' and his new buzz words of innovation, quality, and profit into a search engine, he discovered that certain ranches in Texas USA were running trials on hybrid cattle breeding. Mixing breeds to get a super breed with traits suited to their environment.

This was the innovative new way he was looking for.

He printed out all the information and rushed home to show it to Fergus. 'The principle isn't patented,' he told him. 'So we can use it too!'

He immediately put together a business plan and before long, he was back pitching his idea to the Enterprise Committee, complete with genetic charts and coloured pens.

He projected profits based on a home-bred policy. He showed how to maintain hybrid vigour. He told them how research had proved that low birth weights meant easier calving and lower vet's bills. He said he was going to turn Scottish cattle breeding upside down with his futuristic plans.

They gave him what they called 'serious consideration' and then asked him to show evidence of his research. He pointed to the research done in Texas and the next thing he knew, he had been offered a bursary to study cattle farming in the good old United States of America.

'Good luck to you, Laird Buchanan,' he was told by the Committee. 'Go over to America and see if your ideas will work, and if they do, come back to Scotland and save our beef industry!'

Such a trip was well timed too, Innes decided, as it would allow things to quieten down with regard to Davina and their abruptly annulled engagement.

It would also give Fergus the opportunity to get closer to Davina. The idea of being thousands of miles away from both her and her angry parents after he had plucked up the courage to tell them he had changed his mind appealed to him greatly.

'I'll be away for four months,' he told Fergus. 'It's up to you to manage the farm as best you can. Look after mother and make absolutely sure that Davina falls madly in love with you before I get back. Are we agreed?'

'Right!' Fergus approved.

'I'll expect you to keep in touch with me. I've set up an e-mail account so you can let me know how things are going, especially with your wedding plans.'

Fergus, grinning like a wild thing, nodded his agreement.

So, back on Scottish soil four months later, Innes had no choice but to make his first stop Castle McKenzie because, to his disappointment and dismay, all of the wedding plans he had been delighted to hear about via trans-Atlantic email had turned out still to be his own.

Davina had apparently dismissed his refusal to marry her as poppy-cock. 'She thinks you're trying to prove yourself to her before you come home.' Fergus was forced to admit, as he spoke to Innes on the phone after he had landed at the airport in Glasgow. 'I did my best but she won't even give me the time of day. I hate to say I told you so.'

Poor Fergus was distraught. He had kept the truth from Innes for as long as he could, but having made no progress and his brother due home, he had no choice but to break the terrible news. He had wondered what he would do. Would Innes decide to marry Davina after all?

He could hardly bear to think about it.

Innes entered the imposing old McKenzie pile through a window that had no doubt left open to encourage some heat inside. These old strongholds were always cooler inside than out. He found Davina arranging flowers in the great hall.

She rushed forward to welcome him wearing a brown twill skirt and a beige sweater trimmed at the neckline in lace. 'Innes, my darling, you are home safe and sound!'

Innes kissed the side of her cheek and looked about cautiously. He had thought that before leaving for Texas he had had made his intentions, or his lack of them, quite clear.

Although, looking back, he had thought it strange that she had shown no anger towards him. Davina was known for her fiery temper. He should have realised then that he had been misunderstood. She had used words like chivalry, independence, principles, and values. She had even shed a little tear.

Now, with Orley almost arriving on the next flight, he had to make sure there was no misunderstanding.

'I have to speak with you Davina,' he said. 'It concerns something that I couldn't say in a letter or on the telephone.'

She stiffened in his embrace.

He suspected a tantrum.

'It seems you are still under the impression that we are to be married when I am not, I mean, under that impression or indeed, intending to marry you. I'm afraid it's off.'

Davina went a strange shade of blue. Presuming that she was holding her breath, he spoke insistently.

'We are the best of friends and that's all. I could not condemn you to a marriage based purely on friendship. You should marry someone else. Someone who loves you....'

'But Innes, it is *you* that I....'

Innes turned away. He removed her from his arms and set her aside. He could hardly bear to look her in the eye. He felt like an absolute cad. 'I believe have made my position clear.'

She twirled her pearls between her fingers and watched him leave. Only when he had gone did her heart - like her necklace - break apart.

During his absence the Kirk had been booked. The service and hymns decided upon. The flower arrangements and bouquets ordered. The bridesmaid's dresses chosen. The perfect wedding dress awaited only a final fitting. A five-tier wedding cake had been commissioned and a brand new tartan had been designed for their own twenty-first century dynasty. She was damned if he wasn't going to marry her. Handsome, eligible and titled men were hard to find these days and the fourteenth Laird of Clar Innis was, without question, still very much her man.

She watched him through the window as he walked across the perfectly manicured lawns. He took the shortcut through the rhododendrons in order to head up to Glencorrie on foot. It struck her how much he had altered in these four long months. He was, dare she even think it, more attractive with his cowboy boots and deep American tan. She found herself quoting Lady Macbeth: *'He hath honour'd me of late: and I have bought golden opinions from all sorts of people. Which would be worn now in their newest gloss, Not cast aside so soon....'*

Lady Buchanan had already sent out all the invitations for that evening's gathering in anticipation of her eldest son's return.

Fergus noted that they mentioned nothing of a party.

'Parties,' she insisted to her youngest son, 'are vulgar occasions that suggest drunken behaviour, lack of etiquette, and loud music that only serves to suppress intelligent conversation. This is not a party,' she maintained, 'this is a simple gathering of Clans.'

'Which means there will be no fun and probably no food!' Fergus muttered.

Innes tried to look grateful but he was far from thrilled at the prospect of spending his first night at home entertaining the masses. 'I hardly expect the McKenzie's will want to come,' he mentioned glibly, a comment he then had to justify with an explanation.

'I cannot believe how selfish you are being!' his mother shrieked on being told of the cancelled marriage. 'You have ruined everything!'

Innes thrust a tumbler full of whisky into his mother's hand and insisted that she was over-reacting. 'Davina is fine about this mother. I have already spoken with her.'

'The poor girl has already picked out her wedding dress and set up a list at Jenner's!'

Lady Buchanan tipped back her head and finished the dram in one gulp. 'We will probably have to sell up and live on that dreadful sink estate at the back of the village and all because of your utter *utter* selfishness!' she cried.

'That will simply not happen mother. I have a plan. I have a plan to secure our livelihoods and the estate's independence.'

His mother fell silent at last. If this had been Fergus, she would not have believed a word of it of course, but this was her strong dependable Innes, and if he said he had a plan then she could be sure that it was a good one. 'So be it,' she said, in almost a whisper.

'And now, you can tell us more about this lovely American girl you've invited over here!' Fergus enthused, before quietly congratulating his brother on his resourcefulness. 'What a genius you are - bringing a girl back home is a sure-fire way of getting Davina to really hate you…!'

Chapter Five

A pile of wedding invitations, neatly addressed and stamped, mocked her from a nearby table and Innes's words rang in her head: *'I could not condemn you to a marriage based only on friendship'* As if that was ever a reason not to marry someone. Her mother and father had been married for thirty six-years. They were the best friends before they married. They still were.

Davina dabbed her eyes and stifled a sob. She told herself that Innes had simply lost his perspective and, after four long months in another country, that it was only to be expected. Perhaps if he saw her with fresh eyes, as she had seen him, his interest in her would be rekindled and before you could say *Lady Buchanan-McKenzie* their engagement would be back on.

Feeling inspired by her plan, she flung open the doors of her vast wardrobe and began to haul out all of the drab tweeds and plaids. Then, crushing a new blue velvet gown against her svelte figure, she giggled and did a twirl.

Tonight,' she told her reflection, 'is a night for dressing up.'

Innes's choice of attire that evening was the Buchanan Highland hunting plaid. A tasteful blue and green kilt worn with a dark-blue gillie shirt slashed halfway to the waist and laced with leather. He also wore a sporran and a large buckle displaying the family crest. With his leg hose complete with flashes and soft leather brogues on his feet, he descended the staircase like a man set to conquer his enemy, rather than a man greeting his guests.

'Dressed To Kilt,' Fergus observed, having chosen to wear his own kilt with a Scotland rugby shirt.

Innes grinned at him and then noticing his mother emerged from the drawing room. 'Mother, you look absolutely beautiful tonight.'

Lady Buchanan acknowledged his compliment with a proud tip of her head and a pinched smile. In the dress tartan of red, yellow, and green plaid, she wore a full length evening skirt and a silk jabot blouse together with a sash and a brooch that displayed the Clan crest. This was her favourite outfit. One that her late husband had bought at great expense so many years ago. Of course, monetarily, things had been much better then.

At that moment, the McKenzie Clan arrived and Innes went to greet them.

Daphne and Gregor, Davina's parents, were distinctly frosty with him but thankfully, Davina had no such reservations. She kissed Innes on both cheeks before progressing gracefully toward Lady Buchanan, who had her lips pursed in order to greet a girl she was still quite determined to see as her daughter in law.

'Davina, darling...' Lady Buchanan gushed. 'How lovely you look tonight and Gregor, Daphne, how delightful to see you again.'

'If it was up to me, we wouldn't be here!' Gregor McKenzie confided, 'but my daughter managed to convince us otherwise.'

'*Thank you.*' Innes mouthed to Davina.

'*You're welcome.*' She mouthed back.

'Fergus, do take Lady McKenzie's coat. Davina, my dear, your eyes look terribly red. Have you perhaps been crying?'

Fergus was already in the sitting room pouring drinks for a toast. 'To my brother who has returned to us safely from America,' he declared.

'To Innes!' They all chorused.

Innes walked into the sitting room after taking care of Daphne McKenzie's coat. 'Thank you Fergus. I too would like to propose a toast.'

'And from a man whose proposals mean not a jot,' Gregor McKenzie growled under his breath.

Innes charged his glass and looked straight at Davina. 'To friendship....'

'To friendship!' Lady Buchanan seconded quickly and everyone raised their glass. But it was clear that from then on, even with Innes attempted elucidations, the atmosphere for the whole evening was set at a very frosty zero-degrees.

Despite their housekeeper's best efforts, the food on offer was as disappointing as the whisky, which, because of its Japanese origins, Fergus declared was not legally entitled to be called Scotch. The meagre buffet consisted of a couple of platters of tasteless cheese cubes speared with cocktail sticks and a quantity of rather limp looking toast squares heaped with haggis. The latter no doubt being the tight fisted version of blinies and caviar.

Several neighbours and friends popped in during the course of the evening to enquire on Innes' trip and to hear of his adventures. He told cowboy anecdotes to amuse them but with the unspeakably disgusting whisky and the lack of food on offer, no one stayed very long.

The McKenzie's were so determined to shield their daughter from Innes, that they managed to keep poor Davina trapped in a draughty corner with various phenomenally boring people until almost ten o'clock, when proclaiming that she could just do with a nice cup of tea, she managed to sneak off on the pretext of putting the kettle on.

She found Innes in the garden. He was watching the sun disappear over the hills. 'A penny for your thoughts...' she said, approaching him.

'Ah Davina, you have finally been allowed to speak to me.'

'Not really. Daddy's furious with you. And mummy, well, you know how it is...'

She tried to smile but it didn't really happen so instead she bit down on her lower lip.

'Davina, you will make someone a truly wonderful wife, but....'

She could taste blood on her lips. 'And you will make a wonderful husband....'

'Come on, we had better go inside,' he whispered, 'before your father comes looking for me with his shotgun.'

Davina gave a nervous laugh. She knew he wasn't joking.

At ten thirty, when the McKenzie's announced they were leaving, Lady Buchanan tried to revive the revelry by suggesting that Innes play his bagpipes.

'Another time perhaps,' Gregor McKenzie said curtly as his wife feigned a polite yawn. 'It's getting late.'

Innes caught the yawn and apologised for his complete exhaustion.

'I think you may be suffering from jet lag.' Davina suggested.

'Such concern is to be found in a good wife, Innes….' Lady Buchanan applauded.

'Oh mother, please!'

'But it's true...' Lady Buchanan insisted.

The McKenzie's beat a enraged retreat and when the last guest had been seen to the door, Innes went straight up to his room, so livid with his mother that he left her to put the lights out alone.

Chapter Six

To work legitimately in the United Kingdom, Orley needed a work permit visa and although she could certainly travel to Scotland without one, it would mean only a short stay, so she spoke with Innes on the telephone, completely forgetting about the five-hour time difference. What would he suggest? Would he want her on a trial period?

He had sounded so different on the phone.

He sounded so formal.

Was she to be his employee – or his girlfriend?

Innes said she should apply for a full permit.

She was elated. She tried to keep her excitement under control and to make her voice sound as business-like as his but it was almost impossible when her heart felt like it was bursting out of her chest. Neither was it a good connection. She strained to hear him. His words kept getting broken up. She was just about to hang up when the line came clear and he said: 'Do hurry and get over here Orley, I miss you.'

So that was it. Proof. She was his girlfriend after all.

Orley was glad no one was around to hear her whooping like a coyote and dancing around the cottage like a Red-Indian or leaping on the sofa and hugging the cushions.

But then frustration and worry set in.

Frustration that a full visa permit would mean another two or even three weeks of waiting: and worry she still hadn't had her passport approved. She wondered if her criminal record might hold things up.

To distract herself from feeling totally morose during this time, Orley set about restoring Martha's cottage. The newlyweds had gone off to Florida for a week and so she had no interruptions or distractions. She started with the roof, replacing shingles and flashings, then worked downwards, eventually re-decking the whole of the front porch. There was no stopping her. There was no respite. The only breaks she took were to replenish materials at the local hardware store, to eat, or to fall exhausted into her bed, too tired to dream of Scotland, Innes, or how much she missed him.

After another seven exhausting days and lonely nights, the mailman arrived with her visa and passport. In excitement, she shopped and packed her case.

Her father and step-mother arrived back from honeymoon in an extremely generous mood and gave her money to boost her savings.

'This is only a loan,' Orley insisted, telling them she intending on paying them back with interest someday.

Then she cried again.

'All these tears. I've never seen the likes of it before,' her father told her affectionately.

'I've never been away from you before and I'll miss you.'

'And I'll miss you but I'm in Martha's good hands. Go and see Scotland. Go to Edinburgh castle and look out over the battlements like your mother and I did all those years ago. It was the place we first declared our love and promised ourselves to each other until death do us part. Go there and remember her. Lay some flowers for me.'

Orley spoke to Innes again about what to pack, and then she re-packed her case. Scotland was still warm at the end of August he told her, and the heather on the hills is in full bloom. 'It's beautiful here and I'm waiting for you' he said.

So she had her hair done: a perm and a colour, after all, no one had naturally Pre-Raphaelite red hair. Did they?

Then just as she managed to complete the decoration of Martha's cottage, Innes sent the airline ticket: Galveston to Glasgow none stop and one way.

It had been just three weeks since Orley had stood in this very same spot at Galveston's International Airport and seen Innes onto his flight. The time between then and now had passed in a blur of soul searching, form filling, and bag packing, but now she was beyond all of that and simply beside herself with excitement.

'Phone us as soon as you land in Glasgow,' advised her father.

'Look out for Tanya!' yelled Martha, who actually thought Scotland and Switzerland were neighbours.

'I will, I will!' She blew kisses into the air and suddenly, she was passed the point that said 'passengers only'.

Once through the x-ray machines she was singled out for a bag search but she didn't mind one bit because, although she had flown many times before, it had never been on such a huge aircraft and never transatlantic. Once on board, she was shown to a seat that was both spacious and comfortable.

'A drink before take off, madam?'

With all the excitement, she was only too happy to have her thirst quenched with a glass of chilled champagne.

Champagne - in a crystal glass...

It soon became apparent that she wasn't sitting in the economy section at all and whilst being served caviar and smoked salmon she hurriedly re-checked her ticket. 'You have been chosen for an upgrade, madam,' the attendant assured her. 'Enjoy your flight.'

Take-off was exhilarating. Orley found herself giggling with excitement from the very first roar of all four engines until they levelled off at thirty five thousand feet. Then feeling more relaxed than she had in ages, she settled down to imagine what Glencorrie might be like.

A pile of old rubble in the country, was how Innes had described his home. This left plenty of scope for imagination and Orley had plenty of that.

She wondered how many horses they would have and what the stables might be like: she imagined herself galloping and laughing through the heather with Innes in hot pursuit.

'Would you like to choose dinner from the menu, madam?'

She chose the salmon and broccoli bake with cheesecake for desert. It was delicious.

'Would madam like to partake of an after dinner drink?'

Surely, it would be rude not to...?

'Would madam like another glass of champagne with her after-dinner mint?'

Mmm... Gone to heaven on a 747.

Not surprisingly, Orley slept for remainder of the flight.

One minute she was sipping a champagne cocktail after combining the after-dinner brandy with the after-dinner champagne and really looking forward to watching the brand new remake of *Gone with the Wind* and then, opening bleary eyes, she realised it was breakfast time.

A lavish tray was being laid out in front of her. Set with lots of little china dishes with tiny amounts of delicious foods. Freshly squeezed orange juice, warm croissant with butter and jam, a selection of fresh fruits, and a platter of cooked meats. *Oh dear.*

'Excuse me,' Orley apologised to her steward, 'do you possibly have a vegetarian alternative?'

The offending tray was quickly removed, even though Orley had already started to butter her croissant.

'Would madam prefer a section of cheeses or perhaps our purely vegan option?'

'Cheese,' she said gratefully, 'would be lovely.'

She was delving into her complimentary toiletries bag when the pilot's voice came over the intercom to say they where approaching the southern tip of Ireland and beginning their decent into Glasgow. Orley's stomach churned with nervous excitement.

In no time at all, she would be with Innes again.

It was not so much a touchdown in Glasgow as a splashdown. The sky was leaden and it was raining heavily. As she disembarked she was shivering. She had chosen to travel in jeans and t-shirt, topped with a pale blue sweater that she had purchased in the end of season sale at Sears, but after queuing for an hour in a draughty customs hall and waiting at a perpetual luggage carousel, she was frozen to the core and wishing she had worn a fleecy sweatshirt.

When Innes suddenly appeared in front of her however, the colour soon returned to her cheeks.

'Orley, it's so good to see you!' He wrapped his arms around her in a bear hug and lifted her cleanly off the floor.

In joy, she flung her arms around his neck. 'You're not wearing your kilt or playing your pipes!' she giggled, 'and I thought it was compulsory over here!'

Innes held her out at arms length to take a good look at her. His dark eyes were shining and his beautiful mouth set in the widest of grins. 'Come on,' he said, 'let's get you home. I've had our wonderful housekeeper, Mrs Mackie, make you some of her delicious soup.'

Bizarrely, a small tartan army with their faces painted blue and white strode past them wearing kilts.

'They are off to the football,' Innes explained. 'Rangers and Celtic are playing. How was your flight?'

'It was great. I got upgraded and drank champagne all the way across the Atlantic.' She was grinning widely too. She had wondered what she would do if, heaven forbid, he had merely shook her hand and formerly welcomed her to Scotland.

'Is that all the luggage you have?' he asked, looking down at her small suitcase and flight bag.

'Yeah. I thought I'd just get more things when I got here.' *Warm things,* she thought with a shiver.

They headed out of Glasgow on a busy motorway but soon the road ahead wound through open countryside. They travelled for more than an hour across moorlands until eventually, descending a steep mountain ravine, they passed waterfalls and grazing sheep.

'This is the Nith Valley,' Innes told her. 'We are almost home.'

The hills around them were rocky, peppered with sheep and vibrant purple flowering heather. The gorge was green with woodland copses and fertile grazing.

They left the grey skies behind them and as the sun shone through the mist, a rainbow appeared, spanning the valley and making everything look as though it was being presented in Technicolor.

Orley was bubbling with excitement. After travelling thousands of miles she would soon get to see Glencorrie for herself and meet Mrs Buchanan and Innes's younger brother, Fergus. She almost had to pinch herself to check if she was dreaming.

Turning off a black tarmac road onto a dirt track, they drove through a country gate and then on still further, rattling over a cattle grid and through two large stone gateposts, until eventually, they passed a large sign that proclaimed 'Glencorrie of Buchanan Estate'.

'What a lovely house!' Orley gasped at a solitary stone cottage in the far distance. 'I just knew you would live in place like this.'

'Actually,' said Innes, peering over the steering wheel and into the remoteness ahead, 'I don't think we can see the house from here yet.'

They ambled past the stone cottage without stopping.

Orley was shocked to see that it was uninhabited and in a bad state of disrepair.

'Bet you're glad I don't live there now, eh..?' Innes laughed loudly.

They headed on towards an altogether more impressive and much larger house further up the hill.

'You haven't actually told me anything about yourself have you?' she broached, 'and you live in a castle not a house. This isn't exactly a farm either. It's an entire Scottish estate....'

'I'm not rich if that's what you're thinking,' Innes assured her. 'And everything I've told you is true. We have traditionally always farmed sheep here but you and I are going to change all that when we introduce our herd of composite cattle.'

'Does this mean that *you* are the Buchanan of Buchanan estate?'

'Erm, yes, I suppose I am.'

Orley was reminded of the time she caught him pretending to have a Glaswegian accent and felt suddenly uncomfortable. 'And what do I call you, traditionally?'

'You, Orley' he said with a glint in his eye, 'can call me anything you like.'

The track had become potholed. It twisted and turned until it eventually became a gravel driveway flanked with old yew trees and flowering shrubs. They swept towards a magnificent stone house which stood high and proud against a backdrop of tall pines. Innes stopped the Landrover in front of an entrance porch.

Orley climbed out tentatively. Her gaze fixed on the date carved into the ancient stonework before her. Slowly her eyes were drawn upward to follow the masses of green ivy that climbed over the walls, softening the hard aspect of the gothic architecture and growing wildly in every direction, covering tiny windowpanes and clambered up three stories over tall chimney pots, turrets and roundels. She thought the house looked more like a French Chateau than a Scottish Castle.

Despite the fact that it was mid-summer, a cold wind whipped round her and in the rolling skies overhead, large black ragged-winged birds circled like dark predators.

Orley shivered. It felt cold to be in the shadow of such a very old house.

Innes led the way with her luggage towards a studded oak front door which was carved with what had to be the Buchanan Clan motto: *Clarior Hinc Hondos.*

Orley decided she must ask Innes to help her find the MacKenna family motto. Her father would love that.

Then emerging from the shadows within, a tall woman, with a kindly smile and a floral dress awaited them.

'Mrs Buchanan!' Orley gasped, rushing forward to embrace Innes's mother.

'Och, no, not me, my dear. I'm just the housekeeper!'

'This is our wonderful Mrs Mackie.' Innes said with obvious affection.

In the shadows, a small figure dressed entirely in tweed, silently lingered. She tipped her birdlike head to one side and blinked her black eyes with innate interest at Orley, who knew without a doubt, that this woman was indeed Innes's mother.

'This is Orley.' Innes said. 'Orley, this is my mother, Lady Buchanan.'

Lady Buchanan. Oh my goodness, that must mean Innes is actually a Lord or something...'

'Welcome to Scotland. Come inside. Lunch is almost served. Innes, take Orlene's bag to her room.'

Then without embracing or being embraced, Lady Buchanan led the way.

Once Orley's eyes became accustomed to her surroundings, the features of the hallway became apparent, and directly in front of her was a vast oak-ballasted staircase which Innes was striding up two steps at a time with her luggage. Secretly, she hoped her bedroom would be in the tower she had seen right at the very top of the house.

'This way my dear,' said Mrs Mackie. 'Do come into the family sitting room.'

All around on bare stone walls, animal head trophies and ancient portraits stared down. On passing beneath a pair of lethal looking crossed swords suspended precariously above the doorway, Orley shivered again as if someone had just walked over her grave. Lady Buchanan was already pouring drinks.

Orley, who had never felt so cold in her life, gravitated towards the small fire burning in the huge fireplace, although she doubted that the tiny flames licking lazily at the thin green logs, could possibly warm her.

'Sit here Orlene, and take a wee dram.'

Orley did as she was told.

Then like sunshine bursting into the room, Innes appeared with his younger brother, Fergus.

'How wonderful to finally meet you, Orley.' Fergus said, striding towards her and offering first his hand and then his embrace. 'Innes didn't mention you were a very beautiful cowgirl as well as a very capable one.'

Orley blushed.

'Fergus, you are flirting,' Lady Buchanan snapped.

Orley immediately liked Fergus. Not because he was just as tall and handsome as his elder brother but because he made her feel so welcome. Not that she had taken a particular dislike to Lady Buchanan, it was just that she found her to be somewhat, detached. 'It's nice to meet you too, Fergus' she replied and then turning to Lady Buchanan, she said, 'thank you for welcoming me to your beautiful home My Lady. It's so generous of you to have me stay.'

Fergus hung onto her every drawl. 'Wow, Orley, I just love your accent!'

Having finished her whisky, Orley felt warmth like hot sap rising in her cheeks. It felt good. 'And I love the way y'all talk too,' she laughed. 'I guess I'll be soon be talkin' Scotch in no time, an' y'all be talkin' Texan!'

Their laughter was silenced by Lady Buchanan's terse comment that they happened to be Scottish *not* Scotch.'

'Aye. Just like this whisky.' Fergus said, winking at Orley.

Innes refreshed their glasses as Mrs Mackie announced that lunch was being served in the great hall. They walked through a series of cold stone hallways into a very beautiful dining room which had a bright tartan carpet on the floor.

On the walls, tapestries gave a warmer furnished look and the fireplace, with its fire basket of burning coals, actually seemed to be generating some heat. Either that or the whisky was doing its job.

A huge table was laid with soup bowls and spoons. A loaf of bread sat beside a steaming tureen and delicious aromas filled the room. 'How appetizing, Mrs Mackie.' Orley remarked, her stomach suddenly aching with hunger.

'And what do we have for lunch today?' Innes asked.

'It's an old family recipe, handed down to me by my mother and by her mother before her.' Mrs Mackie answered proudly.

'Then it's got to be rabbit and lentil broth!' Fergus declared.

Mrs Mackie's cheeks glowed with pleasure.

'Oh!' Orley said in a small voice. Her face burning like a furnace.

'Oh dear,' said Innes. 'I forgot to tell Mrs Mackie that you don't eat cows, sheep, birds, pigs, or in fact, rabbits.'

'Doesn't eat meat...?' Lady Buchanan queried.

'Orley must be a vegetarian.' Fergus clarified.

'I'm sorry,' Orley professed, 'But I'm happy just to eat the bread. It looks so delicious.'

Ten minutes later, thanks to Mrs Mackie's quick thinking, she was eating a hot and comparatively delicious commercially produced tomato soup and the embarrassment was forgotten.

After lunch, Innes showed Orley her room in the tower at the very top of the house. They climbed a turning narrow stone staircase until they reached a wooden door. Inside was a deceptively large room with a queen sized bed, a wardrobe and a very pretty dressing table. 'This is your room,' he told her. 'I hope you like it.'

'It's amazing. I adore it!'

'The bathroom is down one flight of stairs and along the corridor. I'll show you....'

'No its okay, I'm sure I will find it myself, later.'

'Then, I'll let you unpack, shall I?'

'I don't expect it'll take me long. Why don't you stay?'

In two strides, his arms came around her and his mouth down on hers. He kissed her so passionately that neither of them wanted to come up for air. 'God I've missed you!' he proclaimed, burying his face in her neck and hair, 'I'm so glad you are here.'

In his arms, Orley sighed with relief. His warm body, encased in a thick wool sweater, felt hard and so wonderfully real. Happiness washed over her.

'I've missed you too,' she told him, recalling the anguish of their parting.

Thank goodness nothing had changed between them.

Her feelings and seemingly the way he felt about her was just the same. They really had been able to pick up exactly where they left off....

Chapter Seven

'What was that you said, Fergus?'

Davina stopped grooming her horse and spun round.

'That Innes's cattle expert from America is a woman. Didn't you know?'

No she didn't know and Fergus knew that she didn't, yet for some sadistic reason, he appeared to be relishing her astonishment.

'Yes, I think he did mention it,' she lied. 'What's her name again?'

'It's Orley, short for Orlene. Her family are MacKenna's.'

'I can't say I've ever heard of them,' she told him dismissively.

Bloodline was important to Davina. Unfortunately for Fergus. She insisted upon it not just for her horses and dogs but also for herself.

Davina continued to groom her horse. She was dammed if she was going to marry a nobody. Fergus was a nobody. He might be attractive but he had no title. The Lairdship of Buchanan belonged to Innes.

Fergus supposed most men his age longed to be taller, better looking, or massively endowed: all he longed for was a title more important than his elder brother's with which to impress the delightful Davina.

'I wondered if you might like to go to the theatre tonight?' he asked her tentatively. His fingers flicking nervously over the two theatre tickets in his corduroy trouser pocket. Tickets that Innes had bought at great expense for the greater good. 'She loves Macbeth. She read English Literature at St Andrews. You can't fail.' Innes had assured him. 'It's a sure thing date'.

Davina shrugged. 'I don't know. Is Innes going?'

Fergus kicked stray wisps of straw from under his boot. 'He said not. Orley is really jet-lagged and so he's staying behind.'

Davina flinched. 'Then I don't think I'll go.'

'But the tickets are for Macbeth. At the Playhouse.'

Her head jerked upward. 'The Scottish Play?'

Fergus nodded. She had been swayed. Just like Innes said she would be. He sighed with relief. What he didn't know was that Davina had been trying to get tickets for weeks but they had all sold out.

'Great. I'll pick you up at six,' he said.

On that premise he was gone before she could change her mind.

Davina sat down on an upturned bucket and thought hard about Innes and Orley MacKenna. On the few occasions she had seen Innes, accidentally-or-otherwise, he had made no mention of another woman. He had been evasive but then he would, wouldn't he, if he was and had been having an illicit foreign affair.

He had talked about his cattle project and had mentioned a cattle expert coming over from Texas to advise him on a breeding programme. Yes, that's exactly what he had said, Cattle Expert NOT American cowgirl.

It was all lies and deceit. No wonder he had behaved so defensively. He must have been riddled with guilt and thought it easier to call off their engagement than to admit his mistake.

She began to laugh. Did he think she was naive or stupid? All men make mistakes. That's what men do. Her mother said so. They begged forgiveness and promised never to do it again. That was the way it worked. It was the way marriages, like her parent's, had lasted more than five minutes.

There were rules of course. Discretion must always be maintained. Neither spouse must upset the status-quo by allowing an indiscretion to get into the public domain. So what on earth did Innes think he was doing- humiliating her in this way?

She shook her head and sighed.

One way or another Orley MacKenna was going to back to Texas – and, as Lady Macbeth might say, - *to alter favour ever is to fear. Leave the rest to me....*

That evening, when the curtain went up at The Playhouse, Fergus noted how Davina's knuckles were set white and clutching the burgundy velvet covered balcony rail in front of her. Her face too was white.

As the first witch began to speak, thunder rumbled from the back of the theatre and lighting cracked from the Gods, and Davina whispered each line with all the rapture and excitement of knowing what was to come.

When shall we three meet again, in thunder, lightning or in rain...?

He ate his ice-cream but most of it ended up on his knee.

Scene two, in the Kings headquarters, had him girding his loins in excitement. *The brave, worthy gentleman - worthy to be a rebel, for to that, the multiplying villainies of nature do swarm upon him.*

Modern day villainess, he decided, were the taxmen. The worthy Gentleman reminded him of him and Innes.

'It's all as relevant today as it was then,' he told Davina during the interval.

Act three, scene two, Davina trembled and wept as Lady Macbeth justified the death of Duncan. She also piercing the skin on Fergus's thigh through his trousers with her sharp nails but he didn't dare complain.

Where our desire is got without consent. 'Tis safer to be that which we destroy. Than by destruction dwell in doubtful joy....

You are absolutely right, she told Fergus later, while thinking about her all consuming desire for Innes and the wedding she had arranged apparently without his consent.

'It's all so bloody relevant.'

Orley awoke after an incredible nights sleep to find it was already late morning. Leaping out of bed in a panic she rifled through her suitcase, grabbing underwear, clean jeans and her most substantial of sweaters, before tearing down the stairs to the bathroom where she searched eagerly for a shower.

She had been warned that European plumbing was often just a draining point, without even a curtain, so she looked about, hoping to see something that might remotely resemble a showerhead. Nothing seemed apparent.

How odd..?

She ran water into the bathtub instead but then couldn't seem to locate a plug for the plug hole. She looked everywhere. Plenty of ancient looking cobwebs in corners but still no plug. This morning, she decided, she would simply have to have a strip wash. Nor was there anywhere to hang her dressing-gown so she had to let it drop to the floor as she stepped into the bath to splash herself with water that seemed to have come straight off a glacier. She bit down on her spongebag to stifle her shrieks.

A short time later, she bounded into the kitchen with an exhilarated look on her tanned face and bade good morning to Mrs Mackie, who was stood at the stove cooking.

Delicious aroma's wafted towards her as the housekeeper flipped small golden pancakes on the griddle. 'And good morning to you, Orley. Did you have a nice sleep?'

'Yes I did, thank you.'

'And are you hungry, dear?'

'Oh yes, I'm starving.'

'Eggs then. A couple of nice poached eggs on toast...?'

'Oh, yes please, Mrs Mackie.'

'And some of my drop scones with jam...?'

Orley nodded even thought she wasn't quite sure what jam was.

Whilst eating her eggs on toast and a whole plate of drop scones, with what turned out to be a delicious blackcurrant jelly, in an environment that seemed so turn of the previous century, she was amused to see Mrs Mackie sending out a text message on a snazzy looking mobile phone.

'His Lairdship said I was to let him know when you were at breakfast,' Mrs Mackie explained, as one stiff finger stabbed at the buttons on the mobile. 'I imagine he's looking forward to showing you around the estate this morning.'

Orley almost choked at the use of Innes's title and wondered if, as an employee, she was expected to use it too.

Glancing at the clock, with a stab of guilt, she realised that the morning had almost passed her by.

Soon, in a shaft of sunlight, Innes appeared in the kitchen doorway. He removed his outdoor coat and muddy boots before padding over to Orley in thick socks, old jeans, and an even older sweatshirt. He looked more like a farm hand than landed-gentry. 'How's that jet-lag?' he asked.

'Oh Innes, I mean, *Laird* Innes, I feel so badly about sleeping in so late on my first day.'

Innes grinned. 'Not at all. I slept in late for two days when I got back from America. Didn't I, Mrs Mackie?'

'Och aye,' Mrs Mackie agreed. 'It must be a terrible thing that jet-lag although I've never had it myself. Just as well I say. Tea, your Lairdship?'

'Yes please, Mrs Mackie.'

Innes sat down opposite Orley and locked eyes with her over the mug of steaming tea placed in front of him

'You okay?'

'I'm ready for anything,' she assured him.

'Good. Then when you've finished your breakfast, we'll go for a nice walk over the hill. And by the way,' he said, lowering his voice to almost a whisper, '*you* don't need to use the trade name.'

Going for a walk involved being kitted out in heavy waterproofs. Orley was offered a pair of green rubber boots and a waxed jacket. 'These are Fergus's but he won't mind. We need to get you some wet weather gear of your own next time we go into the village.' Innes told her.

Orley peered outside. 'But it's not even raining?'

'Oh but it will. It's forecast.'

A large black dog with his tail dutifully swishing joined them and they headed out over the fields together. They walked for a while before stopping to catch their breath at a vantage point from which it was possible to see for miles over the grazing lands and onto the mountains in the distance. Orley could make out the road they had travelled along the previous day. But in place of yesterday afternoon's dazzling hue, the morning light was so much softer and the pastel aspect made everything appear somehow, even more beautiful than before.

As they walked on, Innes took her hand.

Orley was so happy she thought she might burst. Her fears about taking up his offer had all been unfounded. She had worried endlessly while waiting for her passport - about arriving in Scotland to find him behaving differently toward her - or worse, indifferently. But she needn't have worried.

He began to tell her about all his plans for the estate. He explained how important the new cattle project was to their future. He told her how he wanted to be open with her about his responsibilities as a landowner. 'Laird' in Scotland just means landowner,' he told her. 'It's not like Duke or Earl or Baron. It's just a name.'

Orley listened and bubbled with happiness while holding his hand as they walked across the fields together.

'No one has yet bred composite cattle in Scotland. I think it will give us the advantage. It will attract further support and funding from Europe'

'Which breeds are you thinking of combining?' she asked. This was her subject. Her forte. She had experience of breeding composites in Texas.

'Highland with Hereford, Red Angus, and Simmental.'

Orley was quite taken aback. 'Three-way breeding is well-established,' she told him, 'so why are you adding the Highland to the mix?'

'To make it ours. Cattle that are steady on their feet here.'

'You do know it will affect vigour and that the calves will be small when they are born?'

'And less stress with calving means fewer birthing problems,' Innes added.

'Okay so you've done your homework. How will you import the composites?

Innes shook his head. 'I wish we could import because I saw some fantastic cattle in Texas. Import restrictions in the UK due to BSE scares and the aftermath of Foot and Mouth unfortunately won't allow it.'

Orley thought quietly for a moment.

Innes continued to explain. 'I have projected it will take five years to establish the core herd. This is a long term venture but I have the full backing of the Enterprise Committee. They funded my trip to the States.'

'Those restrictions you spoke of. I assume they apply to live cattle but not to frozen embryos?'

Innes smacked his forehead with the palm of his hand 'Why didn't I think of that?'

She laughed. 'You knew that. You were just testing me.'

Innes flung his arms around her and swung her off her feet.

'See, I just knew you were the cowgirl for me!'

'If we implant Highland heifers this season, in less than two years, we will be calving your four-gene composites.' She told him. 'You will have your herd in half the time.'

He was holding her so close now.

Was this all too good to be true?

They walked on. Innes had his arm laid lazily across her shoulders as they made their way through swathes of lush grass. *Was he too good to be true?*

Then as if she had willed it herself, he said: 'Orley, there is something I must tell you. It's not all good....'

Oh heck. Any moment now he was going to tell her he was married or something. She coldly abandoned his warm hand and shoved her hands deeply into the cold pockets of the oversized waxed coat she was wearing.

Oh, dear God, please don't let this be the moment when I find out I got it all wrong, again....

'The Estate is struggling financially,' he said glumly. 'Unfortunately, both my grandfather and my father died within a very short time of each other.'

Orley looked at him and didn't know what to say. Poor Innes. He was obviously still in mourning and she had not even noticed. It must be down to that British stiff upper lip of his. 'I'm so sorry. I didn't realise you had suffered such a terrible loss so recently. That's so terrible. Your poor mother and brother too....'

'It's okay, really,' Innes assured her. 'It's just that we have been crippled with inheritance tax bills.'

Money? What is that compared to loosing half your family?

He was clearly embarrassed about his financial status. Then it occurred to her that maybe he was asking her to work in lieu of payment? Or, worse, expecting some kind of financial investment? Fat chance. She should have 'fessed up to being broke first. 'Innes, I'm sorry, I don't have the resources to invest in your....'

'No.' He interrupted. 'That's not it at all. I just want you to understand what's to be won or lost here. This venture will either make or break us....'

'Why didn't you tell me all this in Texas?'

'Because I thought if things were too complicated you might not come. I'm an impoverished farmer remember and not quite the cool cowboy you thought I was.'

Orley began to laugh. 'So you lied?

He looked coy. 'No. I am perhaps guilty of misleading you, slightly, that's all.'

'You offered me a job and I accepted. I think you should know that I'm not interested in your money – or indeed your lack of it. I'm here because I want to be. I've always wanted to see Scotland. I suggest you pay me what you can and when you can. As long as I have a roof over my head and a meal at your table – I will be happy.'

Innes looked meek. 'I shall pay you a regular wage. I wouldn't hear of it any other way. I do have ways of raising cash.'

He explained as they started to head back. 'I could put up the rents of my tenants and charge tourists at the gate but then it occurred to me that all the cottages need upgrading and no tourist in their right mind would pay a penny to visit this pile of old rubble.'

'Well I'm glad your not the sort of Laird who would put up the rents of his poor tenants,' she told him supportively. 'And I think it's exciting to start something from scratch and to be challenged by all that is at stake. What do you want me to do first?'

'Establish our feed suppliers,' he said with his enthusiasm matching hers 'You need to check that everything complies with the strict organic farming criteria. Do you think we can make it work, Orley?'

'How can we not?' she said as they stood amidst the endless acres of ungrazed lands. 'I mean look at all this fabulously rich grass. If was a cow I'd sure wanna' live here.' Innes gaze followed hers and she noticed with relief that the cool cowboy twinkle was still there.

Innes had spent a lot of time looking into every grant, subsidy and loan that might be available to farmers and landowners in order to raise all the capital he needed. But he couldn't wait any longer. He was running out of time. The only option was to go back to the bank. His home was the one asset he was loath to mortgage but the only other alternative was to sell up, and as Scottish Heritage had already made him an offer, he preferred to use its valuation to tempt the bank into offering up more than the figure first discussed .

Orley entered his study just as he was checking over his paperwork one final time. 'Is it okay, if I come into town with you today?' she asked. Her jet-lag was finally abating. 'Only I thought I'd do some shopping.'

Innes gave a low whistle. 'No problem. You ready now?'

She grabbed her purse. 'I sure am, cowboy.'

Orley's first impression of the small Scottish village of Thornfield was one of delight. There were two high streets. One north and one south and they crossed at the site of a stone column. At this cross stood a pub called The Duke. There was also an array of small shops, a supermarket, a newsagent, a hairdresser, and lots of tourist type shops that sold fishing gear, country clothes and knitwear. Innes stopped the Landrover outside the Bank.

'We'll meet up later,' he told her, peeling a clutch of notes from his wallet. 'You'll need some pounds, they don't take dollars here.'

'I have money and it's all in Scottish, look...'

Innes continued to hold out his cash and Orley continued to refuse to take it until they were both acutely embarrassed.

'Well, if you need an advance on your salary, just let me know. It won't be a problem.' He stuffed the money back into his wallet.

'Well good luck to you. I hope your meeting goes well,' she said brightly.

He nodded. 'Thanks. I'll see you in the Duke. Don't worry if you are there before me, as Fergus will be in there.'

Davina was just stepping out of the newsagents with a copy of *The Lady* tucked under her arm when she spotted Innes's old Landrover. In the passenger seat she could see a woman. She watched as the vehicle stopped outside the bank. Diving quickly into the gift shop doorway, she pretending to look inside at tartan-clad dolls and heather-pattern china, as Innes and the woman got out.

The woman, whom Davina assumed to be Orley MacKenna, had long curly red hair and even longer legs. She wore tight blue jeans and a fringed jacket with strange high-heeled boots. Davina decided that Orley MacKenna looked ridiculous. Who did she think she was – Annie Oakley?

Innes went into the bank. Orley walked down the street.

Davina followed at a discreet distance, only to be stopped by Mrs McDonald, who wanted to interrogate her about wedding plans. She was damned if she was going to tell that her the wedding was off because, with the support of her mother, she had decided not to tell anyone just yet as it hardly seemed fair when it would be back on again very soon.

'I heard the wedding's off. You must be devastated...' Mrs McDonald professed.

Davina was furious but tried hard to look merely affronted. If there was a spy in their midst it had to be their housekeeper, Maud, another devious McDonald.

'Has it ever occurred to you that you might be spreading malicious lies and rumours, Mrs Mac...?' Davina declared, with her head as high as she could carry it.

She hurried away, leaving Mrs McDonald protesting her sources.

The damned American woman had disappeared. She had to be inside one of the boutiques. But which one?

Orley suddenly reappeared. Striding down the street with her fringed jacket flapping open. Her limbs long and slender, her movements lithe, her hips narrow and her legs willowy, her long red tresses bouncing like springs down the entire length of her back. Davina decided that Orley MacKenna looked absurd. She followed her into the Cashmere shop and pretended to browse through a rail of pastel pashmina while observing and listening to the awful American drawl.

'You are new around here aren't you, dear? she heard the shop assistant ask.

'Yes, I'm from Texas.' Orley replied chirpily whilst browsing.

'Then you must be the cow expert from America that everyone's talking about, except that no one expected a woman, which explains a lot in my book.'

'I'm sorry?' said Orley, detecting a note of malice. 'I don't understand…?'

'It explains why at least a dozen decent local men didn't get offered the job.'

Still smiling, Orley held up a cashmere sweater. 'Can I try this one please?'

'And what a pretty bracelet if you don't mind me saying. Och, look, a wee silver piper playin' on the pipes….'

Orley lifted her wrist and shook the charm bracelet she was so proud of. 'Yes. Isn't it sweet. Innes gave it to me….'

As the shopkeeper's eyes creased into another knowing smile, Orley blushed and then there was a loud crash and a rail of sweaters fell to the ground. A woman lurking amongst them muttered apologies and stumbled out of the shop.

Davina arrived at the hairdressers ten minutes late for her appointment and immediately burst into tears. Shona, her hairdresser and confidant, poured her a large whisky. 'Och, here's a wee somethin' ta settle ya' doon, hen!' she said, listening to her clients distress with genuine concern.

'I've just had a terrible shock,' spluttered Davina, whose incoherent raging was preventing her from sitting still and from Shona getting a comb through her quivering head.

'She's come over here, disguised as some kind of cattle expert and what she's really up to, is with *my* Fiancé!'

'Cattle expert? More like expert cow!' Shona agreed, tucking a fluffy towel around Davina's rigid shoulders. 'I do hope you're planning how to get rid of this yankee-doodle-dandy?'

After another whisky, Davina lowered her voice and confided that she had, indeed, concocted a clever plan to ditch the bitch.

'Although,' she told Shona, who had lowered her dark spiky head to hear more, 'revenge is a dish best served cold....'

Chapter Eight

Orley had watched Innes go into the bank. In this strange pallid Scottish light, he seemed to have completely lost his tan. Perhaps he was anxious. She was sure anxious for him.

But as there was nothing she could do to help, she set off down the street in earnest; her mission to buy warm clothing.

In the first boutique, the clothes seemed more suited to older women, as drab tweed skirts and fussy blouses in garish colours dominated the rails. Further along the street, Orley was delighted to discover the Cashmere Store, which had the softest looking sweaters in the most gorgeous colours imaginable displayed in the window. She went inside. The sales assistant soon warmed to her and was incredibly helpful when it became apparent that she might make a purchase.

'I simply cannot decide between the amethyst blue or the rose petal pink!' Orley had breathed quite helplessly in the midst of such heavenly soft sweaters.

'With your auburn hair they both suit you,' the sales assistant had told her. 'Surely, you should take them both?'

In a rush of retail spontaneity, Orley decided that she would.

'That will be two hundred and forty pounds please....'

Orley hurried back down the street in a rush of retail shock, having just spent what almost equated to five hundred dollars on just two sweaters.

Then in the next store she saw a pure lambs wool sweater in a very nice shade of blue, which looked substantial enough to accommodate her through the approaching Scottish winter, for sale at a mere twenty-five pounds.

Inside the bank, Innes was signing the paperwork and handing over the deeds to the family home in return for a whopping big mortgage advance. It was now definitely sink or swim. The branch manager was delighted to be overseeing such a massive transfer of funds. It was, to his certain knowledge, the first time that the Buchanan business account had been in credit during his entire lifetime.

'You have certainly done your homework this time, Laird Buchanan. Your analysis of American cattle breeding has paid off for you. I am most impressed.'

Innes waited while the manager added his signature to the deal. A small muscle twitched in his jaw as he recalled being told just six months earlier, how his cock-a-hoop plans not only lacked commercial vision, but a viable market.

'Your sponsored visit to Texas was a big advantage,' the manager maintained, 'and the Enterprise Committee will be pleased to know they have backed a winner.'

The deal was complete. Innes was led back into the banking hall and offered an outstretched hand as a concluding gesture.

'I'd like to be the first to wish you luck, Laird Buchanan.'

'Thank you sir, although I do believe that we all make our own.'

The pub was incredibly busy. Everyone was shouting. Fishing rods were propped everywhere. Walls were lined with huge fish in glass cases. Antique fishing tackle and shotguns, ancient antlers and stuffed birds, all competed for space with the customers who, in their drooping tweeds, plus fours, and enormous waders, looked like exhibition objects themselves. Orley picked her way through the throng in the hope of finding Fergus.

Although friendly, the local dialect in Orley's ears sounded as if it was a foreign language. That she could comprehend so little of it, she found unsettling and strangely isolating, as she had not expected a language barrier. It was with relief that she spotted Fergus sitting at the bar next to the empty seat he had managed to save for her.

'A drink..?' he suggested, as she settled beside him and tucked her purchases away between her ankles. She would have loved a cup of coffee or even tea, but instead, Fergus ordered two large whiskies. She picked up a bar menu. The smell of food in the air was very enticing and people all around were tucking into traditional fare.

Tatties and Neeps, Haggis and Champers.

Oh dear. What sort of food could it be..?

The door swung open and she looked up eagerly hoping to see Innes, but it was another fishing party arriving. They noisily took up the last remaining table and ordered drinks as if they were out on a Saturday night bachelor party.

A barmaid put whiskies down in front of Fergus and Orley. 'On yer tab then, Fergus?'

'Aye, that'll do, Aileen,' Fergus replied. 'An one fer yer sell.'

'Ken.' she replied, flipping a couple of coins into a large glass marked 'tips' at the back of the bar. The glass was almost full of cash.

'So, ken, this is ya American gal, ken?' Aileen queried, gesturing towards Orley.

Orley blushed. The only word she recognised was 'American'.

'Aye, this is Orley MacKenna from Texas.'

'Aye, hen, its guid ta' meet wit'ya, ken...'

Orley shook the barmaid's hand and couldn't help but wonder why this woman called everyone Ken. 'It's nice to meet you, Aileen.'

Aileen returned to pulling pints from the shiny brass pump levers and pouring large measures of scotch for her customers while Orley sipped on her drink and contemplated the large glass of cash on the back of the bar.

'Big tips,' she remarked to Fergus.

'Aye, bloody enormous!' Fergus agreed, laughing loudly.

In the midst of the affray, Innes was making his way towards the bar. He could see Orley and over the bedlam around him, he could distinctly hear his brother's raucous laughter. Eventually, he reached them and wrapped his arms around Orley in a warm embrace.

'Get the drinks in, Fergus,' he said, kissing the side of her cheek.

Orley seriously wondered if she would be able to take another whisky on an empty stomach but as Innes's meeting had obvious gone well, it would have been rude to refuse. In return, she decided to offer to buy them a meal to soak it all up. 'Neeps and Tatties anyone..?'

'Did the meeting result in all we had hoped for?' Fergus asked Innes with a shrewd nudge and canny wink.

'Aye. Very much so,' came the equally astute reply.

'Then let's celebrate!' Fergus roared.

Several more whiskies and a good few hours later, the three of them left the pub, spilling out into the late afternoon sunshine. Innes, who seemed to be the soberest amongst them, managed to flag down a taxi. Orley confessed to feeling 'all fuzzy' and then slept in Innes's arms as they made their twenty minute journey back to Glencorrie.

Under normal circumstances, Innes might have considered this to be an absolute pleasure, but with her snoring and Fergus in fine voice, he just wished they both had volume control.

Once back home, Innes put Orley to bed. Managing to carry her up the steep stone staircase and tuck her up, fully clothed, between the sheets.

She was shivering and complaining of cold. Innes put this down to the effects of the alcohol. As it was still a pleasant ten degrees centigrade it could hardly be considered cold at all.

Orley felt incredibly ill at the breakfast table the next morning. She had never drank so much whisky in her whole life and as a result, was unable to face her porridge. To make things worse, she had already brushed her teeth four times but could still detect the taste of stale liquor and bitter vomit in her mouth.

So when Innes suggested they ride out and check the estate boundary fences together that morning, she keenly agreed. Fresh air and a fast gallop were just the things to blow away the thumping head and the sickness in her stomach. 'I'll get changed and we'll saddle up,' she enthused.

Only on leaving the house, she had to race back indoors again quickly. Fergus was waiting to use the bathroom when she came out.

'Good morning,' she said to him weakly and then immediately ran back inside again. Through the door she could hear him laughing as she wretched.

'I think I'll use the one upstairs instead!' he shouted.

A while later in the kitchen, as she helped herself to a glass of water, she overheard the sound of raised voices in the next room. She also heard what sounded like crying. The room next to the kitchen was the study. She stopped the water running from the cranky old and noisy tap to listen.

'It is proper to give at least three month's notice!' She heard Lady Buchanan's voice saying in a clipped tone.

Orley tiptoed to the kitchen door and strained to hear what was going on.

Mrs Mackie seemed to be pleading with Lady Buchanan to be allowed to leave Glencorrie.

'But madam, please?'

Orley could hardly believe her ears. Mrs Mackie was in distress. Lady Buchanan was in a great strop. Thoughts of being held prisoner in this dark spooky house flashed through her mind and her blood ran cold. The lyrics to the song *Hotel California* played in her head. She held her breath and crept down the hallway to listen at the study door.

'But you don't understand, madam. My sister needs me!'

'Then you shall go without your severance pay, Mrs Mackie!'

More sobbing.

Orley burst into the study. Mrs Mackie was sat in a chair, her face buried in a handkerchief. Lady Buchanan was stood at the window. She turned at glared at Orley who rushed to the housekeeper and asked, 'Mrs Mackie, what on earth can be the matter...?'

'This is nothing to concern yourself with, Orlene!' Lady Buchanan insisted.

'Miss Orley,' said Mrs Mackie, 'My sister Agnes is sick and I have to go away to care for her.'

Distracted by poor Mrs Mackie's plight and Lady Buchanan's apathy, Orley soon forgot about her own sickness. 'Oh dear, I hope she's better soon.'

'That's just what Lady Buchanan said,' Mrs Mackie replied stiffly, 'but that's because she doesn't want to pay me my severance pay.'

'Enough!' yelled Lady Buchanan, 'Orlene, go at once and tell Laird Innes to take Mrs Mackie to the station.'

Orley glared in Lady Buchanan's direction and was just about to object to being ordered about when she saw a cheque being written for Mrs Mackie.

Her silence had better prove golden.

In the yard, she explained to Innes about Mrs Mackie's sick sister and then watched him disappear into the house to organise a train ticket and take poor Mrs Mackie and her belongings to the station in Thornfield.

'We'll miss you until you get back,' Orley told Mrs Mackie as she helped her into the passenger seat of Innes's Landrover. As Innes was putting her suitcase on the back seat, Orley kissed on the side of her florid cheek, and popped a hastily wrapped gift in her lap. 'A little something. It's not much.'

'Oh, Orley, thank you, dear. That's so very kind of you, although I'm afraid it's unlikely that I'll be able to return any time soon.'

'Does she live far away, your sister?'

'She lives in Kent.'

Orley was not sure where Kent was but assumed it must be quite far away.

Lady Buchanan appeared just as the Landrover was drawing away. She watched it for a moment as it ambled down the driveway and turned to go back inside.

Orley felt she had to say something under the circumstances. 'Lady Buchanan, I can help with the chores and some of the cooking. I don't mind. Just until you get another housekeeper.'

The response from Lady Buchanan was cutting.

'I'm afraid we won't be replacing Mrs Mackie. We can no longer afford to keep a housekeeper at Glencorrie. It's not about wanting or needing. It's about affording and we could little afford that severance pay.'

Orley felt her face colour up until it was burning hot.

Things must be much worse than she first thought.

If they could not afford a housekeeper then maybe they couldn't afford her either?

'I do think, Lady Buchanan, that you could have been a little more friendly towards Mrs Mackie, Orley braved. 'She was obviously very upset about her sister and about leaving your employment.'

'Mrs Mackie was an employee not a friend. I believe that business and friendship should never mix - and that is perhaps something that you should remember while you are here, Orlene.'

And with that, Lady Buchanan walked away.

Orley was flabbergasted but in a last ditch attempt to get on her good side, she called out, 'we could take it in turns to clean and do kitchen chores. I can do potatoes and other vegetables - and deserts. I do a good cheese cake, I am told!'

Lady Buchanan turned only to impart a final shot. 'And while you are doing cheese cakes or whatever *they* are, who do you expect will see to the beasts?'

Orley was furious, especially as she did not yet have any 'beasts' to see to.

It was well into the afternoon before Innes returned from the train station. While he was away, Orley avoided going back into the house and instead, she searched the whole farm and all of it's derelict buildings, for the horses they would ride out on to check the boundary fences.

She was becoming more and more frustrated at not finding any. It was obvious the horses could not be kept in the dangerously dilapidated barns and so they had to be outside somewhere but there were none to be found - only a couple of sick ewes and an old tractor.

Puzzled, she headed back to the yard, just as Innes appeared astride a four-wheeled motorbike at full throttle.

'I am looking for the horses,' she shouted to him.

He swung his leg from the bike and patted the roaring beast's fuel tank with the palm of his hand. 'Sorry Orley, but we don't have any.'

Orley could hardly comprehend it. 'What do you mean – we don't have any?'

'In Scotland, these are our workhorses.'

Before she could stop herself, she had stamped her booted foot in exasperation. 'You have got to be kidding me?'

Innes looked taken aback. 'Horses need feeding and shoeing and sometimes a vet. These bikes are far more practical on a hill farm like ours.'

'So you are telling me that these bikes don't need fuel, tyres, or sometimes even a mechanic?'

Innes began to walk away. He'd obviously inherited that nasty little trait from his mother. 'Where do you think are you going?' she yelled after him.

'To get another,' he replied.

Orley shouted. 'How many do you have? A stable full perhaps?'

He did not answer.

In the time it took Innes to collect the other bike, she had managed to calm down a little. Having reasoned that in the current situation, there was nothing to suggest that after acquiring their herd of cattle, horses could not be introduced to Glencorrie. She would have great pleasure in choosing them all herself.

She and Innes rode the quad-bikes for miles. They toured the boundaries of the vast Buchanan lands looking for breaks in fences or holes in stonewalls and then, at the far side of the estate, where they came across a hamlet of small cottages, Innes stopped to introduce her to some of his labourers and tenants.

To Orley's embarrassment, she found it almost impossible to understand what was being said to her. The heavy local dialect sounded like an entirely foreign language.

'Och, it's a driech and dour dae, hen', she was told over and over.

This, according to Innes, was a rolling comment on the inclement weather.

Orley found herself nodding her head like a dim-wit and saying, 'it's so nice to meet you, Ken,' over and over again, as inexplicably they all seemed to be called Ken, even the women.

It was past seven o'clock when they returned to Glencorrie. The evening light was still holding.

Lady Buchanan was settled at the fireside reading a paperback book and without looking up, she informed them that their dinner was in the warming oven. Orley thanked her and admitted to feeling very hungry, as a matter of course, she asked of their meal.

'It's liver and tatties,' came the reply.

'But Orley doesn't eat meat, mother. Can you please try to remember that?'

'I did and it is not meat, it's liver and tatties....'

'It's perfectly okay,' said Orley, scraping her potato onto a fresh plate. She was far too weary to complain.

After their meal, Orley was still hungry. So while Innes answered a telephone call, she ventured outside and pulled an apple off an old tree in the garden. It was a calm evening and although the air was chilly and damp, she was feeling cosy and warm in the big blue lambs-wool sweater she had bought in Thornfield.

She sat on the garden bench and nibbled at the sour tasting fruit, whilst watching an apricot coloured sun setting over the burnt-umber shaded hills around her.

'That was Mrs Mackie,' said Innes, joining her on the bench. 'To let us know she had arrived safely at her sister's house in Kent.'

'Oh, I'm glad. It was such a long journey for her.'

'I thought it was very decent of you to give her that beautiful cashmere sweater as a leaving gift, Orley.'

'How did you know about that…?'

'She couldn't wait to open it and see what you had wrapped up in this weeks copy of *The Scotsman*.'

'I have to say I'm confused over your mother's treatment of poor Mrs Mackie. She practically refused to pay her any severance and then she let her go without so much as a thank you.'

Innes looked sad. 'Mrs Mackie was here a long time and I'm sad to see her go.'

'And how is it that your mother doesn't know about you mortgaging the house and the money in the bank account?'

Innes stiffened. She suddenly felt sorry for him. He had such a lot of responsibility and it wasn't his fault if his mother was an absolute bitch. He had the enormous tax demand to pay and, from what she could tell, plenty more bills on his desk. For all she knew, his mother might be the type to blow the lot on whisky. 'I'm sorry, Innes. Its been a long day and I'm just feeling crabby.'

He looked at her and grinned. 'You're crabby?'

'Yes, I am.' She met his smile and straight away the tension between them ebbed away. 'You were thinking of the Crab Shack in Baytown, weren't you?'

He put his arm around her. 'Aye, I was.'

She was hoping it might lead to a kiss but he stood up and beckoned her indoors. 'Come on, we had better go inside before we get bitten to death by the midges.'

'But I was hoping we could sit here and watch the sun go down together?'

'It's too dangerous.'

'What are the midges?' Orley looked about the garden, although she was not sure what she was looking for. 'Are they the same as haggis?'

Innes laughed at her. 'Do you mean to tell me that in all your father's stories of old Scotland, he never once mentioned the famous Scottish midge...?'

Chapter Nine

Fergus took a walk over to Davina's house with a picnic basket containing two hardboiled eggs, two pork pies, a jar of pickles and a bottle of sparkling pink wine.

It was a celebration picnic. In his pocket, he also had a very special something that he had received in the post that morning which he hadn't yet shown it to anyone. He wanted Davina to see it first.

The mist was clearing the turrets of McKenzie Castle as he approached the long driveway. He stopped to pick the last of the late summer flowers from the border. Pink orchids, which he decided were the exact colour of Davina's smooth skin. Tiny sprigs of speedwell in the exact shade of her beautiful eyes. He wound them together into a posy with a strong stem of grass and popped them inside the picnic basket. Girls loved men who brought them food and flowers - he'd read it in one of his mother's magazines.

He found her grooming a magnificent horse at the back of the house where the stable block was as beautiful as she was. She was wearing slim-fitting black jodhpurs and a pale-lemon sweater. Her hair was neatly pulled back into a short pony tail and she looked, for all intent and purposes, like a bright ray of sunshine in an otherwise grey sky.

'Hello Davina,' he said.

She looked at him with a raised brow and, lowering her eyes, she spotted the picnic basket. 'Hello. How are things, Fergus?'

'Things are fine,' he replied.

This was progress. She had asked about him before mentioning Innes.

'How's Innes?'

'Innes is – busy.'

'I know he's busy. What's he busy with. Has he got his cows yet?'

'No. Not yet. He's busy with this and that.'

The speedwell-blue eyes narrowed. 'Really. Just one cow then?'

Fergus's eyes widened.

Davina dropped the grooming brush. 'I mean cow*girl* of course. A mere slip of the tongue.'

'It's a lovely day for a picnic,' enthused Fergus, waggling the basket in a way he hoped might be tempting. 'What do you say?'

'What an absolutely lovely idea. I'm famished.'

Fergus was thrilled.

'I'll saddle up Misty for you and we'll ride up over the hill.'

Fergus hesitated. He hated horses. Horses hated him. He had learned to ride on a wooden rocking horse and had been shocked to find out that real ones had hidden agendas. 'Why don't we just walk?' he suggested nervously. 'It's a lovely day for a walk.'

'Because if we ride we won't have to lug the picnic basket ourselves and we can go further over the hill where no one can disturb us.' Davina explained, almost playfully.

Suddenly wild horses couldn't have stopped him. 'Great, let's go!'

They started up the hill at a slow pace for which Fergus was grateful but when his horse bounced into an uncomfortable trot, he heard himself yelling, 'whoa there - we don't want to pop the cork too soon!'

'Oh, you do spoil me!' Davina gushed. 'I do so love champagne.'

Fergus then wondered, considering the occasion, if he should have chosen the Clicquot over the Cava.

When they reached the brow of the hill, the land levelled off and the ground was covered with soft moss and lichen.

Large rocks anchored clumps of heather in a purple haze and on the carcass of an old fallen tree, they tied up their horses and laid out an old Buchanan tartan rug. They sat together. Fergus polished off the eggs and the pies and Davina drank the fizz.

'It's eleven and a half percent,' he told her immodestly.

'It's very tart,' she replied, swallowing it quickly. 'You should recommend it to Innes's cowgirl.'

'I have something to show you,' Fergus said, fiddling in his trouser pocket.

'Oh Christ. For God's sake. Not now. Put it away, Fergus.' Davina snapped.

Fergus produced a document. 'This was sent to me and it says that I am the direct descendant of Fergus of Galloway and heir to The Kingdom of Galloway. It says they have been trying to trace me for years and that the title is mine by birthright.'

Davina cast a brief eye over the document and could hardly suppress her laughter. 'Well, it certainly looks old. As old as something can look stained with beer and kept in a smelly pair of trousers. Oh Fergus, you are so much fun, but if it was genuine - then surely Innes would inherit the Kingdom of Galloway, not you?'

Fergus was crushed. Yes, Innes had said something months ago about 'getting him a title' and he had forgotten about that. In his desperate quest for Davina's love he had foolishly been taken in. It was typical of Innes to set him up like this. 'But it is addressed to me and I'm meant to reply to the Scottish Chancery,' he said feebly.

'You are so gullible. Anyone can buy fake titles off the internet for ten pounds. It doesn't mean a thing. Someone's having a joke and I think we both know who that person is, don't we?'

Fergus blushed scarlet with embarrassment. He would say nothing more about it. Not to Innes and not to anyone. He would pretend that he didn't really think he might be the Lost Fergus, Baron of Galloway, which was a title far more important than a mere Laird. He screwed up the letter, rammed it back into his pocket and ate another pie.

'Do you have any whisky, Fergus?' Davina chirped as she emptied the remains of the fizz into her plastic cup.

Fergus also had a hip flask in his pocket. He handed it over. 'Never knowingly under supplied,' he said far too optimistically for his own good.

'Oh goody!' giggled Davina. 'Now, tell me more gossip about Glencorrie and why Mrs Mackie felt she had to leave. Was it all to do with that filthy cowgirl?'

They finished the whisky between them. It was clear to Fergus that Davina was enjoying herself. If he told her lots of juicy gossip she listened to him without interrupting. She sat close. So close that he was overwhelmed by her perfume and the heat from her body. He had to cross his legs for fear of embarrassing himself with excitement.

She opened a packet of crisps and fed them to him. 'I know I can trust you implicitly, my darling Fergus', she began to say, as she allowed him to lick the salt from between her fingers, 'to tell me the truth, the whole truth and nothing but the truth....'

And she had called him 'darling.' This was a development of monumental proportions.

Fergus almost wanted to run back down the hill and report this to Innes forthwith.

'Of course you can t-trust me,' he spluttered, 'I always tell the truth. I'm known for it.'

'I want to know what's happening between Innes and the cowgirl. I want you to keep me informed. You will be rewarded, obviously', she said a tad clinically. 'If it's over and he's sorry then I am prepared to forgive him. All he has to do is send her back to Texas and all will be forgotten. You don't have to protect him anymore. You just have to tell him. Are we clear...?'

Fergus wasn't clear. He hadn't anticipated this at all. Forgive him? All will be forgotten? Until now, she had been playing the woman-scorned so well that he had forgotten she had a forgiving side.

There was nothing else for it. He would have to tell her more – and invent stuff if necessary. When she knew about Innes's illicit Texan affair she wouldn't want to forgive him - she would want to forget him for sure.

'Yes. They met in Texas and fell in love. I'm sorry Davina....'

He had hoped she might cry on his shoulder and then he could legitimately put his arm around her and kiss her all better again.

Unfortunately, when he finished telling her about the Great American Romance, there still wasn't a tear in the tormented blue eyes.

'And what, in your opinion, does she have - that I don't?' Davina demanded.

He took a deep breath. There was no point in stopping now. It might be brutal but whatever it took to get the juices flowing.

'Well, in my opinion, you are far more beautiful than Orley - but Innes thinks differently. He likes the way Orley dresses. He thinks she's sexy. He also says she's clever. He absolutely loves her long red hair.'

Davina didn't collapse into sobs. She got angry. She began to rant and rage. She even swore. Fergus had never in his life heard Davina swear. Okay, she had once said 'bloody,' - and he had been shocked then, so he gazed at her in absolute astonishment as her rosebud lips moved in sync with words he expected might crack open the hills around them and cause the seven horsemen of the apocalypse to appear. Surely it must be the drink talking?

'What do you mean, he prefers *her* looks to mine? I'll show him. I'll bloody-well show him. He won't get rid of me so easily.'

Then she leapt to her feet and began tightening up her horse's girth.

The horse groaned.

So did Fergus. He began to pack away the picnic rug and all the empties. 'I don't understand it either. I much prefer a stylish sophisticated woman, like yourself, Davina,' he assured, 'but Innes has gone mad for a wilder woman.'

But Davina wasn't listening. She was already in the saddle and heading home at a pace that Fergus, unfortunately, found himself obliged to follow.

'You haven't forgotten that it's Rural Night, dear?' Lady Buchanan tapped her foot and waited for an answer impatiently.

Orley looked blank.

'It's the first Tuesday of the month. The Rural meeting. Tonight?'

The Rural..? Orley tried to say it. 'The Roo-er-al' but she failed miserably. She found it impossible to roll her R's effectively enough.

'I'm sorry, I don't remember you mentioning it. What is it, exactly?'

'It's the Scottish Women's Rural Institute,' Lady Buchanan barked. 'And tonight I am to introduce you to the ladies. I suggest you go upstairs and get changed.'

Orley did as she was told yet again, even though her whole body ached from riding the 'squat bike' all day long.

Also, she was so warm in the clothes she was already wearing that she was loath to remove them, even if they were dirty and smelly, because it was bitterly cold in the tower room. She braved an icy wash and put on almost every item of clothing hanging in her wardrobe. Layering was the only way to feel warm again.

She brushed her hair, which was now frizzy in the damp Scottish air and scowled at the exhausted face in the mirror.

Buck up, she told her reflection, *you could at least make an effort....*

Lady Buchanan, wearing a hairy tweed shawl around her shoulders with matching bonnet, waited in the hallway for Orley. 'We will need to hurry,' she said, waving the narrow beam of a torch towards the open door.

Orley hurried down the stairs in a jacket with buttons that wouldn't meet due to the numerous clothes beneath it.

Innes grinned at her sheepishly, looking both amused and apologetic. 'See you later. Have fun.'

'I could drive us there couldn't I, Innes..?'

'Aye, take the Landrover....'

'Nonsense.' Lady Buchanan snapped. 'We can walk. It's only five minutes away. Don't forget the shortbreads on the table over there....'

Orley picked up a rusty biscuit tin and gave it a rattle.

'If you break them we will not win tonight's competition!'

Mumbling an apology and gripping the tin, Orley followed both Lady Buchanan and her torch beam down the darkening driveway, taking long strides to keep up with her short fast ones, as they hurried towards what had to be the social highlight of September.

In a large wooden hut that smelt of damp mothballs and camphor oil, the local meeting of the Scottish Women's Rural Institute was already underway. Orley walked in tentatively, feeling sick with nerves. The fast walk had caused her face to glow and now they were inside this warm room, she was starting to perspire beneath her numerous garments.

The women were all chatting and drinking tea from bone china cups and saucers, but once they saw Lady Buchanan and Orley, they all stopped to stare.

Lady Buchanan cleared her throat. 'I would like you to meet Orley MacKenna. She is an American who has come over here to help us with our cattle.'

Orley smiled. She had been introduced as a farmhand. At least she knew exactly where she stood with Lady Buchanan. 'Howdy,' she said. She didn't often use the word but thought it might be expected.

'Hello.' Everyone chorused.

'Nice to meet you, Orley.'

A silver-haired lady approached with a tea-tray. She had a soft lyrical voice and was elegantly dressed in tweeds and pearls. 'I am Moira McMorran, the Ministers wife, and I believe you are a real cowgirl from the State of Texas?'

'Yes, ma'am, I am. It sure is a pleasure to meet you.'

Both Lady Buchanan and Orley took a cup of tea from the tray just as another lady approached, whose pursed-tight expression made her appear less than friendly. Lady Buchanan looked flustered.

'So this is the American cowgirl. How very interesting?'

'Do let me introduce Lady Daphne McKenzie.' Lady Buchanan gushed at Orley.

'Ma'am.' Orley said politely.

Lady McKenzie glared through incensed eyes.

Orley's teacup trembled in its saucer. She was rescued by a voice booming from the long table at the top of the hall saying, 'ladies, shall we convene?'

They all took their places on benches that had been placed in militant straight lines facing the long table where a select few were seated.

Orley sat uncomfortably, trying to pay attention to the proposals for the upcoming harvest festival event. It was so hot and so stuffy that after a while, she was struggling to stay awake. An old lady next to her was already asleep, with a full set of false teeth in a lather of spit on her lap.

When they broke for refreshments, Orley dashed to the ladies toilet and locked herself in a cubicle, wishing that she could stay there until it was time to go home. However, when others entered the room, that seemed unlikely.

'Did you see the look on Daphne McKenzie's face when she was introduced to the American girl?' A voice suddenly said. Another woman giggled. 'Yes, I thought for a minute she was going to slap her!'

Both the voices giggled together.

Orley held her breath.

Slap her? Lady McKenzie really had hated her on sight.

'Well, can you really blame her?' The first voice said. 'The church was booked for her daughter's wedding and the dress already bought from Jenners.'

'And now we all know why he jilted her….' said the second.

Orley stayed where she was until it seemed safe to come out. She mulled over the overheard words again and again until her head ached.

Tenaciously, she crept back into the room and tried to avoid eye contact with anyone, especially with Lady McKenzie and whomever the dreaded daughter might be.

She was offered a tiny sandwich with her second cup of tea but found it too hard to swallow. Her throat seemed to have a lump in it the size of a baseball.

On their way home, Orley trotted dutifully behind Lady Buchanan and the torch beam, which attracted all the midges out from the cold damp evening mist.

Chapter Ten

The next day Orley rose especially early. She had promised to help Fergus move sheep across the glen to their winter grazing lands. At the time of offering, she had been most excited about seeing his sheep dogs in action. But now, in the cold morning light and weary from lack of sleep, all she could think about was Innes's ex-fiancée.

Should she ask him outright? Was it even her business?

She walked into the kitchen to find the only sign of Innes was his emptied breakfast bowl on the table. She was relieved.

'Don't worry. We saved you some breakfast.' Fergus jabbed his spoon towards a pot of porridge on the range cooker. 'It's still hot.'

'Where is Innes off to so early?' she asked.

'A meeting. You know, Laird stuff.' Fergus watched as she helped herself from the pot of grey lumpy gruel. 'You okay this morning Orley? Only, you look a little peaky.'

She sat down and sighed. 'Yes. I'm fine.'

Fergus grinned at her. 'Bet you're looking forward to Friday then, eh?'

'Friday?'

'I believe you and Innes are both going off to Edinburgh?'

'Oh Edinburgh. Of course. Yes, we are.'

She smiled and pushed away her bowl.

'Not hungry? Don't worry I'll finish it off.'

'Innes has sourced the new herd at last,' she said. After trawling through a mountain of sale catalogues and spending hours on the phone talking to breeders and suppliers, they planned to attend a cattle auction in the Capital. 'Only,' said Orley wistfully, 'it's gonna be business rather than pleasure.'

Fergus looked at her with surprise.

'I just meant that we won't get to do any sightseeing this time, or visit Edinburgh castle. I do so want to see the castle, you see it's where my dad proposed to my mom.'

'I'm thinking of getting tickets for the Edinburgh Hogmanay street party.' Fergus told her. 'Do you think you and Innes might like to come? I'm planning to ask Davina and she's more likely to say yes if you two come along too.'

'It sounds wonderful. I'll ask Innes. Is Davina your girlfriend then?'

Fergus blushed furiously and stammered. 'Erm, yes, she is.'

'And are you planning to get engaged sometime soon?'

With his face even redder, Fergus shrugged and muttered something vague.

Orley giggled and decided it must be something he was working on. 'Only I did hear that Innes was engaged until recently. I think, her name was Jenna....'

'It's news to me!' he said with an obvious confusion. 'I've never heard of Innes being involved with anyone called Jenna.'

This pleased Orley immensely. This Jenna person must have only been a wannabe and with him being a Laird, she suspected that there might be plenty of them about.

She breathed another great sigh of relief and resolved to be less jealous in future. It was, after all, her least attractive quality.

She spent the morning astride a quad bike, herding the Buchanan flock from one side of the valley to the other and, in the afternoon, she pressed on with her explorations of Glencorrie.

Thanks to an old midge repellent recipe found in a *Scottish Women's Rural Institute handbook,* advising a blend of Eucalyptus oil, talcum powder and starch together with a dram of whisky, she managed to do so in relative safety. While dressed in waterproofs and smelling like a distillery, she headed out into the rank undergrowth and steady afternoon drizzle towards the eastern corner of the house where from her tower room window, she had spotted a disused courtyard.

It had looked to be very overgrown and untidy from her high vantage point but at ground level the shabbiness was shocking. Robust weeds and knee-high thistles grew through the ancient cobbles of what was once a very grand old stable yard. The dilapidated old steadings were in a dangerous state and one building even had a tree crashed right through the middle of it.

Orley could not understand how *not* repairing these buildings could ever be a viable option on a farm.

It was no wonder, she muttered to herself, that Innes was looking into hybrid breeding with Highland Cattle, as they wouldn't need shelter in severe weather. She sighed despondently at the neglect and dearth around her. Yes, Highland's were a good choice in the circumstances.

A lichen covered long neglected pot of dahlia flowers at the side of a slimy old stone water trough provided the only bright spot around. They nodded their golden heads, offering hope that it might be possible to bring horses back to these stables and Glencorrie.

Amongst the derelict debris, she discovered what might have once been an ancient tack room and clearing through overgrown thistles, found that all the original building materials were still on site. Large sandstone blocks had long tumbled from walls and now lay covered with moss but they could be cleaned and reused. Timbers and roof slates would need to be replaced with new here and there but the whole project, although extensive and daunting, would probably cost less than she first thought.

She intended to speak to both Innes and Fergus, to get their approval for her renovation plans, but first she had to get herself cleaned up. Unfortunately, on returning to the house, she discovered there was still no hot water coming from any of the taps.

For the second time in as many days, Davina sat in the hairdresser's chair sipping complimentary whisky and flicking through a well-thumbed copy of *Trash* magazine.

Prince William – who will he marry..? shouted the headline.

'Perhaps we should let the Prince know you're free again,' Shona whispered into her ear.

Davina's body stiffened as Shona ran her fingers expertly through the sleek bob, as intimately as perhaps only a hairdresser could. 'So you don't like this style then, hen?' she said.

'Don't call me hen, Shona. I'm not a damn chicken. The hair's too ditsy. I want it to be wild. I want to be a force to be reckoned with. I want to turn *his* head and break *her* heart. I need to be a fiery red head.'

Shona's inky eyes crinkled. 'But isn't she - a red head?'

'Yes. Which means he likes red, does it not?'

Shona suggested hair extensions too. 'Let me give you lovely waist length red tresses....'

Davina agreed. She wasn't going to give him up without a fight. She wasn't going to be upstaged. She wasn't going to be robbed of a husband by a fiancé-pinching-fancy-pants American girl.

So five hours later, with flame-coloured hair extensions that curled down to the small of her back, Davina was transformed. She was empowered. She looked fabulous.

Orley, exhausted from her endeavours in the old stables and blackened from head to foot with dirt and grime, finally tracked down Innes. She tersely suggested to him that he go and tinker with the huge old range cooker that was supposed to provide a full tank of hot water several times a day.

'I have had no more than a tepid bath or a cold shower since I arrived here and, believe me, I need a hot one now.'

'Don't worry,' he promised. 'I'll get you a bath full of piping hot water in no time at all with lots of bubbles. Here, have a drink while you wait.' He pushed the whisky bottle towards her and opened the cooker door. 'I'm pleased to say that there is definitely some heat in here.'

'Then lets have a nice cup of tea.'

Innes lifted one of the huge round lids off the hotplate and put the kettle on.

Twenty minutes later, when the kettle had still not boiled, Orley was drinking the whisky. She scowled at him in misery and frustration. She knew she was stinking. Her hair, which she had tied back into a long plait to keep it out of the way, was completely filthy. Aside from the simple need to feel clean again, every part of her body was in pain, aching from pulling up weeds and stinging from all the nettles and thistles. 'Oh Innes,' she pleaded when it was apparent that it would be at least another twelve hours before the water was hot enough to empty into a huge cold cast iron bath and then remain warm for more than two seconds. 'I need a hot bath!'

At that moment Lady Buchanan appeared, dressed in a dressing gown and with a towel wrapped turban-style around her head. 'Oh, I didn't expect you two back for a while yet,' she said somewhat nonchalantly. 'Dinner will not be ready until seven.'

'And what are we eating?' Innes asked, as nothing had seemed apparent inside the oven.

'Haggis. Yes. It'll be haggis tonight.'

He looked satisfied until Orley happened to question the ingredients of a haggis.

Lady Buchanan looked flummoxed. 'Erm oats, isn't it Innes? Yes, I think its oats and spices.'

'And meat,' declared Innes despondently.

'Did you enjoy your bath this evening, Lady Buchanan?' Orley asked with a stiff smile.

Lady Buchanan said that she had and that she took her bath as she took her whisky, one each morning and one each evening.

Orley did not say a word but her eyes piercing through Innes like lasers, spoke volumes.

'I have a plan.' Innes said suddenly. 'Get your things together Orley and I'll meet you outside.'

She did as she was told while praying to God that he was not going to suggest that she bathed in the stream as he did, because she suspected that the water that crashed down the hill, was only prevented from actually freezing by its own violent torrent. Why it should be known as 'a burn' was beyond her.

She packed a towel together with a set of clean clothing and in the Landrover they headed out into the pale evening light. After ten minutes or so they drew up in front of a rather grand looking country house. Innes climbed out of the Landrover to be greeted by a very glamorous looking woman. 'Thank you for helping us out,' she heard him say to her. Orley looked on curiously as Innes kissed the woman on the cheek.

Both women then looked at each other. Orley climbed out of the Landrover. She realised that she was shaking.

Was this gorgeous creature Innes's mystery fiancée?

Before he could introduce them the woman spoke.

'Hello. I'm Davina and I believe the old boiler is causing you trouble?'

Davina smiled kindly and Orley smiled back with relief.

This must be Fergus's girlfriend. Thank goodness for that, because Davina had very long shiny red hair, soft features, and an incredibly sleek figure. Orley didn't know if to be impressed or envious. 'Yes. She is. It's nice to meet you. I'm Orley.'

Davina hooked her by the arm and swept her through an old stone porch entrance.

'Come with me, Orley. I have drawn you a nice hot bath....'

Orley immediately noticed the impressive Latin carved deeply into the stonework above them: *Hostem Apud Nos Est.* 'Wow. Another clan axiom - what does it mean?'

Davina considered the words for a moment. 'In translation, it means that the enemy is amongst us....'

Then she laughed lightly, her laughter sounding like a peel of bells as she led the way inside the magnificent house. Davina's skin, Orley noticed, as they moved into a softer light, was flawless. Her eyes, ice-blue and expertly smudged with grey eye-shadow, looked like they belonged to an exquisite cat. This was a woman, Orley decided, who bathed in asses milk and had hand-maidens dry to her off with ostrich feathers.

'I'll let you two ladies do whatever ladies do and come back later.' Innes called out from the bottom of the staircase.

'Don't be silly.' Davina told him. 'No sense in rushing off. Pour yourself a drink while I show Orley up to the bathroom. I'll come down and join you. We can catch up on gossip.'

Orley watched as he walked toward the drawing room.

She on the other hand didn't need any encouragement to do as she was told. The house was beautiful, and, in anticipation of a bathroom fit for a lady, she thanked Davina profusely as they swept up the rest of the staircase together.

'Not at all,' Davina insisted. 'Isn't that exactly what friends are for?'

Orley smiled. *Friends.*

The bathroom was a lavish marble affair. The tub deep and already filled to the top with steaming water. Towels had been laid to one side and were fluffy and aired.

Orley was in heaven. 'Oh thank you!' she gushed for the twentieth time.

'Innes and I will have a little drink downstairs. There's no rush. You just relax and enjoy. The hot water is plentiful and the evening still new.'

Orley undressed and sank beneath the soft fragrant water.

She considered how it was only when deprived of something that it was ever fully appreciated. And tonight she had not only managed to get a nice hot bath but also acquired a nice new friend. It would be so lovely to have another woman around to talk to and luckily for her, Davina, who was Fergus's girlfriend, lived right next door.

Davina paused to smooth her hair and run her hands over her clothes as she hurried downstairs. Innes, darling Innes, who looked gorgeous tonight in black jeans and roll neck sweater was waiting for her in the drawing room. She entered the room and closed the door gently behind her in an attempt to appear relaxed. Inside her heart and soul was in turmoil. One half of her wanted to rush back upstairs to hold the cow-girl beneath the bathwater for a good five minutes. The other half wanted to collect her father's twelve-bore from the gun cabinet and blow Innes's devious brains out or, at the very least, run through his cold heart with the poker.

He was standing by the fireplace. A flickering light cast a warm shadow across his face, outlining the clenched jaw.

'Had a hard day?' she enquired, while pouring whisky from a decanter that cast refractions as sharp as the look she was giving him.

'Aye, one way and another. Thanks for helping out, Davina. I'll get a plumber to sort out our boiler problem first thing in the morning.'

She sauntered towards him. 'It's no trouble at all to run a bath....' *Of course it was trouble. He had tricked her into helping his American slut. She had thought it was he that needed the bath.*

She smiled and recalled a verse from The Scottish Play:
Bear welcome in your eye. Your hand, your tongue; look like the innocent flower, But be the serpent under it....

'Why don't you pop back later yourself, Innes?' she breathed. 'In a couple of hours the water will have reheated.'

Innes stared into his glass. 'No, thank you. I much prefer to shower.'

She ached with longing. With desperation. If only he would look at her. Tell her what he thought of her new look. Her new long red hair. Her tight black cashmere sweater and even tighter Black Isle plaid trousers...?

As if by the sheer force of her will-power, he dragged his eyes upward over her body and stared at her for a moment before adopting a perplexed expression. His voice was deep when he said, 'somehow, you look a little different tonight, Davina.'

'Different?' she queried lightly. 'Oh, you mean my hair. I needed a change. Change is good. Don't you think?'

The black eyes looked at her coldly. 'Yes. Red looks good on you.'

Nervously, she raised her glass and proposed a toast.

Then let's drink to change....'

They drank. She didn't see his frown. His confusion.

She was too busy thinking that 'a little different' was not nearly different enough. That 'good' simply wasn't good enough. She wanted a much bigger reaction than this. She wanted to knock him off his feet. *She wanted him down on one knee....*

Chapter Eleven

Despite having had the lovely warm bath and the delicious hot toddy that followed it, Orley awoke next morning in her tower room feeling incredibly tired.

Not only was she tired but she was shivering. Her joints ached terribly. Her head hurt too. Her nose was streaming and her throat was raw. She sat up and felt dizzy. She had been ill before, of course, she had caught chicken pox as a child which had been pretty uncomfortable and, about five years ago, she had a nasty bout of cryptosporidiosis which she got from infected cows - but even that was nothing compared to this.

She was sweating hot and then freezing cold.

She didn't know whether to put on a jumper and wrap around a duvet or tear off everything and combust. She was burning up. She was chilled to the bone.

Great waves of sickening heat rose up from her stomach and passed through her only to leave her soaked in an icy sweat and hardly able to breathe. She contemplated crawling out of bed but did not have the strength. So she decided to lay there for a while. How long could she be there before she was missed?

Lady Buchanan rarely rose before ten o'clock. Fergus certainly wouldn't look in on her and Innes might have already gone out on business. Heck, she could be there all day.

It upset her that Innes was never around in the mornings, but she would never have the nerve to say so. Just a quick rap on her door and a 'good morning' from him would have been sufficient - but no, she rarely saw him until later in the afternoon. Sometimes not until supper time. He was preoccupied with 'Laird stuff' as both she and Fergus called Innes's all encompassing and relentless estate duties.

She listened. The house was far from silent. It creaked and groaned in the wind. Windows rattled. Outside the ragged black birds screeched as they circled her tower. If she died, which she suspected she might, they would no doubt pick her bones.

Hauling the blankets around her shoulders, Orley climbed out of bed and made her way to the kitchen. It seemed to take forever to get down the narrow spiral stone steps and, when she did finally make it, she felt so weak, that she could hardly lift her arm to fill the kettle.

While she waited for it to boil she shivered and clung to the range cooker for support. She was quite alone in the house or so it seemed. A loneliness descended upon her. In her weak state she felt vulnerable. A wave of homesickness, every bit as strong as the fever that had washed over her earlier, hit. It took massive effort for her not to burst into tears. *I could die here and no one would know except for those in this house that are already dead.*

And there were plenty of those.

Orley could sense the ghosts of the house. In her nightmares, the ancient plaid-clad ancestors bearing swords and murderous expressions, climbed out of their gilt edged frames and came up the steps of the tower get her.

She crawled back to bed clutching her tea and a piece of toast. She tried to relax. Perspiration trickled from every pore. Her brow, her hair, her whole head dripped with sweat. Throwing the blankets aside, in desperation, she leant across the bed to open the casement window, only to find that it wouldn't budge. The old wooden frame had long ceased to yield. She pressed her steaming forehead against the thin pane of cold glass and gasped. She could see a man far below her, in the stream. He was swimming. No, he was bathing, then he rose up, waste deep in the water, washing himself. It was Innes.

She knew she would never be able to attract his attention from so high up in the tower, so once more, she dragged herself out of her bed. Taking the blankets with her, she padded down the stone steps, through the kitchen and out into the yard. An icy blast almost knocked her back. Around the corner towards the east side of the house, directly below the tower window, in the stream, she found him.

'Are you coming in?' he asked, suspecting he might be declined. He smiled and stood waist deep in the water. 'Although I have to warn you, it's a bit fresh this morning.'

Orley shook her head. 'Innes, I really don't feel very well today.'

He took one look at her and he waded from the stream, his face full of concern. He was also oblivious to the fact that he was standing in front of her completely naked. He pushed hair away from her eyes with a cold wet finger and said, 'lets get you back to bed.'

'You should dry off first,' she said to him. Trying not to stare. 'And get dressed.'

She had seen his upper body before on the beach in Baytown but never like this, wholly unclothed. His body was incredible. His skin was paler where his shorts had been and the Texan sun hadn't, which showed off the dark hair around his manhood. He looked like a Greek sculpture.

Innes wrapped a towel around his waist. Quickly, he collected his clothes and guided her back to the house. He pressed a cold hand on her hot brow and told her she had a raging temperature.

'That's hardly surprising after what I've just seen,' she told him with a giggle that came out as a hacking cough.

'I'll 'phone the Doc. You get back to bed,' he insisted.

She did as she was told, struggling to catch her breath.

Davina was in her bedroom listening to the new *Deep Vein Thrombosis* album on her brand new iPod while practicing putting on her eye make up the way Shona had taught her. Dark grey smudges for her eyelids, thick black kohl for her eyeliner, two coats of multi-lash mascara, and a solid slick of vibrant lava-red lipstick that exactly matched the shade of her hair. In the mirror she looked like someone else entirely. All she needed now was the right clothes to complete her new image.

The fashion pages of *Alter-Ego* and *Rich Bitch* lay open on the bed. A pile of clothes, dowdy tweeds, pleated skirts and pie-frill collared sweaters, lay on the floor after being cleared out her wardrobes in anticipation of leather and lace.

She shopped on the internet, embracing the whole cyber couture thing and pounded the Buy It Now buttons on eBay and eRetail.

She was interrupted by her mobile phone bleeping a text message. It was Fergus again. She sighed. He was becoming nothing but a damned nuisance.

'Cairn tonight? Pick u up at 7?' His message said.

The Cairn was an annual traditional harvest celebration held in the village hall. It was not the kind of 'do' that Davina relished. The drink, the food, and the entertainment, was provided traditionally every year by the landowners and always taken advantage of in the extreme by the farm workers, who having worked themselves silly 'gathering in' for the past few weeks of shortening days, let themselves go with wild abandon. Binge drinking on the free whisky and gorging on the 'champers,' (a traditional, if modest, dish of mashed potato) all of which was always thrown up afterwards behind the village hall or in the hedgerows of the road back to Thornfield.

The McKenzie's and The Buchanan's took it in turns each year to provide for the Cairn. This year it was up to the Buchanan's to provide both the goodies which meant that Fergus would man the bar and Innes would play his bagpipes.

Davina wondered if Lady Buchanan would have Orley peeling the potatoes. With a smirk she imagined her sitting in the cellar, like the maiden in the Rumplestilkin story, only instead of a pile of straw and a spinning wheel she would be surrounded by a mountain of Maris Bard and have only a blunt peeler.

'I'm Ok for 7pm.' She texted back to Fergus.

The village hall was a rough and ready venue, so Davina dressed for warmth in tight black jeans and a dark green velvet fitted jacket. As she was looking forward to knocking the breath out of Innes's bagpipes, she made sure her that her new long shining red hair, which she had spent hours straightening and polishing, gave her an entirely decadent look.

The sound of Fergus's rusty old Landy blaring its horn outside, told her that it was time to go. It was bang on seven o'clock and already quite dark.

Davina climbed into the Landrover. Crisp packets crunched under her bottom as she sat in the passenger seat. The butt of a shotgun nudged painfully into her side. She pushed it to one side. 'Oh for goodness sake Fergus, couldn't you have cleared all this before picking me up?'

'I did but I'm still eating those crisps. You've just squashed my dinner.'

She had to slam the door three times to get it to shut. Then, encased in the filthy old vehicle, with Fergus, who she doubted had even taken the time to wash never mind eat, and the stench of damp dogs and dead rabbits, she tried to roll down the window. 'How does this bloody window open,' she yelled.

'Sorry. It doesn't,' came the reluctant reply.

'Why am I not surprised?' hissed Davina under her breath.

'You look lovely tonight,' Fergus said handing her a posy of flowering heather.

She snatched it off him. 'Where's Innes? He's supposed to be playing tonight.'

Fergus turned on the radio and drove off towards the village. 'He's had to call off, I'm afraid. Orley's got the 'flu. The doctors been out and she has to stay in bed.'

'It doesn't mean to say he has to stay in it bloody-well with her!'

'He's trying to get her to eat some supper. She's very weak.'

Davina was seething. She had gone to all this trouble with her makeup and hair only to end up spend the evening with a load of farmer's boys and Fergus.

It began to rain. The windscreen wipers didn't work. She was just about to tell him to turn round and take her home when *The Prom's* on the radio faded to silence and so did the Landy. They rolled to a halt. 'What's wrong? Why have you stopped?'

'I haven't. It has. Must be something wrong. Damned alternator probably.'

Davina screeched. 'What do you mean probably?'

Fergus swore under his breath and turned the ignition key a couple of times. Nothing happened. 'We'll have to push it off the road or it could be a hazard for someone driving back in the dark.' he said.

'Push it - we?'

'Aye.'

'No. I'll sit here while you look at the engine and decide how to fix it.'

'Can't fix it without a new part.' Fergus apologised but it didn't do him any good. Somehow, yet again, he'd managed to blow his chances with Davina.

'It's not a new part you need - it's a new bloody Landrover!' she yelled as the rain pelted down nosily on the metal clad exterior. She knew she had no choice but to get out and push because it was almost pitch black.

There was no moon either. The rain lashed sideways in stair rods.

She climbed out reluctantly.

Eventually they managed to get the Landrover onto the verge and walked back up the lane. Fergus continued to apologise but she refused to forgive him. When they reached Castle McKenzie she stormed inside.

'Goodnight Davina,' Fergus said, to the door slammed in his face.

All Davina could think about was Innes in Orley's bed. Walking back from the abandoned Landrover, all she could think about what she could do to get him out of it. She took a shower, dried her hair, and dressed.

Then she went into the kitchen and searched the larder for a tin of soup. She tipped the contents into a pan and slammed it onto the Aga hotplate and rummaged through the medicine cabinet until she found a liquid laxative, which she added generously to the soup.

'That'll keep her in the bathroom rather than the bedroom', she muttered while pouring the whole lot into a vacuum flask.

She drove over to Glencorrie in the Range Rover. Peering thought the rain dashed windscreen with her wipers on full pelt. Then crunching to a halt outside the porch, she dashed inside, where she found Innes halfway up the staircase.

'Davina!' he said with surprise.

Davina launched into the spiel she had already rehearsed. 'Fergus told me that Orley was sick. I was so sorry to hear it. I made her some soup.' She held out the vacuum flask with a steady hand.

Innes eyes softened towards her. 'That is so decent of you,' he said. 'Orley will be delighted. Would you like to go up and see her?'

'Oh no, best not. Not if she has the 'flu. I don't want to catch it. I must go. It's getting late after all.'

'But surely you must have time for a drink? Fergus told me what happened. How you both had to walk back in the rain. Damned vehicles are always breaking down.'

He took the flask from her and led her through into the sitting room.

Davina looked round. The fire was burning in the grate but the room was empty. Happily, she settled herself on the sofa and watched Innes. She noted how tired he looked of late. She hoped he had been working too hard.

'Fergus went onto the Cairn after all,' he went on to say. 'He took mother in my Landrover. He didn't want to miss it. Besides he'd promised to play the pipes in my place.'

'Oh. I hadn't realised that.'

'He said you were soaked to the skin and covered in mud, so he didn't dare call for you again tonight, Davina.'

She tried to laugh but was feeling so tense that it came out like she was being strangled.

Innes poured two glasses of whisky. 'To your bravery tonight', he toasted.

'Oh, it wasn't bravery,' she objected. 'I'm afraid I was very cross with Fergus. I don't suppose he told you that we pushed and pushed that bloody Landrover, while all the time getting wetter and muddier, before he realised he had left the hand-break on!'

Innes laughed heartily.

Davina finished her drink but he didn't offer a refill. He just stared at her like someone would stare at a jigsaw puzzle with a missing piece.

'Anyway, I must be going. The chicken soup will still be hot in the flask so make sure Orley drinks it all up,' she instructed.

Innes assured her that he would. But he left the flask on the kitchen table as Orley didn't eat chicken. But Davina hadn't known that and, in any case, it wouldn't be wasted, as Fergus would be glad of it when he came home from the Cairn.

It was two days before Davina found out that her little plan to sabotage Orley's well-being hadn't worked. She heard it from her mother first, who had seen Lady Buchanan shopping in Thornfield. She had said a mystery stomach virus had struck Fergus: that he had been sitting on the toilet since the night of the Cairn. 'It could not have been the champers,' Lady Buchanan had told her, 'because I had that and I've been all right. It has to be that same sickness brought to Glencorrie by the American girl, only mutated, and, by rights, we should be informing both the environmental health and the Scottish agricultural department about it....'

Boldly, Davina rang Glencorrie, her brightly polished fingers tapping out the numbers with delight. She must not let her voice betray her. Silently she quoted from *Macbeth*. *'I am one, my liege, whom the vile blows have so incens'd that I am reckless what I do to spite the world...!'*

Lady Buchanan answered the telephone and, after saying how delightful it was to hear from her and how caring a person she was to even bother to call, revealed that Fergus had been prescribed electrolytes by the doctor who was confident that there was nothing too seriously wrong.

'He's lost a little weight though,' she said.

'And Orley, how is she now?'

'Oh recovering, but still confined to bed.'

Davina gritted her teeth. Never mind. Like her noble ancestor Robert the Bruce she would try and try again. She would make more soup and, if necessary, she would spoon feed it to the little cow-bitch herself. It would be mushroom soup this time. The meadow at the back of the stables was full of wild mushrooms at this time of the year. One didn't even have to get up early to pick them: they simply appeared like 'magic'.

This time Davina set off on horseback. The thermos of hot mushroom soup in a saddlebag. It was a glorious Autumnal day. There were more leaves on the ground than on the trees. The few remaining aloft were blood red and trembling in the cold northerly breeze. Davina trotted along quoting *Lady Macbeth*. '*Was the hope drunk wherein you dress yourself? Hath it slept since?*'

There was no one around at Glencorrie when she arrived. The yard deserted. Davina went inside and stood in the hallway shouting for Lady Buchanan and then for Innes. She peered into the kitchen. Unwashed plates and cups lay abandoned on the table with remnants of porridge.

Davina collected up a single bowl and spoon and scraped them before rinsing them quickly in the sink and heading to the tower room. As she climbed the stairs, she could hear Orley coughing.

She stopped and listened for voices, just in case Innes was inside there too. She didn't want to see them in the act together. Imagining it was bad enough. She knocked at the door. 'Orley, it's Davina. Can I come in?'

'Oh yes, Davina. How lovely, please come in.'

Davina peered inside. Orley was sitting up in bed reading a magazine. She looked dreadful. Her eyes were red. Her nose looked swollen and raw from being blown so often on cheap paper tissues.

'I've brought some hot soup for your lunch and a couple of magazines in case you're bored', she said, putting copies of *Trash* and *Celebrity Tosh* down on the duvet next to *Farmer's Weekly* and *Cattle News*.

Orley patted part of the bed beside her. 'Thank you so much. Sit down Davina. I can't tell you how nice it is to see you. I've hardly seen anyone in almost a week. Lady Buchanan won't let me out of the room just in case I'm contagious.'

'You're not contagious are you?' asked Davina, holding her breath.

'No. I'm much better. What's the soup?'

'Mushroom, I made it myself.'

Orley smiled. 'My favourite.'

'Well I can't stop. Must be going. I'll see you when you are back on your feet.' *'Go bid thy mistress when my drink is ready. She strike upon the bell. Get thee to bed....'*

Orley looked disappointed at her leaving so soon. 'Oh, okay, well thanks for the soup. What do you say if we all go out somewhere together as soon as I'm better. What do you think? You and Fergus, me and Innes?'

Davina forced a smile. 'Yes. We should. As soon as you get better.'

The next day Davina heard from her Mother, who had seen Lady Buchanan at Bridge Club, that Orley had taken a turn for the worse.

'I have done the deed – didn't thou not hear a noise?'

With great satisfaction, she rang Glencorrie to express her concern.

Fergus answered. 'She's had a relapse,' he confirmed. 'Innes is still with her. He is very worried because Orley has had terrible hallucinations. She woke everyone last night with her petrified screaming. Although she's calmer now, thank goodness, but our mother insists that Innes wears a full face mask when he goes into the room. The doctor has promised to drop in later....'

Davina put down the telephone and screamed with manic laughter. She threw herself onto her bed, Orley MacKenna, she vowed, would rue the day she came to Scotland and tried to steal Innes from her.

Chapter Twelve

A mere week after her recovery from the 'flu and from being given the all-clear to go out again, Orley was sitting beside Innes in the cab of his brand new Landrover as they made their way across country.

Together they had identified the cattle. They had searched for animals raised on organic grazing that were suited to receive the composite embryos they would ship over from Texas. 'This auction is the place to find the best Highland Cattle,' Innes explained. 'It's held in Edinburgh at the Ingleston showground.'

'When will we get to go and see the castle?' Orley asked with a squeak of excitement as a road sign welcomed them to Edinburgh.

'Not today but I promise you that we'll do the whole tourist thing together very soon.'

She told him it was okay, that today was the day they stocked Buchanan lands and founded their herd.

'Buchanan Beef will be from a traceable source,' he told her. 'People are willing to pay top money for that kind of quality.'

Orley hoped for all their sakes that he was right.

They arrived at the market in plenty of time for the sale and went over to the area where they had arranged to meet a seller from Argyll. Once they found him, Innes introduced himself.

'So you are The Buchanan?' the seller remarked.

He looked Innes over with narrowed eyes and reticence. Orley heard him mutter something about expecting a much older man.

'Aye' replied Innes, 'and this is Orley MacKenna. My cattle manager.'

'Howdy' said Orley, slipping back into her native tongue. She had meant to say 'hello' but the market with its ripe smells and chaotic noise pulled her straight back to her roots.

A broad grin spread across the seller's face.

'American, an' Texan at that!'

'Sure am. Born and raised,' Orley whooped proudly. 'Working for Innes Buchanan an' lookin' to establish a new Highland fold. Might just be lookin' for your help on that score, sir.'

'Och, none of that sir with me, the name's Macleod.'

Innes listened to the banter in amazement.

Apparently, Macleod had connections with a ranch in Texas that Orley knew well and suddenly, they were getting on like a barn on fire. 'I'd like to see your heifers, if that's alright with you, Macleod?' Innes heard her ask.

'I'd be delighted. I can tell you the life story of each and every one of 'um...'

And he did.

Innes stood on the sidelines and watched Orley in action. She certainly knew her stuff.

'I've got another twenty ladies in the next pen. Would ya' like to see 'um too?' Macleod teased.

Orley was behaving like a girl with a litter of kittens rather than a woman amidst twenty nervous cows. Even when Innes lost sight of her, he could still hear her whooping with laughter at Macleod's rude cowboy jokes.

Before the auction had even begun, Orley had managed to strike a firm deal to buy the twenty fifteen-month olds, ten two-year olds, five three-year olds, and a burley yearling bull called Hamish. They had their fold.

All Innes had to do was count out a great wad of money into Macleod's large and very filthy hands.

'I promise you that very soon indeed we will be producing the finest beef in the world.' Orley told Innes in great excitement as they made their way home.

'I think we need to celebrate,' he said. 'It'll be a while before the transporter catches up, so let's stop off somewhere for lunch.'

They pulled off the road and into the car park of the *Tam O'Shanter* pub and Innes, being a gentleman, rushed round to open her side of the Landrover. Then ambling and laughing, with their hands entwined, they walked into the lounge bar to a warm and welcoming waft of beer infused air.

'Mmm, sure smells good in here...' enthused Orley. At the well polished bar they were asked if they would like to see the lunch menu.

'Yes please,' they said together.

'And what would you like to drink?' Innes asked. He opened his wallet and even the low light of the bar she could see it was still stuffed with cash. 'I'd like a glass of Champagne please.'

'We have sparkling wine by the glass, madam.'

'No. We'll take that bottle over there.'

Innes gestured towards a bottle of Moet and Chandon on a high shelf.

The bottle retrieved and a bucket of ice arranged, they were escorted towards a small table next to the glowing log fire.

The barman pulled the chair out for Orley. 'Madam....'

'Whay, thank you, kind sir,' Orley said, in her deepest Texan drawl.

The barman looked totally smitten. Innes could only assume that sophisticated American women with a taste for champagne didn't come into this bar very often.

'You are such a contradiction, Orley,' he told her with a smile, as he poured the champagne and dismissed the competition. 'A cowgirl that doesn't eat cow. A tomboy with long pretty hair. An American that prefers Scotland. I've never known a girl like you before....'

'But you have known girls before, I mean, you have had a girlfriend. A fiancée, even?'

Innes took a sip of the bubbling liquid and cast an eye over the menu.

'One in particular, perhaps?' Orley pressed.

'I'll tell you about mine if you tell me about yours?' Innes said bluntly without meeting her eye.

Orley hastily studied her menu. 'Mmm, I'm famished.'

But the eager barman was never far away. Orley waved him over.

'Excuse me. But do you have a totally free-range, organic, grass and grain raised, perfectly marbled piece of beef on your menu...?'

The barman traced a wavering finger down the listing.

Innes leaned back in his chair, stretched out his legs and looked both amused and perplexed. 'Is the cowgirl about to eat cow?'

The barman looked a tad embarrassed.

'Erm, now let me see, madam....'

Orley shook her head. 'Perhaps I might have a word with the chef...?'

He scuttled off and brought back the chef.

'Madam,' the chef assured her, 'we only serve the highest quality of meat in this establishment. I guarantee, you will find no better in Scotland.'

'But totally free-range, organic, grass and grain raised, perfectly marbled beef, would be better, would it not?'

The chef sighed.

Orley patted the empty stool next to her. 'Have some champagne with us,' she said to him whilst summonsing another flute. 'And I'll let you in on the biggest secret in Scotland.....'

'Our first advance order!' Innes said in astonishment ten minutes later and once the chef had retreated happily back to his kitchen.

'Buchanan Beef has a real ring to it, perhaps you should look into making it the official trade name,' she suggested, before realising she had said 'ring' and 'trade name' in the same sentence. She blushed and hoped Innes wouldn't pick up on it.

They enjoyed their lunch, talked about cows and sheep and horses, and Innes promised to take Orley back to Edinburgh soon to see the castle.

'We'll do the whole tourist thing soon, I promise.'

Then after arriving back at Glencorrie, they drank lots of coffee, and prepared for the imminent arrival of their cattle.

'I have to admit to having a soft spot for Hamish,' Orley confessed.

'Do you always fall for the bull then? Innes asked.

Realising what he had just said, Orley laughed.
'Yeah I do. Apparently I have a real talent for it....'

For Innes, the past few weeks had been challenging. The Estate matters that Orley called his 'Laird stuff' had taken up so much of his time that he felt badly about leaving her alone, especially while she had been ill, but it could not be helped. Winter was fast approaching and so much had to be done before the first snows fell. He had been given no choice but to replace the old Landrovers. Fergus's ancient vehicle had been towed away for scrap-metal as it would have cost far more than it was worth to fix it. His own Landy had been a faithful friend but it would never have passed its next MOT test. So he had negotiated a half-decent part-exchange deal for two new Landrovers.

Then he had bought a new computer with internet access, dragging Glencorrie into the twenty first century, although, he was still unable and unwilling to tell his mother the truth, about how and why he had mortgaged Glencorrie.

He had casually mentioned money coming in from cattle grants and farming subsidies to cover his spending, although she might have guessed that the amounts received wouldn't have stretched to their new vehicles, the new computer, and the new Aga cooker. Still, they needed these things and thankfully the budget had just allowed for them.

Then the roof of Gillie Cottage collapsed.

Innes received a call on his mobile phone about eight thirty that morning. He rushed over to the cottage to find the roof, together with the whole chimney stack, inside the cottage. Thankfully the occupants had all got out unhurt.

'Aye, we're lucky to be alive, ken,' the Gillie told Innes, whilst sucking air through his teeth.

'Aye, ken,' the Gillie's wife explained. 'We were all aboot early 'an the weans where outside doing their chores a'fore school, feedin' chucks and chopping the logs, when the whole thing came doon.'

Innes looked over the scene, to see that the only spot not piled with rubble and slates was a small area in front of the range cooker where Mrs Gillie must have been standing, stirring the porridge. He felt truly terrible while she gathered up her children and kissed each grubby little head in front of him. 'Well, thankfully no one was hurt,' he said, whilst contemplating the horror of being responsible for so many deaths. 'I'll have the cottage surveyed and the repairs made straight away.'

'Aye. An' we'll stay at my sisters hoose 'till then, ken. An' we'll all be hopin' to be back home in time for Christmas, mind. I'll fair break the wean's hearts if Santa canny cum doon our own lum.'

Innes contacted the Estate's underwriters immediately and an inspector was despatched. Unfortunately, he pointed the finger of blame upon the recent high winds and the fact that the ancient cottage was riddled with woodworm.

'I'm afraid we cannot payout on your claim, Laird Buchanan. Property neglect. It quashes our liability.'

'Quashes!' Innes exclaimed. 'We have maintained our policies with your company for decades and now you tell me you cannot payout. We'll see about that!'

Innes went to the very top. He threatened to do things he would never have done in a million years, like go to the national press, but still it didn't cut much ice. His approach however, did prompt a hurried damage limitation review of all the Estate properties.

As a result, sixteen cottages were identified as having similar problems to Gillie Cottage. The fact that the first incident could have resulted in a terrible tragedy made the repairs so pressing that all the cottages had to be immediately vacated.

Some families had nowhere else to go and Innes had no choice but to temporarily re-house them in a hotel in Thornfield, all expenses met, while renovations were made.

Only then, was it agreed with the insurance company that future Estate claims and liabilities would be covered.

Innes suddenly realised, to his despair, that the hole in the Buchanan bank balance had become a lot bigger than the one in the roof of Gillie Cottage.

The past few weeks had also been extremely hard work for Orley, who was busy with the cattle that had arrived in a stressed condition from being transported all the way across country. The bull seemed the most upset and Orley was worried that he might stop eating and fall ill.

'They didn't like being penned so close together in the transporter,' she told Innes. 'It made them nervous.'

Still concerned about Hamish, she insisted they got the vet out. 'We don't want to risk colic'.

But the panic was over when it turned out that the majestic brute just needed a bit of tender loving care. The vet was very complimentary about him and told Orley that they should consider showing him. 'I've seen a lesser bull win at the Royal Show,' he said running his hand along Hamish's firm back.

'Really?' Orley hadn't realized he was a potential champion.

'Yes. See the way the horns come out strong and level from his head, slightly inclining forwards and slightly rising towards the points?'

'Yes, I certainly do.'

'Well, that's good. It means he has a strong back, see...'.

'This is fascinating. The Royal Show you say?'

'Aye. He's bound to win. I'd put money on it.'

When Innes appeared, Orley went into great detail on how Hamish was going to be famous and win them lots of prizes. 'If Hamish wins the Royal Show, he will be on the cover of every farming magazine in the country.'

Innes looked unimpressed. 'I try to avoid publicity,' he told her.

'It would be free advertising!' Orley spelled out.

'Oh. I see. How is he. It wasn't colic was it?'

'No, but I'm really glad I called the vet out.'

Innes frowned. 'Let's hope he doesn't add the cost of his advice to the bill.'

Orley continued to brush the bull's long flowing red hair and polish the sweeping horns. While she did so, she chatted to him and called him 'darling'.

As they had no budget for advertising, Innes had to agree that parading Hamish around the Agricultural Shows would be a good way to promote their business.

'Okay,' he said. 'We'll try a couple of small events first. The Nithshire Show is always held on the last Saturday in September. I'll look into it.'

'Help!' Orley yelled, 'he's gone asleep. Bless him.'

Innes could not believe his eyes. Whilst being groomed Hamish burley bull had actually fallen asleep, with his huge head resting on Orley's shoulder.

Chapter Thirteen

When she was not attending to the cattle, Orley was working very hard at restoring the old stable yard. Tall weeds and prickly thistles had been pulled from the cobbles. Fergus had been helping and between them they had managed to clear away all of the debris and sort building materials into neat piles. It had been backbreaking work. When Innes returned from his estate meeting, she had expected him to be impressed with all they had done but for some reason, he appeared less than enthusiastic about their project.

'We have almost finished restoring this yard to its former glory. Do you think you might buy us some horses to put in it?' Orley had asked.

Innes looked rueful.

She had wanted to throw down her shovel in frustration.

'I know you want horses here Orley, but there is a reason we don't keep them at Glencorrie,' he said.

She looked from Innes to Fergus and wondered why this valid reason hadn't been mentioned before. Innes then explained how a long time ago all of the horses at Glencorrie had been lost to the 'Scottish Disease'.

Fergus apologised. He knew how keen Orley was to have horses in these old stables and how much she missed riding 'the great clumsy things'.

'I had forgotten all about it,' he said, 'but Innes is right. I was only very young - but I do remember now. One after the other they all died.'

Orley was horrified. *A Scottish Disease? Surely there could be no such a thing?*

Innes looked uncomfortable. 'All I can say is that horses do not do at Glencorrie.'

Do not do....? As an experienced horsewoman, Orley refused to believe in such an outrageous and location specific phenomenon and was determined to prove them wrong. She would find a way to bring back the horses.

She went onto the new computer that Innes had bought so they could all access the Internet, the World Wide Web, and the e-mail from home. It was a wonderful resource, especially appreciated by Orley, who until it was installed, had been unable to contact her family in Texas as often as she would have liked.

She searched on line for a disease that didn't exist in America yet was prevalent in Scotland. She expected to find nothing but, to her dismay, she found it all to be true. There was indeed a disease of which there was no explanation or cure, that killed hundreds of horses every year and mainly in Scotland, hence the name *Scottish Disease*.

This cast a mood of despair over Orley and dowsed all her enthusiasm to continue with the stable renovations.

Later that afternoon, feeling entirely miserable, she drove into Thornfield to collect the supplies that were needed. She was grateful to get away as a walk over the fields wasn't going far enough.

Fergus asked her to collect drugs for a sick ewe. Innes asked her to get fuel for the quad bikes. Lady Buchanan pressed a 'wee' shopping list into her hand that focused entirely on the off-licence. It seemed to Orley that once Lady Buchanan had got a sniff of a bit of money in the bank, she had abandoned her supermarket special offer priced whisky in favour of her favoured single malt. She wished she was feeling half as generous with the grocery provisions, which were only ever ordered in once a week and then kept in a fridge so old that it wouldn't keep fresh for more than two days.

For the errands, the Buchanan's had credit accounts all over the village. All the locals did. It was a system, Innes explained, that encouraged local loyalty and kept money in the village rather than the outlying towns. Orley opened an account for herself at the Chocolate Box. She didn't normally have a sweet tooth but her meals at Glencorrie were so very different to those she was used to in Texas. Here she found she was craving energy inducing sugars and, having discovered chocolate and candy bars, every excuse for going into town became her opportunity to buy some.

On her way back to Glencorrie, she pulled over onto a grass verge to enjoyed the view of the hills whilst also enjoying a couple of bars of chocolate. The packs that she hid in her pockets were to be saved for moments of extreme hunger, which usually happened mid-morning and mid-afternoon. She told herself that she was doing a manual job in a cold climate and therefore she needed the energy.

Later that afternoon however, guilt ridden and also feeling a little sick, she left the quad bike in its shed and walked across the fields to check on the fold. The exercise would help to burn off those extra bars.

She walked briskly uphill until she got out of breath and then, at the place she called Hilltop, she rested. Today she could see the fold. Sometimes they grazed much further afield. She did a quick headcount, observing them for a while to ensure they were well.

She was just about to make her way back downhill again when she spotted a horse and rider in the distance. They were exercising in a white railed paddock on neighbouring lands. The land adjacent to Buchanan land belonged to Davina's family and it seemed, to Orley's excitement, that Davina kept horses.

By the time she had reached the white railed paddock she was out of breath again and both the horse and rider had disappeared. Determined to get to the bottom of the situation concerning the Scottish Disease, she walked around the house, following neat gravel pathways until she found the entrance. Orley pulled on the doorbell handle and waited.

A housekeeper came to the door and invited her in.

Orley looked round. The house was just as beautiful as she had remembered it from her bath-night visit. It was an ancient place, just like Glencorrie, but unlike Glencorrie the rooms were furnished with very expensive carpets and elegant furniture.

On a highly polished table in the centre of the hall was a huge amount of lilies in full flower. Their pungent aroma filled the room. Orley was admiring them when she heard a shrill voice.

'I just adore lilies, don't you?'

Orley looked up to see Davina wearing stylish British riding clothes descending the staircase. 'I'm sorry to call on you uninvited,' she gushed.

'No invitation needed for friends or neighbours.' Davina declared with a wave of an elegant hand.

Orley, flattered at being considered a friend said, 'I would like to ask your advice on something, Davina, if I may?'

'I do hope that you and Innes are not having arguments already.'

Orley was surprised at this comment. Why would they argue? Was Innes more difficult than she knew? Did Davina know something about him that perhaps she didn't?

'Come through into the drawing room. We'll have a drink.'

Orley followed her into an incredibly beautiful room where Davina poured large measures of whisky into sparkling glass tumblers. Edinburgh crystal glass tumblers, to be precise. Orley recognised the cut. Her father and stepmom had received a set as wedding presents. She accepted the drink and took a sip. The whisky slipped warmly down her throat.

'So what sort of advice do you need? Romantic or practical?' Davina asked.

'I wanted to ask if you have ever lost horses to home-sickness?' said Orley, still captivated by the pattern of the cut glass.

'Home sickness..?'

'I'm sorry. Gosh, I meant to say grass-sickness.'

'Heavens no. Why would you ask?'

'Because I am told that horses don't do at Glencorrie, since one winter about twenty years ago when they all died.'

'They call it the Scottish Disease, you know,' warned Davina.

Orley nodded. 'I know. I have asked Innes to restock the stables at Glencorrie and he tells me that it would be unwise to do so.'

'So you and Innes *have* been arguing.'

'No. Not at all. It's just that I cannot understand why you can keep horses here and yet, in adjoining fields, we cannot...'

Davina smiled but did not elucidate. 'You seem angry Orley. Would you like another drink?'

'I'm not angry, and no, I won't have another as it is only three-thirty in the afternoon. I can hardly believe how much you people drink!'

Davina raised her pencil thin eyebrows and tentatively replaced the crystal stopper.

'Oh I'm sorry Davina. I didn't mean to be so rude. I'm upset. I love horses and horse riding and, well, I had thought there would be horses at Glencorrie.'

Davina's perfectly made up eyes narrowed. She spoke sympathetically.

'So you are disappointed, and Scotland is not all you hoped, I knew it. I think we all did. It's not the end of the world for you to admit that you and Innes have nothing in common. Actually, he hates horses.'

'Innes doesn't hate horses!' Orley protested. 'He told me that he learned to ride in Texas and he loved being on horseback. I know Fergus doesn't like to ride horses but that's only because he is afraid of them.'

'You could just go home again, you know, if you were too unhappy here....'

There was a moments silence and then Orley smiled at Davina. 'You're right, of course.'

Davina smiled back. 'Yes. I know. It's been lovely having you around Orley. And I for one will miss you when you are gone.'

'Thank you. You are such a good friend. It would be so easy to quit, wouldn't it, - to get on the next flight out of here and say goodbye to Innes and all of his problems. Well, you know, I have never been one of life's quitters and I want to say thank you for reminding me of that, Davina. And for making me realise how selfish I have been. Innes is feeling financial embarrassed at the moment and I need to be supportive of him - not demanding.'

Orley walked down the lane back to Glencorrie with her thoughts on Innes and the problems he was having with money. Having borrowed heavily from the bank, he still had to find mortgage repayments every single month until they made a clear profit. He must be disappointed in her, she realised to her shame, because she hadn't exactly turned out to be the cattle manager or the support he had hoped. She had actually been a drain on his resources by being ill and complaining about the house being cold, the food being strange, the air being damp. What must he think of her? She had to buck up. There was no other way.

It started to rain. It had looked fine earlier and she had not taken a coat. Take your coat, Innes had advised, the forecast is for rain. He said it everyday and everyday he had been right. Darned rain. Scotland must be the wettest place on earth. And there she was again - complaining about stuff that she nor Innes could do anything about.

Arriving back at Glencorrie, she went straight up to her room and stripped off her wet clothes. She was shivering violently. An icy blast blew from between gaps in the sash windows onto her goose-pimpled skin as she scrambled frantically with a fleecy pair of track bottoms and a roll neck sweatshirt. Catching a glimpse of her reflection in the dressing table mirror caused her to recoil. She moved in for a more detailed personal appraisal and her heart sank when she saw that her tanned skin had turned pale yellow and her face was strangely bloated. Her lips were cracked and blue. Her eyes were bloodshot from walking in the cold wind and her hair was the most disturbing sight of all. Gone were the golden Pre-Raphaelite tresses that hung in coils almost to her waist. It hung now in drab rats tails. The climate in Scotland had turned her curls to an ugly frizz.

She searched through her toiletry bag for the bottle of intensive hair care that she had previously used to prevent sun damage. She rubbed it through her hair before tying it back into a single plait. It was all she could do for now. Davina's hair, she remembered, had looked fabulous. Orley looked in the mirror again and sighed. *You'll have to do something - and soon - or Innes might change his mind about you and then you'll be on the next flight out of here....*

It cheered Orley up immensely, when one of the first e-mails to come through on the shiny new computer was for her. She had emailed out to her father and Martha, who had obviously passed on the email address of Orley's new electronic mail status, to Tanya.

'Oh wow, it's for me, and it's from Tanya!'

'Tanya? Do we know a Tanya?' Lady Buchanan muttered as she hovered over this machine that offered a window to the world.

'My sister,' said Orley proudly.

She didn't like to say half-sister because it didn't sound proper and, besides, she had always wanted a sister, and Tanya wasn't half a person, was she?

Now they were in communication with each other they would be like real sisters. Orley felt better. Less homesick. All of a sudden the world felt like a smaller place. She settled down to read Tanya's email.

I have a new job in Paris. I'm a nanny for two gorgeous children and live in an apartment close to the centre of Paris. I also do a bit of film work. Did you spot me in the Da Vinci Code? Hoping to pop over and see you if I get time off over Christmas - but cannot promise at this stage. Do email a reply soon and tell me how you are and what you are up to in Scotland. Mom sent me photos of the wedding. You are so very pretty. Lots of love from your new sister, Tanya.

Orley giggled with delight. The way Tanya had signed off made her think they both felt the same about each other, even though they had never met. She replied straight away. Funny things emails. Informal things. So unlike letters.

She typed. *Wonderful and exciting to hear from you. I am a cattle manager here on a Scottish estate and we are establishing a new herd of composite Highland cattle. Scotland is very beautiful and very different to Texas. When will you know if you can visit me? Love from your very excited sister, Orley XXX*

Chapter Fourteen

Hamish the bull was standing in blissful repose with his eyes half closed, dozing in the morning sunshine, as Orley rubbed off the mud from his horns with a big soapy sponge in preparation for his first agricultural show. It was the last Saturday of September but remarkably, after the torrential rain and howling gales of late, the summer seemed determined to return for one last curtain call.

It couldn't have been a better day for the Nithshire Show. The wind was light and from the south. Swallows gathered and chattered on the telephone cables in preparation for their long flight south. Butterflies warmed their wings on the walls of the big house and bees worked busily on the last of the buddleia in the borders. Orley hummed along as she worked on Hamish, whom she decided, was without doubt, going to win The Best Of Show.

It was mid morning when Innes swept into the yard. He looked quite the part of a Laird today in a tweed jacket and fawn moleskin trousers. He strolled towards her. 'I do love the wet look,' he declared rather wickedly.

Orley's hair had escaped from its plait and was clinging in wet strands over her jean–clad hips. 'It'll soon dry in this sunshine,' she told him while taking a brush to the bull's long wet red coat and kissing him affectionately on the end of his nose. 'You can see that he's starting to fill out and that means he's happy here.'

Innes observed that Orley's body was also much curvier of late.

She turned to see he was looking at her in *that* way again.

She blushed when she realised that his gaze had dropped to her soaking wet t-shirt. She said something about bulls having commendable manners. 'This one for instance, listens when I talk to him and doesn't make rude or suggestive comments.'

'Doesn't mean he's not thinking them,' Innes added jauntily.

Orley threw the sponge. It landed with a wet splat, soaking his chest.

'Now you're in trouble!' he yelled, removing his jacket and lifting the shirt over his head.

She heard herself groan. There wasn't an ounce of excess flesh beneath his well-cut clothes. His body was hard, still tanned from southern Texas sunshine, and rippling with defined muscle. Dark hairs in the middle of his chest trailed downward, narrowing to the line past his navel, and disappearing into his trousers. Orley remembered the sight of him walking out of the burn totally naked on the morning she had became ill with the 'flu.

If he only knew what he did to her.

From the challenge in his eyes she could see he was planning some sort of revenge attack and fearing it might involve cold water and the hose pipe, she fled, squealing loudly as she ran towards the meadow.

'You can run, Orley,' he shouted after her, 'but ya' canny hide!'

She didn't dare look back but she knew he was following. So she ran as fast as she could, which to her disappointment was not as fast as she would have liked, because the grass was long and tough. The sprawling clumps of heather were woody, the stems tangled and impenetrable, the going steep and the muscles in her legs were burning. She was also terribly out of breath.

How had she ever 'gotten this unfit?

She fell down into a soft patch of grass, giggling to herself with excitement while staring upward into the clear blue sky and allowing her breathing to slow. Was that her heart thundering or Innes coming up the hill?

She trembled with anticipation. Above her a large brown buzzard hovered on the high thermals. She watched and felt a certain affinity with the bird. Was it faith or hope that kept him aloft? She watched the bird soar until Innes cast a shadow over her. He stood, breathing heavily, with his hands on his narrow hips. His body, still stripped to the waist, shimming like a golden Texan plain.

He looked down at her just as the bird had done and for a second, the doubts crept in.

Might she only be potential prey?

'You got me…' she said softly from her grass bed.

He sank to his knees.

The buzzard cried from high above.

Orley cried from within.

Innes lay down and stretched out beside her. He supported himself on one elbow and studied her lazily.

He smiled and spoke her name softly.

She could smell the lemon scent of his cologne rising off his body. He kept his eyes fixed on hers. His eyes were the blackest she had ever seen them. She looked to his lips and instinctively licked her own. He was going to kiss her.

She closed her eyes as his fingertips reached out to touch her face. If she opened her eyes, would he see the love she had inside of her for him? If eyes were after windows to the soul would they convey all she found impossible to say?

His fingertips trailed downwards across her neck.

He said her name again, whispered this time, and he asked if he could make love to her.

Why did this surprise her? He was a gentleman after all.

She ached to be with him. For weeks now, the longing for physical contact with him had been agony. In the house it was almost impossible to be alone together and she felt continually uneasy there because his mother was everywhere and nowhere. Innes was often out on estate business anyway and when he was around the telephone always rang for him at opportune moments.

Did she say yes – or only think it?

She arched her back as he tugged her shirt over her head. He pulled loose the belt buckle on her jeans and removed them in one swift movement. In that moment they looked into each others eyes and their bodies crashed together. He kissed her the way she had dreamt of night after night. She kissed him back until they had to break off only to beg each other to continue.

'Relax,' he breathed, his voice heavy with longing, his hands reaching out to touch every part of her body, leaving a trail of ignited passion. 'There is no need for us to rush. There is no one around to spoil this....'

Orley opened her eyes. It was true. Even the buzzard had left them alone and the only sound she could hear was the wind gently whistling through the heather and the bracken.

Afterwards they didn't speak. They just grinned at each other coyly while he buckled up the belt on his trousers and she quickly dressed. Walking back down the hill holding hands, Orley said, 'that was even better than I imagined.'

He laughed and said something that made her heart soar.

He said, 'thank goodness this love of ours isn't just in my imagination. I was starting to wonder....'

Her breath caught in her throat. *This love of ours.*

'I believe love should always come from the heart and not the imagination....' she assured him.

The air between them sparked all afternoon. Long lustful gazes and ridiculously wide grins were exchanged all the way to the Nithshire Showground. They held hands like their lives depended on it. Orley's fingers intertwined through his even when he had to steer the Landrover and she had to pitch in with the gear change.

Orley was deliriously happy. The boundaries of their relationship had been crossed and there was no going back.

Her fears about his complicated lifestyle, his real motives for bringing her to Scotland, and the mystery behind his cancelled engagement had all been unfounded. They didn't matter anymore. Innes loved her. He wanted her in Scotland for all the reasons she wanted to be there. For him. She was happier than she ever thought anyone had a right to be.

Orley finished preparing for Hamish's showing class once they arrived at the show ground because Innes had agreed to judge several early afternoon classes and they were already late. As he hurried off towards the small pet marquee, she couldn't take her eyes of him. Once he reached the other side of the paddock, he turned round to wave. She waved back and blew a kiss. It was as if they were sending smoke signals to each other.

She sang heartily as she gave Hamish his final polish and then the tannnoy crackled to life to announce the Best

Highland Bull class. Orley gave Hamish's halter rope a gentle tug. Fergus spotted them and came over to offer his support. 'They are calling your class,' he told her. 'Good luck!'

Hamish held up his polished horns and his pink nose sniffed the air. He gently butted Orley to let her know he was ready and then moved off slowly, past all the hot dog stands and the family picnics that he could smell but not see because Orley had brushed his heavy forelock of hair right over his eyes. He bellowed in a deep baritone and everyone turned to watch him go by as he ambled along with his long coat shimmering like burnished gold in the late afternoon sunshine.

'Yes Hamish.' Orley assured him. 'We're off to collect your first prize.'

Once in the white fenced ring and surrounded by the flapping flags of St Andrew, it seemed quite apparent to Orley that none of the other bulls had half the presence of Hamish the Magnificent. He must have sensed it too because he was on his very best behaviour.

They had to walk in a circle around the steward who in a suit and a bowler hat looked more like a banker than a countryman. He signalling for all the competitors to form a line and then he examined each animal in turn. He had a small notepad and pencil in his hand and he looked incredibly serious as he scribbled onto it.

He asked everyone questions on blood-line, history and health, and Orley rehearsed in her head what she would say in reply as they waited.

'What age is this bull?' The steward asked her when it was eventually their turn. 'He looks terribly young for this class. She was about to answer when all his other question were fired. 'Where was he bred? What are your plans for him? Does he have a valid British passport?'

Orley thought this man, Geoffrey Sinclair, as it said on his badge, was the rudest man she had ever met.

'He is one year old and when he reaches his peak he will be used to sire the new Buchanan fold of composite cattle.' Orley declared.

Geoffrey Sinclair, looked at over his spectacle frames and shook his head. 'I doubt that this particular animal has the stamina and I do believe that inter-breeding will weaken vigour and encourage all sorts of diseases back into the industry. It shouldn't be allowed.'

Orley was furious. This man was incompetent. None of his statements were founded. She was just about to give him a piece of her mind – and tell him how ignorant and bigoted he was – when she had a change of heart because that is what the old Orley would have done. She was the new Orley and as such she would be calm tempered and easy going. She could smile and take criticism however unfounded because everyone was entitled to their opinion, right?

Hamish was eventually given fourth position out of four entrants and a rosette with *Reserve* printed on it.

Orley thanked the steward with a smile even though her teeth were gritted which made it very hard to do.

She pinned the ribbon onto Hamish's halter and smiled nicely again for the press photograph. Then she led him out of the ring and bought two ice creams, one for her and one for Hamish.

She looked about for Innes while Hamish raked the ground and scoffed his ice cream. He was considerably less fazed by his lack of success than Orley was. Poor Hamish, she thought, hadn't even been allowed grass that morning in case it had stained his teeth green and it had all been for nothing. At least it was easy to tempt him back into his trailer with a handful of the green stuff.

Fergus, who had been asked to judge the Oddest-Shaped Vegetable competition, was keenly making his escape following riotous applause.

'Should have been called the rudest-shaped vegetable competition really,' he told Orley, as he helped shove Hamish's overly-large posterior into the trailer. 'The winner was a phallic parsnip - the biggest I've ever seen!'

He stopped laughing when Orley told him what had happened with Hamish and how prejudiced the Steward had been against Buchanan Beef but he didn't offer any sympathy, as he was far more interested in what was going on in the show jumping ring.

'I thought you didn't like horses much?' Orley said to him.

'Next to jump is Davina McKenzie riding Camilla,' the loudspeaker announced.

Orley laughed. Although Fergus didn't like horses very much - he certainly liked Davina - especially in jodhpurs.

'Go Davina!' he shouted as the bell rang and Davina and her horse entered the ring at a canter.

'Oh, how wonderful she looks. I do envy her with her horses.' Orley said to Fergus.

Davina made every jump look so easy.

'She is a super rider. She is sure to win,' enthused Fergus.

A moment later they were both groaning, as the top rail of the last jump clattered to the ground.

Davina must have been galloping past the umpires microphone when she swore because her expletive was heard loud and clear echoing across the paddock.

'Oops,' said Fergus. 'I should have kept my big mouth shut.'

'So should Davina,' Orley said, noting the outrage of fellow bystanders.

'Terrible language and she calls herself a lady,' said one.

'Aye. Lady Muck,' said another.

Fergus and Orley dashed over to the collecting ring only to be almost trampled to death as Davina and her horse, both with eyes rolling and teeth barred, thundered past to the loud thwack of the whip.

'She's beating up her horse!' Orley gasped in astonishment.

'Horse must deserve it,' Fergus replied. 'Camilla may have bolted. She's famous for it. She was blacklisted by the hunt last season for overtaking the Master of Foxhounds.'

Davina had dismounted by the time they reached her.

Orley patted the mare. A huge fresh welt was clearly evident on her flanks. Fergus kept his distance from what he considered to be a very dangerous brute. 'Well done, you were in second place. You should be in there collecting your ribbon with the others!' he told her.

'I only collect firsts.' Davina replied dismissively.

Camilla's sides were heaving like a set of giant bellows.

'It looked like a very difficult course.' Orley said, offering commiserated to Camilla rather than to Davina.

'Look!' Fergus said pointing to the placings board. 'And you had the best time.'

Davina gave Camilla another slap with her whip. 'We should have won. She's such a bitch and she should go for dog meat.'

Orley was horrified. 'Don't you think you're being a little hard on the horse? What do you think, Fergus?'

Fergus was too busy watching Davina tap her whip menacingly against her leather boot to care about poor Camilla. Orley noted the double-bit bridle and the blood pouring from the horse's tongue. She felt an overwhelming urge to punch Davina in the mouth so she might know just how it felt, but instead, she took a deep breath and told herself to walk away.

This is none of my business, she told herself.

'Well, if you'll both excuse me, I must go and find Innes,' she said instead.

'I think Orley really misses riding horses,' Fergus confided to Davina as he accompanied her back to her horsebox. A vehicle that the entire British Equestrian Olympic team would have been proud of. 'You see, she used to be a proper cowgirl in Texas.

'I think it's Texas she misses most.' Davina replied. 'She came to see me the other day and said she was finding life here very difficult. I think she might pack up and go home soon.'

'I can't see that happening,' Fergus refuted. 'Innes is mad about her.'

Davina's face turned a shade of pale green.

'Well I can't see him remaining so,' she said waspishly, 'if Orley continues to pile on the weight. I mean, the girl was slim when she arrived and look at her now....'

Fergus had also noticed that Orley had put on rather a lot of weight recently. He attributed this to all the empty chocolate wrappers he had found in the old Landrover but then – suddenly - he had a thought.

'I shouldn't really tell you this,' he said to Davina while trembling at this risky new tactic. 'But....'

Davina practically gave herself whiplash. 'What? What shouldn't you tell me?'

Now he had her full attention and with it an opportunity to turn her head and her heart away from Innes for good.

'Oh, I really shouldn't say...' he continued.

'Come on Fergus. Say?'

'It's just that I don't actually think Innes knows yet....'

Davina grabbed Fergus by the lapels as if she might strangle him. 'You have to tell me,' she snarled.

She was breathing heavily and her top lip was beaded with sweat. Fergus was giddy with excitement. The thrill of horse sweat, whisky, French perfume, and from the riding whip pressing against his leg.

'As long as you absolutely promise not to say a word,' he whispered.

'You have my word. Now come on spill the damned beans, Fergus!'

'Orley is pregnant.'

Davina released her grip on Fergus and tried to walk away. She only managed a few steps when her legs buckled and Fergus caught her.

They sat together on the ramp of the horsebox and he offered his hip flask. 'Here, have some of this.'

'Are you sure?'

'Yes. It's whisky.'

'I mean are you absolutely sure she's pregnant?'

'Oh yes. Mood swings, one minute she's angry and the next she's as sweet as apple pie. Morning sickness, chucking up her breakfast, and everything.'

'Oh my God! What am I going to do now?'

Orley entered the Pet's Corner tent to find Innes pining a third place rosette on a mouse's cage. She watched in amusement as he tried to decide between two identical rabbits for second and first place.

'What does your rabbit like to eat best?' he asked one of the young owners: a little girl with a cute smile and a dimple.

'Lettuce' the little girl answered clearly. 'Collected from our own vegetable garden. It's organic lettuce too.'

Everyone clapped. Indicating that this surely merited the red ribbon.

'And what does your bunny like to eat, Joe?' Innes asked the little boy, who was wrestling with his rabbit and clearly winning the fight.

'Mostly my mum's knickers,' came the cheeky reply, 'but sometimes it's my socks.'

'Very unusual. I think we have a winner here!'

Innes pinned the red rosette onto Joe's shirt and awarded him a gift voucher. There were gasps of amazement and cries of outrage. Then having spotted Orley in the crowd he made good his getaway.

'That wasn't fair!' Orley complained as they left the tent together. 'That boy was hurting that rabbit and didn't deserve to win. What were you thinking?'

'Joe is the son of one of our shepherds. The poor kid doesn't have much. So, in my opinion, he deserved to win.'

'And what about that poor little girl who actually loved her rabbit and fed it on organic lettuce?'

'Her rabbit won't end up in the family pie. So she can always win next year. How did Hamish get on?'

'The judging was prejudiced,' she told him.

They held hands all the way back to Glencorrie.

Chapter Fifteen

Davina was seething with both anger and fear.

Anger, because Innes had been unfaithful to her by having an affair, and fearful because if Fergus was right and Innes didn't know she was pregnant, once he found out, he would no doubt offer to marry the American slut.

It was the worst day of her life.

It had been agony to see them both climbing into Innes new Landrover and driving away from the show together.

Davina felt cheated. Robbed of her fiancé and deprived of her future. The whole thing was such a shock and had her thinking murderous thoughts and with them, more verses from Lady Macbeth:

What beast was't then, That made you break this enterprise to me?

All her recent and best efforts had come to nothing. She had re-invented herself. She had bought a new and exciting wardrobe. She had the long red hair and the sexy new look that he wanted. She had walked round looking fabulous - and yet he had chosen to ignore her. Perhaps beauty was only skin deep? Perhaps it was time to start digging deeper? Six feet deeper. Davina allowed a smile to play on her pursed lips.

Ay, a bold one, that dare look on that which might appal the devil.

A terrible accident. Like falling from a horse at high speed and hitting her head on a sharp rock could be arranged, for example. One that might just bring about the desired result and then Innes would be free again. The past undone. No one would blame her. No one would know.

False face must hide what false heart doth know.

There was no room for error. To cause the cow-bitch's death or at the very least a miscarriage that warranted a total hysterectomy followed by Innes switching off the life-support system, meant planning everything down to the smallest detail.

So, the next morning, for the purpose of research, Davina went riding with her dear friend and fellow horse-riding enthusiast, Kirsty Wallace.

Kirsty also happened to be this year's Cornet's lass in the annual Riding of the Marches ceremony.

'To be Cornet's lass is an honour that I have dreamed of all my life,' Kirsty told Davina, as they trotted along the hillside together. 'It has meant giving up a lot and even postponing my marriage to remain eligible but it has all been worth it....'

'Such dedication.' Davina said admiringly, as she checked her watch. *What a shame you'll miss it....*

To Davina's surprise, it took a full hour of fast riding before the girth strap of Kirsty's saddle finally gave way.

But when it did it - it was a most effective and satisfying dispatch. Poor Kirsty was tipped off sideways as the saddle came away. She screamed horribly as she hit the ground, with her feet still in the stirrups, and her legs strangely twisted.

Later the same day, Davina paid a visit to Glencorrie.

'I've come over to ask if you might help me out. I'm afraid I'm in a bit of a fix...?'

Innes's face was full of concern as he invited her into the sitting room.

As Davina had hoped, Orley was present, and also offering to help her.

'A fix?' asked Orley.

It seemed the American was unfamiliar with such an expression. 'Yes,' explained Davina. 'I am one of the organisers of The Riding of the Marches this year and unfortunately our Cornet's Lass has taken a nasty fall from her horse. I have been asked to find a good rider to take her place. I immediately thought of you, Orley, because I know how much you love to ride.'

Orley's face lit up. She looked to Innes.

Innes seemed pleased. 'I do hope the poor lass is not too badly injured.'

'Thank you!' Orley gushed.

'What a wonderful opportunity for Orley. The Riding of the Marches is an event of great importance here in Nithshire.' Innes said, giving Davina a warm smile.

She smiled back at him.

Innes then went on to explain to Orley about the ceremony. 'It follows a sequence of events that have been laid down over the centuries, when the Provost and his council rode out to ensure the boundaries of the town were strictly observed.'

'Wow. And all this is done on horseback?' Orley shrieked.

They nodded.

Orley beamed.

'I was also hoping,' broached Davina, 'that you, Innes, would consider being our Cornet as our elected choice has stepped down following the Lass's accident. They are engaged to be married you see and her bone pinning operation has been scheduled for, would you believe it, the very same day as The Ridings....'

'Oh, the poor things. That's so terrible.' Orley wailed.

Davina shrugged. She could hardly believe it herself.

'I don't think so,' Innes said. 'Fergus might do it. I have other plans.'

'But Fergus has agreed to be The Pursuivant. He can't present both the Charter to the Provost and also to himself. We need a Cornet.'

'And a Cornet needs a Lass,' Orley pleaded. 'Oh Innes, please. It'll be so much fun?'

'We know you learned to ride horses in Texas.' Davina goaded. 'You really have no excuse this time, Innes.'

The excitement on Orley's face must have changed his mind. 'All right. If it helps. I'll do it.'

Orley giggled with excitement and hugged him.

Davina hugged him too.

'How many horses do you have?' Orley asked her.

'Four. I have Misty and Heather, mum and dad have Charles and Camilla, although they don't ride so much since the ban on hunting with hounds. Innes can borrow Charles and you are welcome to ride Camilla, Orley.'

'Oh, where are my manners,' said Orley, thinking she should have put the kettle on, 'would you like a drink Davina?'

'Oh, no thank you. It's too early for me. I must be going.'

Innes walked her to the door. 'Thank you for thinking of us today,' he said to Davina with his voice low and his hand placed lightly on her elbow.

Davina shivered. His touch shot through her like a lightning bolt. 'I want to be friends with Orley,' she said. 'I hope you don't mind, Innes?'

'Of course not. She has already told me how much she likes you.'

'Really? Well that's nice.'

'And, she suggested the four of us go out together one evening. Let's arrange it soon.' He smiled and kissed Davina's cheek.

'Yes. The four of us. Sounds lovely.'

Innes watched her as she climbed into her Range Rover.

She waved cheerfully at him and then drove off. Once out of sight she whooped victoriously. Her plan was going to work perfectly. No one would suspect a thing, least of all Innes, who would get to see the whole thing perfectly executed with his very own eyes.

Saturday, the day of The Riding of the Marches arrived and Orley was beside herself with excitement. It was all she could think about. She would be riding with Innes as part of a traditional Scottish village cavalcade.

She would have so much to tell her father!

She was up and about at her usual time of six-thirty. By seven-thirty she had seen to the cattle, eaten her porridge, and was standing in the kitchen in her riding clothes waiting for Innes and Fergus.

Davina had lent her some riding clothes, which had actually turned out to belong to Lady McKenzie, as Davina had said they were more generously sized. They did fit rather well even if they felt a bit strange. The knee length leather riding boots creaked when she walked and the white tight breeches clung to her legs.

Heck, I've just got to stop eating chocolate, she told herself whilst despairing over her reflection yet again.

Innes walked into the kitchen. He was also wearing long leather riding boots and white breeches. Although his dark coat boasted long tails. He looked incredibly handsome and just like he had stepped out of one of his mother's historical romance novels. He also wore a top hat which she wondered how he would ever get to stay on his head.

'You look great!' she told him truthfully.

'You too.' he said, pinning a blue rosette to her lapel. 'We wear these as officiating principles.'

Fergus joined them. He was also looking very smart in riding attire. 'All set? he asked. 'The horses will at Thornfield Cross at quarter to eight. You are both meant to move off with the cavalcade at eight.'

'And what about you, Fergus?'

Orley was still confused over who did what during the ceremony and where. It all seemed very complicated.

'I'll ride up over the railway bridge and meet you for stobbin and noggin.'

'The most lethal concoction known to man,' reminded Innes.

At just before eight, the Provost, who was in real life Angus the pub landlord, and for the purpose of ceremony was also the King's Procurator, arrived at Thornfield Cross.

The onlookers applauded him enthusiastically.

Innes and Fergus moved forward on foot.

Innes spoke boldly for all to hear. 'Sir, I present to you the Pursuivant who brings with him a Charter from our Sovereign Lord to this Burgh'

Everyone cheered again which spooked Orley's horse just as she had a foot in the stirrup. She was not at all fazed by this naughtiness and eased herself gently into the saddle, taking control of the reins, and telling the famously bolting Camilla to behave herself.

Camilla, who was obviously testing out her driver, spun round and did her best to take off.

Innes presented the Pursuivant, who was of course Fergus, with the task of conveying the Kings Charter and all its attendant privileges to the Provost.

Orley listened in amazement to all the pomp and ceremony while being fascinated and confused all at the same time.

'By command of our Sovereign Lord, I bring to you this Charter and desire you to have it proclaimed to those here assembled,' the Provost yelled.

The town clerk, who was really Mr McIntosh of the Chocolate Box, then read out the Charter. 'I give you earth and stone of this town and water from its streams and all rights pertaining thereto!'

And the Minister, who really was the Minister, led the prayers.

Fergus yelled his well rehearsed reply: 'And I accept this symbol of earth, stone and water from your hands,' and then passed the Flag back to the Provost who in turn presented it to Innes.

The whole thing was exhausting and ridiculously flamboyant.

'To you our Cornet, duly appointed and accredited, I give this Flag for its safe keeping and charge you to preserve and defend it, if need be to the extreme issue of death.'

Orley gulped. *That was one heck of a promise Innes!*

She patted her mount's sweat-dampened neck and was grateful to Camilla for standing calmly at last. 'That's a girl. Save your energy for later.'

When she looked up she could see Davina standing on the platform behind the attendants wearing a long white silk gown and a tiara. She looked like a bride. She was staring straight at Orley but wasn't smiling. Probably miffed because I got Camilla to stand still while all other horses are hauling their riders everywhere, Orley thought smugly.

That'll show her horse beating doesn't work.

Thank goodness. Innes had the flag in his hand and they could be off. 'I accept this high honour and the charge of safe keeping this Flag, if need be to death.' He said, mounting his horse, the very classy looking Charles.

Then the Cavalcade clattered off leaving just Fergus standing at the Thornfield Cross.

'Off you go Orley!' he yelled as Camilla pranced.

'What about you, Fergus, where is your horse?'

Someone came along and handed him a bicycle.

'I'm following on this. Off you go!'

Innes was at the top of street by this time. Orley could see his flag waving over the bobbing black velvet capped heads of the riders.

She cantered through the masses and they obligingly parted like the veritable red sea in their scarlet jackets.

This was so very exciting. She was riding again. It felt fantastic. Camilla was a strong spirited ride but she had no worse manners that she was used to when riding in Texas.

The saddle felt a little strange. Small and flat. She kept loosing her stirrups and had to grip with her legs more than she was used to doing but you didn't master a horse with brute strength, or they would undoubtedly win, it took skill and patience. Thankfully, Camilla seemed to recognise that she was in confident hands and calmed down a little.

When she reached Innes she was grinning widely. 'Isn't this fantastic!'

He smiled. 'I'm not sure yet. I'll tell you later!'

Once flanked by his Lass, Innes held the flag aloft and everyone cheered. Then he led the gallop and a couple of hundred galloped in their wake. There were wild-eyed ponies all out of control. Long-legged thoroughbreds threatening to overtake, chunky cobs with no brakes and, last but not least, a bicycle ridden by Fergus.

They stampeded up the hill towards the war memorial where Innes was to lay a wreath. Meanwhile, the spectators waiting in the village, were treated to the spectacle of crowning of the 'Ridings Queen' namely Davina, who waved regally to her public and checked her watch.

Any minute now and they would be at the War Memorial and Innes will be dismounting to lay the wreath.

The pipe band struck up with *The Blue Bell of Scotland* and a dozen decorated floats carrying hundreds of local children began making their way slowly down the centre of the street. Flags waved, pipes piped, spectators yelled and Davina stayed in sight of her audience at all times while discreetly checking her watch.

At the war memorial, the Cavalcade and its followers mustered to say traditional prayers, led by the demonic looking Minster who, wearing a black cloak, was aptly mounted upon a black stallion who Camilla was suddenly quite desperately keen on.

Orley was too busy keeping her in check to bow her head and close her eyes in prayer. Most others, she noticed, had taken the opportunity to tip back heads to take the contents of their hip-flasks, rather than to thank God.

The horses were keen to be off again. Some were lashing out with hooves and teeth in an appalling display of bad conduct. Camilla, who was kicked in the hock by a nasty looking piebald cob, retaliated and put the piebald out of the ride out once and for all. Soon they were off and there was a terrible crush to get through the narrow gate into Kirkview Gallops. Many suffered terrible falls or worse.

The falls were caused by appallingly behaved ponies, who ditched their small riders and, in the resulting mud bath, left them sobbing with disappointment.

The worst was someone who inadvertently left their knee cap on the gate latch. Orley could still hear the screaming almost a mile away but there was no way to stop and help.

The horses, if not the few riders still mounted, were determined in their mission to follow Innes and the Standard.

Orley wished she had worn gloves. The reins she was pulling at were covered in some kind of a textured rubber, which was fine for grip, but apt to pull painful chunks of flesh out of her blistered and bleeding fingers. 'Whoa, Camilla!' she pleaded as the big horse continued to pull like a steam train. Orley could see the flapping colours of The Standard ahead, pinpointing Innes exact location. She marvelled at how he was doing and prayed that she wouldn't find his exhausted body impaled on the damned Standard Flag Pole at the end of the day.

It was at this point that Orley felt her saddle sliding sideward. She pulled on Camilla's reins again to no effect. She tried an old cowgirl trick of hauling on one rein until the horses head was against her leg and couldn't see where she was running. This seemed to be working. Camilla continued under her own momentum for a short while, but could not hold the bit in her teeth, so had no choice but to slow down.

It was then that Orley noticed that she was riding in a snaffle more suited to a child's old pony rather that a huntress with attitude. The bit in Camilla's mouth on the day of the Nithshire Show had been a Double Hackamore, something that could have stopped the devil's horse in its tracks.

Camilla had not quite slowed when the Minister thundered past on Satan. She ran sideways, clipping Satan and clashing stirrups. Even then, Camilla managed to throw a kick that would have put her successfully on the stage at the Moulin Rouge.

It was at this point that Orley realised they had parted company. Although it wasn't immediately obvious to her because her bottom was still in the saddle. It was the horse that was missing.

There was a moment where the world was spinning round and then there was a sickening thud. One that sent her spiralling into darkness. The world was silent and black while Orley lay on the field.

In the village, Davina was making her speech and judging the best decorated float competition. She could hardly concentrate. It should have happened by now. The cut she had made in Camilla's leather girth strap should have given out at around thirty minutes into the ride. They would all be hurtling over the fastest part of the ride out over Kirkview Gallops.

She imagined the scene. Orley's body lying with several limbs obviously broken, red blood on her white breeches from between her long awkwardly twisted legs. Terrible injuries resulting in her loosing the child and, if she lived, being barren for the rest of her life. Davina smiled and announced the winner of the best decorated float. There was no contest. It had to be The Shakespeare float. She presented the prize of a Pub Grub gift voucher to Macbeth and clapped heartily. Everyone watching the spectacle joined in - and just when she thought the applause might be going on a little too long - she realised that the thudding noise was not entirely attributed to the crowd but to the air-ambulance flying over head.

Orley didn't know how long she had been lying there. She groped at the ground with flayed fingertips. Damp grass. Then sound kicked in and voices could be heard. 'Get an ambulance' and 'call for the Doctor.'
Her head hurt. Everything hurt. She tried to move but it was a bad idea as an excruciating stab of pain seared through her.
She opened her eyes for a few seconds and saw a woman who said, 'it's okay, I'm a doctor.'
Then her eyelids grew heavy and the turrets of Glencorrie appeared. In swirling mists she called out for Innes. She was cold. So cold. Then in darkness she heard a soft voice. It was her mother, who whispered that maybe this adventure had not been so much a journey as a final destination.

Chapter Sixteen

Innes came galloping to the scene. His standard flag abandoned. Deep concern etched on his grey face as he jumped from his horse. 'Someone get a doctor!' he yelled.

'I am a doctor and the ambulance is on its way, Mr...?'

'Buchanan. I am Orley's...' he wondered what to say, was he her boyfriend, her landlord, or was he her employer...?

'Hold this mask onto her face. She needs oxygen.'

'Is she having trouble breathing?'

'She is unconscious.'

Then Fergus arrived on the scene.

'Oh God!' he yelled, falling to his knees next to Innes, 'there's so much blood!'

'Orley! Oh my God, Orley!'

It was clear that her riding hat had split in two and there was indeed a great deal of blood.

'Can you please remember that she might still be able to hear you,' the doctor insisted. 'And do not remove what's left of the hat. It's too dangerous. It must be done at the hospital. I've called an ambulance.'

'Fergus', Innes instructed, 'get on your mobile and call the air ambulance from Dumfries. We have got to get her to hospital now!'

The doctor was busily checking vital signs. 'That's no a bad idea considering where we are. The Thornfield ambulance could take too long.'

Innes took Orley's hand and began to stroke it, but his own hand was shaking almost too much. 'What do you mean, too long. Do you mean she might die?'

He remembered to whisper should Orley hear him.

The doctor didn't answer. She continued making sure airways were clear. She retook Orley's blood pressure and tested her reflexes until the thudding of rota blades could be heard travelling through the valley. 'I'll have her stabilised as soon as we get a back board and neck support,' she said.

Orley then groaned and her eyelashes, caked in blood, flickered. Innes pleaded with her. 'Orley can you hear me? For God's sake please hang in there. I love you Orley….'

But she didn't answer.

The air ambulance landed and the paramedic carefully assisted in transporting Orley inside. There was only room for one other passenger and, of course, it had to be the doctor on the scene.

'Come on,' said Fergus dragging his grief stricken brother away from the helicopter as it prepared to take off. 'I'll drive you to the hospital.'

'How, Fergus, on a bloody bicycle?'

'No, look. There is Davina…'

Innes looked across the field. At the gate was a shiny black Range Rover. They ran towards it. 'Davina, thank God you have come. Orley is being taken to the accident and emergency in Dumfries.'

'Move over,' said Fergus. 'I'll drive.'

Davina did as she was told, sliding across to the passenger seat. Innes climbed into the back. He looked terrible. To Davina's surprise, there were tears clinging to his dark eyelashes. He wasn't openly crying, as perhaps a lesser mortal might do in these circumstances, but he wasn't far from it. 'I hope you are not blaming me for this.' Davina said curtly.

Fergus took his eyes of the road to look directly at Davina. 'How could anyone blame you? You weren't even there?'

'I think she means because it was her horse.' Innes said from the far distance of the back seat.

'Camilla can be a handful, but you did say that Orley was an experienced rider.' Davina replied.

'She is. She's a cowgirl for God's sakes!' Innes insisted.

'And have you ever seen her ride before?'

'No,' Innes conceded quietly.

'Then maybe she lied to you.'

Innes bolted forward and hissed directly into Davina's ear. 'Orley wouldn't lie! We don't know what happened but there is bound to be an enquiry. It was an accident after all.'

Davina went suddenly quiet and they drove the rest of the way to Dumfries.

'Head injuries can be complicated I'm afraid,' the doctor told them after six gruelling hours of uncertainty in the waiting room of the hospital. 'Orley has suffered a depressed skull fracture.'

Innes was on his feet but was shaking so much he hardly looked able to stand. 'You said suffered - do you mean she's dead?' His voice cracked as he asked the dreaded question.

'No. No she's out of danger now. The surgery went well but this kind of skull fracture can cause contusions, bruising in the brain. We will have to keep an eye on her for a while and do some tests.'

At Orley's bedside in intensive care, Innes held her hand and waited helplessly. There was nothing else he could do except trust the doctors and nurses that were caring for her.

The tubes going into her body and the probe going into her head were there to monitor brain damage. The machines blipped and flashed. He stared at them as if mesmerised.

Then, taking her hand, he bend towards her until he was so close he could feel her body heat. 'I wonder if you heard me earlier, Orley? I told you that I loved you and I meant it. I loved you the first moment I saw you on that beach with flowers in your hair and tears in your eyes....'

Innes's own tears fell from his eyes and onto Orley's hand. He rubbed them away from the fingers that felt so warm but lifeless in his and waited for her to wake up.

During the night, having refused to go home, he overhearing concerns about Orley having fluid build up in her brain and he wept again quietly while he prayed.

In the morning he woke with a start. He was sitting in a chair opposite Orley's bed. She lay as before and there was no evidence of her having moved but then he heard it again. A groan. A noise from under her face mask.

'Nurse! Nurse!'

Innes pressed the call button and continued to yell until several nurses rushed into the room. 'She said something. I heard her!'

Thankfully, to prove he wasn't going mad, Orley made the noise again. One of the nurses checked Orley stats. Another took a tiny torch and lifted Orley's eyelids.

'She's not in pain.' The first nurse assured him. 'Try not to worry. She's doing really well. Believe it or not, she's been a lucky girl. She's only asleep so she can rest and get better. Now why don't you go home and get yourself sorted. We can call you if there is any change.'

Innes was still wearing his riding clothes and his white breeches were smeared with dried blood and mud. His boots were also filthy and his face looked even more brooding than usual with its dark shadow of stubble.

'No,' he said. 'I'll go to the washroom and get breakfast in the canteen. Then I'll come back.'

'Suit yourself,' said the nurse.

But he was only half way down the ward when he saw Fergus and Davina headed towards him.

'How is she?' Fergus asked immediately.

'We've brought you a change of clothes and a wash bag,' said Davina.

'She's comfortable. Whatever that means,' he told them, and then uttered his thanks as Davina handed over a small holdall.

When Innes came back out of the men's washroom looking clean shaven, dressed in blue jeans and a clean shirt, they all went to find the hospital canteen. Innes ordered coffee. Fergus bought his brother a full cooked breakfast and had to eat it himself when Innes pushed it away.

Davina sipped tea.

'I think you need to call Orley's family.' Fergus said to Innes. 'No one has called them yet and it's probably better if you explain what's happened.' He pushed a mobile phone across the surface of the Formica table toward Innes.

'What will you say to them?' asked Davina. She bit her lip and narrowed her eyes while searching for insight into the extent of Orley's injuries.

Innes shook his head, picked up the phone and headed towards the exit. Fergus and Davina watched him through the window as he stood outside in the cold October air and dialled up Baytown Texas.

Orley opened her eyes to find that the lights around her hurt her eyes. Everything was white and bright. She had something on her face. She tried to pull it off. It was dark outside and the lights seemed too bright inside. She felt something sharp from her arm. She squealed in pain.
Suddenly, he was there and her panic calmed.
She could see him clearly this time. Innes's face, looking a little dishevelled and tired, smiled down at her. She realised then she was awake.
'How are you feeling?' he asked.
She blinked to focus on him. Tears welled in his eyes.
'I'm okay,' she tried to say. Her voice was croaky. Her throat dry.
'Welcome back. I've missed you.'
'How long have I been - here?'
'Almost a week. I was so worried. We all were.'
He pressed the call button. The nurse would need to know she was awake.

A few days later, with Orley responding to treatment, she was moved out of the high dependency unit and into the general ward. In the meantime, Innes had been desperately trying to get a flight arranged for Orley's father and her stepmother, but there had been a hurricane warning in the Southern States and, after Katrina, the State of Texas was taking no chances. They had battened down the hatches and cancelled all flights. However, once Mac heard his daughter's voice and her assurances that he needn't worry, he was pacified. Orley told him: 'remember that time I got all concussed in that damned crazy rodeo in Pasadena, daddy? Well, it sure ain't as bad as all that!'
Innes smiled and shook his head.
With Orley on the general ward, visiting times were restricted to an hour in the morning and two hours in the evening. No matter what Innes said or how much he pleaded with the ward sister, there were no concessions, not even for

a Laird. Perhaps it was just as well he went home when he did because poor Fergus, who was holding everything together back home, was exhausted too.

'It's harder now that we have the cattle as well as the sheep,' he told Innes. 'It can take me an hour just to locate them. By the way, the slates for the cottages having new roofs are on back-order with at least a six week delivery time, and the roofer says he doubts he can do the work before Christmas anyway.'

Innes groaned. He went inside the house.

His mother was sitting by an unlit fire reading a book from the library. She had a blanket over her knees and a glass of whisky by her side.

'Why isn't the fire lit?' he asked her.

'Because there's no wood and no coal.'

Innes picked up the empty scuttle and went outside to the bunker were they kept the coal. It was empty. He pulled his mobile phone out of his pocket and rang the coal-man.

'Your cheque bounced Laird Buchanan,' he was told.

Innes found some wood, made a fire to warm his mother and, noting the amount of whisky she had drank, told her he would make her a pot of tea.

Unfortunately, he found the Aga cold and, on further inspection, the oil tank empty. He was furious. He stormed across the yard and dragging Fergus off his feet, hauled him over to the oil tank. 'Why the hell did you let us run out of oil? You know it's the only way of cooking and heating water. What's going to happen when Orley comes home - and the place is freezing bloody cold and there's no food on the stove?'

Fergus was equally furious. 'Because all the bloody cheques have bounced that I wrote for the coal, the grocery shopping, and the vet's bill. I didn't dare write another one out for the oil. That's not my fault. Just like it's not my fault that Davina won't fall in love with me – it's all bloody well yours!' They glared at each other. Teeth barred.

Breath came out their mouths in great gusts.

Innes let go. 'I'm sorry,' he said.

Fergus slumped into a sitting position on top of an old and discarded oil drum and put his head in his hands.

'No. Innes, it's not your fault. It's mine. I'm just not as clever as you are. I can't juggle finances. I can't make women fall for me. I can't really do anything. I'm a hopeless cause.'

Innes ruffled his brothers hair and gave him a clip round the ear. 'That's why you need me, right?'

'Aye. Right.'

Innes went to the bank. The October mortgage payment had wiped out the current account. So he transferred funds from the deposit account balance and withdrew some cash. He paid the coalman. He ordered oil. He went to visit the plumber and asked him to install central heating into Glencorrie. 'And it's got to be put in soon,' Innes explained. 'Before Orley comes out of hospital.'

At the hospital, Davina was visiting Orley. She thought it was about time she reaped the results of the damage she had caused and so popped her head around the door of Orley's room. 'This is nice. A room to yourself. This must be costing Innes a fortune.'

Orley dragged herself upward into what might be considered a sitting position. She was still far too sore to put too much pressure on her buttocks which were black and blue from the accident. 'Davina. How lovely to see you.'

Davina offered flowers and went straight to study the clipboard at the bottom of the bed while Orley said something about getting a vase of water. 'Are you on the mend at last?' She asked Orley sweetly.

Orley insisted that she was. 'I think I'll be out in a few days. Just waiting for a MRI scan then I'll be out of here.'

She smiled bravely.

Davina looked perplexed. 'No scars then. My word, you have been lucky - and emotionally, how are you in that department?'

Orley shrugged. 'I'm not put off horses if that's what you mean – it was hardly Camilla's fault. How is she?'

'Unscathed you will be pleased to hear.'

'I'm so glad to hear it!' came the choked response.

Davina smiled but wanted to kill Fergus. He was to blame for all this by deliberately misleading her. Orley hadn't been pregnant at all. If anything, the whole thing had brought the cow and that bastard Innes closer together.

What was she to do now? She had as good as lost him. She was as good as condemned to marry a nobody. Perhaps she should relinquish and consider marrying Fergus after all? Especially as he had tried so hard. It might give her the ideal opportunity to repay him slowly for all the misery he had caused her.

At Glencorrie, Lady Buchanan glared out of the window at the activity in the courtyard. 'What on God's earth is going on?'

Vans were parked and men were working. Lengths of copper tubing were being measured and cut. Innes was talking to the plumber.

'Central heating,' Fergus told his mother proudly.

Several days later, Orley was pronounced fit enough to leave hospital but the doctor in charge of Orley's case had asked for the family to gather in his office with Orley's carers, to arrange for and explain the importance of her palliative care. 'Orley's tests have also shown us that she is suffering a kind of lymphoma disease caused by a lack of protein,' he went on to explain.

The room went quiet.

Lady Buchanan clutched her pearls.

Innes went white.

Fergus looked confused.

The doctor decided the point needed expanding upon when Lady Buchanan suddenly blurted out. 'You can tell us the truth - she has the human strain of Mad Cow disease, doesn't she?'

Everyone, from the consultant to the house doctor to the ward sister to the staff nurse, gasped.

'Mother!' Innes shouted out.

'Well that's what it sounds like to me.'

'I can assure you, Lady Buchanan, that Orley does not have Variant Creutzfeldt-Jakob disease. She will, with the right diet and convalescence, fully recover. Her symptoms are derived from poor diet.'

Innes was shocked to the core and not just from his mother's outburst. He had subjected Orley to conditions some would consider torturous. He had affectively starved her. He expected to be arrested on the spot.

Instead, after agreeing to implement special care and a high protein diet, he had to leave Orley for one more night while he ventured into the sub-zero temperatures of the hospital car park where he stood for a while deeply in thought.

He'd had to deal with so many problems recently. There had been so much to do. The bank. The cattle. The property repairs. The concerns of his tenants. Trying to get them all back in their homes for Christmas. He had simply not noticed the changes in Orley's wellbeing. How could he have been so inconsiderate?

Had he really been amused by her secret addiction to chocolate? Why hadn't he realised that she had just been hungry? Once, he had overheard an estate worker saying that Orley did the work of ten men. Why hadn't he thought about that little comment a bit more?

He had totally let her down.

Chapter Seventeen

At Glencorrie there was a steady procession of cards and flowers as the residents of Buchanan Estate showed their concern for Orley and their relief at the news of her being discharged from hospital. Lady Buchanan insisted that everyone was making far too much fuss. The girl wasn't even home yet, although Innes had gone to fetch her. 'She's coming home from hospital because they need the bed for sick people,' she was heard telling someone who had telephoned for an update on Orley's progress.

'That's not nice!' Fergus told his mother. 'Everyone just wants to know that Orley's getting better.'

As Innes's Landrover approached Glencorrie and the turrets and roundels came into view, Orley's eyes widened. She was home at last and Glencorrie looked so beautiful to her now. She remembered being overawed by the house the first time she saw it, disappointed even, at how ancient and fearsome it looked to her. Now it felt like a friend. A welcome home. As they came to a halt in the yard, she lifted a quaking a hand to her mouth.

'Oh, Innes, this must be costing a fortune. Have I been the one to...?'

'Orley, everybody has central heating these days and it's about time we joined them. I have been assured by the plumber that by the end of today everything will be...'

She kissed him. Had he read her mind and discovered how she had dreaded the onset of winter and not being able to feel warm? She could not find the words to thank him so she kissed him some more.

He grinned. 'And did I forget to mention the new hot water system?'

She kissed him until they were both breathless.

Innes helped her from the Landrover. He carried her bag. He fussed over her insistently. In her tower bedroom, he placed her bag on the bed while she went over to inspect the window casements that had had been fitted with secondary glazing. No more drafts. The large radiator installed on the wall opposite was making loud clunking noises.

'The plumber says it's just air in the system. I'll settle down'.

She felt guilty and thankful all at the same time and couldn't help but worry about what Lady Buchanan would make of it all.

A while later, in the sitting room downstairs, Innes was trying pacifying his irate mother. 'A heating system will add value to the house,' he insisted.

'What for. Are we selling?'

'No. It will prevent dampness and mildew.'

'It will shrink the natural timbers and cause dry rot!'

'Mother, it will keep us warm!'

'So will a warm sweater and a log on the fire. In fact logs will keep you warm twice.'

Innes looked heavenward. He had heard this tale so many times. 'Yes, I know, once when you chop them and then again when you burn them.'

'Central heating indeed. Your father will be turning in his grave.'

'Oh mother. He would do the same. This place is in need of renovation.'

'Innes, this house has stood here for hundreds of years and it's not about to fall down now. We can ill-afford this and you know it. You are simply pandering to the needs of a girl who does not belong here and for all you know, might be already planning to move on!'

Innes spun round. His black eyes burning like coals.

'Don't you ever...'

Lady Buchanan stood her ground and lifted her chin defiantly. 'Ever what, Innes..?'

Innes's eyes narrowed. 'Make me choose - because I'm telling you that you might not win...!'

His mother bit down on her lip. She knew she should have kept quiet. It was best not to push him too far, but as usual, she couldn't help herself. 'And what makes you think she'll stay?'

Nothing prepared her for what he said next.

'Because I love her and I intend to ask her to be my wife.'

Lady Buchanan fell silent except to stifle a sob. If this had been Fergus, she would not have believed a word of it of course but this was Innes, and if he said something, then she could be sure he meant it.

Orley amazed everyone with the speed of her recovery. It had almost been three weeks since her accident. Her headaches had gone and she had the sparkle back in her eyes. She had been eating the prescribed three high protein meals a day, consisting of fresh ingredients bought in daily from the village or outlying farms and she was looking well.

She had just been back to the hospital for a check up and had even managed to convince her doctor that she should go back to work.

'Gently does it,' he had advised but there was no strong objection to her doing so.

This was cause for celebration, Innes told her that evening over dinner.

Orley hoped he meant to take her to Edinburgh. Where they might take in a show, stay overnight in a hotel, and visit Edinburgh Castle at last, but she didn't suggest it in case he had something else in mind.

'This salmon is delicious,' she said instead.

'It is exceptionally tasty,' agreed Lady Buchanan. 'Is it from our river, Innes?'

'No.' Innes laughed. 'Fergus brought it home from the pub.'

'Then I believe it will be from our river.' Lady Buchanan concluded dryly.

'It's time for a party,' Innes declared, once their meal was over. 'Orley needs to meet everyone on the estate informally and it would be good to invite all the people from the village.'

Lady Buchanan's face looked as though it was sucking a sour plum. 'Inviting one's staff only encourages familiarity,' she protested.

Fergus groaned. 'Yes mother. That's the whole point.'

'Anyone for apple pie?' asked Orley. 'The apples are from the garden….'

After their meal, they sat in front of the fire in the sitting room and discussed the proposed party. 'Lets put an open invitation in the village newsletter,' said Fergus.

Lady Buchanan looked horrified.

Orley sat writing their ideas on a pad. 'So, who do you want to invite?'

'The Young Farmers and the fishing club,' said Fergus.

'The shooting club and the Gamekeeper's Association,' said Innes.

'The ladies golf team and the local Scottish Women's Rural Institute,' said Lady Buchanan, 'and could you perhaps pour me another whisky, dear?'

'Just pass her the bottle' said Fergus, getting another from the cupboard.

Orley was amazed at how much they all drank, especially Lady Buchanan, who could handle a measure so large it would knock out a bull. 'Erm, not for me, Fergus,' Orley said covering her juice glass with her hand. 'I intend to be up at first light to check the fold.'

Innes smiled.

'I'm curious,' said Fergus, 'why are those Highland cattle known as folds and not herds?'

'Actually,' Lady Buchanan interrupted, 'it is because in the olden days, in winter time, the cattle were brought together at night in open shelters made of stone, called folds, to protect them from the weather and wolves.'

They looked at each other and Innes declared his mother a source of constant information. She looked pleased and then, taking her whisky, announced it was time for her to head up to bed.

'Goodnight mother.' Innes and Fergus both said in unison.

'Goodnight Lady B. Sweet dreams,' said Orley.

Lady Buchanan stopped in her tracks and turned round.

'What did you just call me, dear?'

Orley's face turned crimson and tentatively she apologised. 'Oh dear, that was so rude of me. It's just that, your title is such a mouthful sometimes - don't you think?'

'It's quite all right Orlene, Lady B was a term of endearment once used by my late husband and you have reminded me of that.'

She smiled and Orley nearly fell of her chair.

Then there was a strange moment, a short-lived one but a moment all the same, when the bird-like glare and the icy demeanour disappeared and in its place there was a softness.

Orley found this heartening and disconcerting all at the same time and looked to Innes, whose eyebrows where as high with surprise as hers.

During the course of that particular evening, Orley had noticed that Innes kept disappearing for a few moments and then reappearing again.

He did this once more time after his mother had gone to bed and when he came back, he announced to Orley that her bath awaited her and then led her upstairs. 'Trust me,' he said, 'and close your eyes.'

She did so and allowing him to guide her down the long passageway and into the bathroom. She heard the door close behind them. 'You can open them now'.

She opened them and gasped. 'Oh, Innes. You spoil me!'

He had lit candles, arranged clean towels, scented the bath full of water with some of his mother's Lily of the Valley bath foam, which he must have stolen stealth-like whilst she had still been downstairs. There was even Celtic music playing softly in the background.

'Well, you deserve it. I don't mean the bath as that's something you need. Not that you *need* a bath, you deserve...'

'Oh, shhh, you deserve to be kissed,' she said as her lips grazed his.

He lowered his eyes and kissed her gently, lightly flicking his tongue over the soft contours inside her mouth.

She sighed with pleasure and he took this as a signal to continue, pulling her closer, until she felt the hardness of his desire against her. She heard herself moan as a the hot line between the inside of her mouth seemed to fuse with the excitement he aroused in her groin.

They were both quite breathless when Innes released her from his grip and sank to his knees. Realising that he intended to remove her clothes, her hands grasped his.

She wasn't so sure. It was many weeks ago that they had made love in the meadow. She was less confident now with him and of herself. She felt excruciatingly embarrassed about all the weight she had gained.

'Do you think we might take a bath together?' he suggested. His voice thick with lust.

Oh my God. Should they?

She tried to remember the last time she had shaved her legs but it was too late to worry as he had her jeans down in less than a second. Then he peeled off her sweater and threw it inside out onto the bathroom floor. She kicked off her shoes as Innes removed his trousers and, with the music playing, it was like a kind of dance.

Orley needn't have worried. His eyes remained locked in hers as they sank into the large cast iron bath with gasps and sighs and, as candle light flickered on the shiny steam-drenched stonewalls, they looked at each other from opposite ends of the bath.

'Come here…' he whispered after a while of staring and relaxation.

Orley twisted round and lay stretched out in his arms. Her body supported by both the warm water and his strong body. She luxuriated in their slippery closeness and delighted in his hands over her skin, cupping her breasts, whilst he kissed her neck and whispered how beautiful he found her to be. Then he made her laugh by nibbled her ears and tickling her until she was shrieking with pleasure. All the time she was aware of his arousal against her, warm and hard, as she lay beneath the bubbles and between his legs.

Outside an owl hooted. It must have been perched on a tree right outside the misted up bathroom window. 'That's a barn owl,' Innes told her. 'It's cry is quite distinct.'

'It sounded so spooky. I think I would find this house scary if I was in it all alone,' she said, clinging to his strong arms as fleeting shadows leapt across the tiled walls like spirits of the night.

'The house is haunted by previous Buchanan's,' Innes told her, 'but I like to think they are looking out for us.'

'I've been woken in the night,' she admitted to him uneasily. 'I thought someone or something might be in my room.'

Innes kissed her wet hair and laughed. 'How do you know it wasn't me lurking in the darkness, lusting after you.'

'Because until recently it was so damn cold up there that I would have heard your teeth chattering,' she laughed back.

'Do you want to know about the first time I ever got really scared?' he whispered.

Orley was intrigued. She turned to face him. Yes, she wanted to hear what would make this brave man afraid. She sat waist deep in the water and looked into his eyes. Foamy scented bubbles ran in rivers down her upper body. Innes gazed at her glistening breasts and dark pointed nipples.

'Only please, don't tell me the story about the headless ancestor that roams the staircase, because Fergus already scared me stupid with that one.'

He seemed too distracted to find that funny. 'It's got nothing to do with ghosts,' he said with his eyes huge black pools of longing, shining through the steamy space between them. 'It was the thought of loosing you, Orley. I was so scared.'

'I was scared too,' she confessed.

A long poignant silence fell between them.

Innes rose up from the water. 'Come on. Let's get you dry. It's getting cold.' He stepped out of the bath first. The water parting and foaming in his wake. He held up a towel for her. All the time his eyes remained locked inside hers.

Orley let the bathwater go and stepped out onto the soft bathmat. She allowed him to dab her dry. He following each pat with a kiss and then, as he reached forward to dry her back and shoulders, she found her breasts pressed against his bare chest. The contact made her gasp. She could feel his erection hard against her. She prayed for his lips to continue but to her disappointment, he stopped to wrap a towel around himself, kilt-like, before collecting her up in his arms.

    She gasped with acute embarrassment. What if she was too heavy for him? What if his mother - or Fergus - saw them coming out of the bathroom like this together?

    Again, she needn't have worried. He carried her effortlessly down the hallway to the privacy of his own bedroom, where once inside, he locked the door behind them. The hallway had proved to be thankfully clear of eyewitnesses, which was just as well, as she had managed to loose her towel on the way.

Chapter Eighteen

Orley's dilemma over her weight gain and the fact that her hair was hanging in dread-locks rather than curls was played on her mind, especially when they talked about the party idea once more. How could she possibly face Innes's relatives, friend's and employee's, when she looked such a mess?

If only she could wear a mask or lots of make-up..?
Then she had an idea.

'What do you think about having the party on Halloween night?' she asked the family brightly.

'What a great idea. It could be a fancy dress!' Fergus added. 'We have never had one of those before. I could go as Batman. That would fit with the Halloween theme!'

'I've never heard of anything so ridiculous,' said Lady Buchanan. 'It's sounds so....'

'Much fun?' Fergus quipped.

'American.' His mother hissed.

But Innes thought it would be fun too.

Fergus whooped. 'I think you would make a fabulous Catwoman Orley, if you don't mind me suggesting.....'

Orley giggled. 'That makes Innes The Boy Wonder!'

'I don't think so.' Innes objected. 'I was thinking of something much more gory like the bloody ghost of William Wallace....'

Lady Buchanan was not at all happy with these ideas until Orley suggested she might look good in a long black spooky dress. 'Like Morticia from the Addams Family'.

'Do you really think so, dear? Yes, I do remember The Addams family. It was one of my favourite old TV shows. I do believe I have a suitable gown in my wardrobe....'

A few days later the invitations had gone out. Orley and Fergus had made them using black card and glitter. They had little bats, moons and stars, stuck onto them. Fergus also helped make up posters to put up in Thornfield's clubhouses and halls and Orley wrote the copy for the village newsletter. 'I need to get this in Thornfield before five o'clock,' she said to Fergus.

'Don't worry I'll take it. I'll pop over and see Davina on the way back with her invitation.'

Orley had noticed he had made a special one for Davina. 'You really like her don't you, Fergus?' she said quietly so that his mother did not hear.

Fergus blushed and nodded. 'Doesn't get me anywhere though,' he said.

'I didn't realise so many people lived in Thornfield.' Lady Buchanan grumbled as she stuck the last stamp on the personal invitations. 'I do hope we aren't going to get all sorts of yobs arriving by the coach load. That's exactly what happened to The McKenzie's last year when they opened up their garden to the public.'

'Yes, but mother, they were being filmed by the BBC'S How Gorgeous Is Your Garden,' Fergus reminded her.

'The lawns were absolutely ruined and they were pulling litter out of the herbaceous border for weeks,' Lady Buchanan declared with a shudder.

'The McKenzie's...?' Orley repeated. 'Where have I heard that name before.'

Her blood ran cold at the recollection. Lady McKenzie had wanted to slap her face at the ladies Rural meeting because her hopes of bagging Innes for her daughter had been dashed by Orley's very presence.

'Of course you have heard of them. They are our neighbours.' Fergus informed her.

Orley stared at him. 'What did you say?'

'Davina. She is Davina *McKenzie...?*' he repeated.

Orley's jaw dropped. All this time and she hadn't put two and two together. It had been Davina's mother at the rural meeting. Orley's face felt like it was burning: as if she *had* just been slapped.

It was a Friday evening and Davina was feeling despondent. Her new outfit, delivered only that morning from *spank.com* was a perfect fit in all the right places but what use was it to her when she had no reason to wear it?

The foursome evening that Innes had promised had never materialised. So she decided to call him on his mobile phone to remind him only to discover that he had swapped his phone with Fergus. She tried to cut short the conversation but he yarned on about how glad he was to hear from her and could he come over? Davina groaned. She was bored with Fergus's attentions and was about to tell him she was busy washing her hair when he said to her that he had something to tell her.

'Something important?' she asked.

'Something important and exciting.'

Davina hesitated. This could be the news she has been waiting for. Fergus might not be able to discuss it over the phone. Orley might be leaving.

'Is it something I've been looking forward to?' she asked tentatively.

'Yes. So I'll pop round shall I?'

'Yes. Come over straight away. I'll pour us some drinks.'

As the phone went down, Fergus raced to the shower and in his enthusiasm, practically scrubbed the skin off his body.

It didn't bother him that the water was no more than a trickle or that the shampoo was burning his eyes, or that shaving so hurriedly had cut the top of the newly erupted spots on his chin. He sang as he rubbed his hair with a towel until it emerged shiny and even more unruly than before.

He sprayed Innes's deodorant under his arms before climbing back into his jeans, and then he paused at the mirror to admire his red-eyed reflection. 'You handsome brute,' he told himself with a smile, only to realise that he still had to clean his teeth.

'Don't forget the copy for the newsletter has to be in Thornfield for five o'clock Fergus.' Orley reminded him, as he slipping a bottle of single malt into the pocket of his wax jacket and headed out.

'Damn!' She heard him mutter.

He had obviously forgotten.

'Damn and blast!' he said again a while later as the Landrover cruised to a halt. He was out of fuel. The red light had been on for a while but in delivering the copy by five o'clock, and getting there by the skin of his teeth, he had missed out on getting to the garage. Everything except the Co-op and the pub closed at five o'clock in Thornfield.

It was a dark and cold night. Not a star in the sky to be seen and no moon to guide his way. No torch either as the battery had packed in. He walked up the lane towards Castle McKenzie. He could see the lights of the castle on his left.

He turned into what he thought was the driveway. He laughed aloud and congratulated himself on knowing the route like the back of his hand. He jumped over the gate rather than bothering to open it and walked confidently into the darkness ahead.

Then he heard a noise. He froze and stopped to listen.

It was behind him. A fluttering of panic rose up from his stomach. Was he being followed?

He held his breath. The hairs on the back of his neck stood on end. There it was again. Nearer. Yes, nearer.

Dear God what was that?

It sounded like heavy breathing. He broke into a run and whomever or whatever was keeping up. No, it was gaining on him!

In terror he picked up speed towards the lights of the castle. The sounds were all around now. Grunting, sniffing, gnashing. He ran one way and then another trying to avoid being caught but they seemed to move with him in the darkness. Fergus's imagined wolves, salivating and snarling, closing in as a pack to rip him apart and gobble him all up.

'Who's there?' he called out, trying not to wet himself with fear.

He shouted again but was struck heavily from behind.

He hit the floor with the wind knocked out of him.

He was terrified.

Because the ground was so soft and muddy, he realised he was otherwise unhurt, so he picked himself up and scrambled forward. He seemed to be travelling in slow motion, every step was like wading through a vat of treacle.

But the beasts were still behind him. He could feel their hot breath as he fled to where he thought the path should be - only to find it wasn't there anymore.

Instead there was a four-bar fence. He must have made a turn to soon for the driveway and must be in the paddock which meant that the beasts must be - *horses. ...!*

He leapt the fence with all the impetus of an Olympic champion high jumper and once he knew there was a barrier between him and *them,* he turned to see that in hot pursuit were Charles and Camilla, blowing through their noses in horsy pleasure and delighted to bump into him on such a dark night.

'You mention this to anyone,' he told them nervously, patting their enormous heads, 'and there'll be trouble....'

He rang the pull cord bell on the door of McKenzie castle and was made to wait for Davina in the hallway. 'You can't walk on my clean floors with those muddy boots, Master Buchanan,' he was told by the housekeeper in no uncertain terms.

He looked down to see he was covered in mud. Spattered from head to toe. He sniffed himself and from the smell rising he suspected it might not be mud after all.

Davina descended the staircase. 'Fergus!'

She was wearing what could only be described as a tight strappy black dress that looked like a leather cobweb. Her long red hair was shining and swinging as she walked. She looked so incredibly sexy that Fergus could hardly speak.

'D-Davina!'

She stared down at him and frowned. 'What on earth...?'

He smiled obliviously. 'So you know!' he gasped.

His aching limbs, his injured back, his mud splattered clothes, the broken whisky bottle that was seeping its contents down his trouser leg and causing a golden puddle on the polished marble floor that gave the impression he was urinating. Only none of it mattered when Davina looked like that.

'How? Did Orley tell you?' he gasped.

'Know what?' she demanded.

'About our Halloween party - I see you already have your outfit!'

'How dare you!' she screamed. 'This is fashion. Now get out!'

He had never seen Davina quite as angry. Well, not since he and Innes had locked her up in the cellar with a couple of ferrets when she was twelve. He fled the house but on doing so, he actually managed to achieve what he had gone their to do, which was to deliver the party invitation. He left it on the hall table.

The end of October was dark and cold. So cold that Orley had taken to wearing a thermal vest under her three bulky sweaters. She despaired at herself for looking something akin to a bodybuilder. It was the day before the party and the postman was delivering a heavy box and yet another handful of reply cards.

'Me and the Misses are really looking forward to the fancy dress party,' the postie told her enthusiastically as he clawed the air with a hairy hand, 'we're both gonna be werewolves.'

Orley laughed. 'We are delighted you are both coming Mister McDoggart.'

She was also delighted that her order had arrived in time.

She had shopped on the internet with her credit card having discovered a fabulous on-line Halloween shop. She had ordered tins of spray cobwebs, fake blood, and an assortment of severed limbs, rubber bats and spiders.

'Let me carry this box into the kitchen for you.' Mister McDoggart insisted. 'It's part of my job so it is, ken,'

He then stayed and drank tea until Orley had unpacked and examined every item. 'Aye, ken, plenty of vampire bats in the air around here so there is,' he said, making strange sucking sounds through his teeth.

'I'll thank you not to scare the poor girl. She's from America you know,' said a stern voice from the kitchen doorway. 'Vampire bats indeed. I think you would be better delivering letters to the poor folk who are still waiting for them, Mister McDoggart!' Lady Buchanan showed the postie to the door.

Orley held up a long black wig. 'I got this for you, Lady B.'

'Ooh!' came the delighted reply. Lady Buchanan snatched the hairpiece and plonked it on her head, tucking in the grey stragglers she admired herself in the mirror. She looked very pleased and Morticia-like.

Orley was reminded of the *mirror mirror* scene from *Snow White*. 'It suits you,' she said truthfully.

'And where is yours, dear?' Lady Buchanan asked.

'Well actually,' Orley confided, 'I thought I'd go for the real thing....'

'I would like it dyed jet-black please,' she told Shona, the trendy stylist at Thornfield's hairdressers.

'We call it Urban Gothic here, madam.'

The girl in the mirror standing behind Orley, had cropped black spiky hair, a pale complexion and very inky eyes, which sparkled wickedly as she gazed over the long auburn locks in front of her.

'Well, I look such a mess and I'm here for you to do something radical about it,' Orley told her in no uncertain terms.

'Then something radical coming up....'

With the thumping music playing in the background, the complimentary glasses of whisky and the Indian head massage, Orley was so relaxed that she was almost comatosed.

So by the time Shona the wacky hairdresser had got around to snipping and shaping, Orley was in no mind to stop her.

'Wakey wakey, I've finished. Whadya fink, ken?'

When Orley opened her eyes and her senses came rushing back to her, it was way too late to scream stop, it was far to late to ask for a simple trim or to request highlights. She was a fully fledged Urban Gothic Ladette.

'Erm, thanks. I think I love it...'

'That'll be eighty quid, then, ken.'

Fergus couldn't stop laughing. Innes said it was a complete shock and he needed time to get used to it. Lady Buchanan said that she had her doubts that such a style actually suited Orley's round face. But Orley thought the new look was wearing well. She only had to wash it and give it a little rub and she was ready for anything. It was the easiest hair she had ever owned. It made her look even paler, which was something else to get used to, but otherwise she felt good. It was as if with a new hair cut, she had adopted a different persona, she was tougher and suddenly less prone to tears than someone who had long curly demanding hair. She felt so much more sexy. Innes would simply have to get used to it.

Chapter Nineteen

On Halloween night it snowed. Not heavily according to Innes, who warned that when it really came down, they could be snowed in for days if not weeks.

'This is just a flurry,' he maintained.

Orley, who was wide-eyed with wonder and had never seen snow before, was so enchanted with the flakes blowing around in the frozen air, that for a moment to two she managed to forget that it was well below zero outside.

'In the great snow of ninety-six,' Fergus told her, 'we were isolated from the outside world for almost six weeks. Storms and drifts cut off the electricity and the telephone. Sheep froze solid in the fields….'

'And how did you manage?' Orley asked nervously.

'Oh we managed just fine,' Innes insisted, 'because we had the generator working, didn't we, Fergus.'

Orley looked relieved.

'Aye. That's what finished it off I reckon.' Fergus added sadly.

'Lets go inside,' Innes said. 'It's time we all got changed before our guests start arriving.

Orley had been busily preparing food and decorating the house all day. Innes and Fergus had spent most of the day gathering logs in the nearby woodlands and had lit and stacked all of the fires in the house and with the central heating chugging away as well, it was nice and warm for the party.

Eventually everything was done. The rooms looked fantastic. The existing ancient cobwebs had been embellished to the point that the whole place now resembled a dark spooky and very haunted mansion and outside, in total contrast, the snow added a sparkling air of white magic to the whole evening.

Orley took one last look over the room before going upstairs to get changed. Everything seemed to be in order. Fergus had turned an antique, wood-worm riddled sideboard into a bar area, which he had loaded with bottles of whisky, brandy, rum, and probably every other alcoholic spirit known to man. No doubt the drinks bill would be horrendous. Next to the bar, on a side table, hundreds of sparkling drinks glasses, all hired for the occasion, twinkled in the candlelight.

As well as the alcoholic drinks, several bowls of light punch on a tomato juice base had been mixed by Orley for those, like herself, who only wanted to drink moderately and for greater effect she had added jelly worms.

Upstairs in her tower room, she struggled into the costume she had been carefully creating all week. It had been inspired by the cover of a novel entitled *The Sexy Vampire* which she had borrowed from Thornfield library.

She was determined to look so sexy that Innes would want to get his teeth into her later. Although she had to hold her breath as she poured herself into it and grit her teeth to get the zip up. She had spiked her short snazzy hair with gel and applied a great deal of face make-up together with a bright red lipstick, before popping into her mouth the essential vamp accessories.

Appraising herself in the mirror, she smiled decadently, which of course, disclosed those vicious-looking long pointed teeth. She felt great. A little too busty perhaps in the tight black body-stocking but she didn't have to worry too much about that, as she would also be wearing a full length black cloak. The outfit beneath was intended for one particular person's eyes only.

At the other side of the house, Fergus was pacing the floor in frustration. He was gutted with disappointment because after waiting around all day, the Batman outfit he had ordered from a fancy dress shop in Glasgow, had failed to show up.

'Not to worry,' Innes told his distraught brother.' I know you wanted to be Batman but if you do the same as me, find an old shirt and kilt, you could also be a ghostly hero....'

'Och, I don't want to look the same as you, Innes.' Fergus complained.

'You won't be. I'll be William Wallace and you'll be Rob Roy.'

After hauling everything from his wardrobe in order to find his very oldest things amongst all his very old clothes, Fergus managed to find an old kilt that had once belonged to his father. 'You're sure this won't put the girls off rather than attract them?' he laughed, slashing the kilt into tatters.

'Do you mean one girl in particular, Fergus, or girls in general?' Innes asked him curtly.

'One in particular, of course,' he assured his brother.

Lady Buchanan was already busy welcoming the first guests and on seeing Fergus, she instructed him to take everyone's coat and pour the welcome whisky. She also insisted that Innes go down into the cellar to bring up more red wine.

'I'll take the coats, if you go down to the cellar,' Innes whispered to Fergus. 'Then, I'm going upstairs to see if Orley's ready.'

But his mother objected. 'Fergus will either break all the bottles or drink more than he can carry. You do it Innes and hurry up....'

The first to arrive were the McKenzie's. Gregor was dressed as a priest and looked very demonic. Daphne, bizarrely, was dressed as an angel and looked like a fairy off a Christmas tree. 'How marvellous you both look,' Lady Buchanan enthused while being entirely satisfied that her outfit looked so much better that Daphne's. 'But where is darling Davina...?'

'I'm here, Lady Buchanan,' came a sweet voice from under a witches hat.

'Oh, my goodness, my dear. I hardly recognised you.'

Lady Buchanan tried not to stare at Davina's pert nipples, which having been exposed to the cold night air, were peeking through the sparse fabric like chapel hat-pegs.

Davina's eyes were sparkling mischievously but her teeth were chattering. 'Lovely dress...' Lady Buchanan declared, 'but I'm most concerned about you catching your death of cold, my dear. Why don't you go into the cellar and collect a cloak?' She led Davina to the cellar door. 'I have a black velvet cape down there that I you are more than welcome to borrow.'

'Thank you, I am a bit chilly. I shall pop it on for a little while.' Davina had no intention of wearing the mouldy moth-eaten cast. She had just seen Innes disappear into the cellar. She followed, making her way tentatively down the dimly lit steps and into the vast room below.

In front of her was a rack of outdoor clothes. She made her way along them, her fingers splayed out to feel for the velvet fabric against her fingers. Her eyes searched for Innes. The cellar was creepy and cold. Its stone walls partitioned into rooms, mimicking the house above it and similarly filled with junk. At the sound of a deep voice, she almost jumped out of her skin. 'Davina, is that you?'

She gave out a high pitched shriek that echoed around the dingy basement surroundings. Then, in the stifled glow of the dirty twenty-five watt light bulb, she saw a bloodied Celtic warrior. His face was deathly white and smeared with what appeared to be the dried blood of a fatal head wound. His clothes were torn and stained. 'Innes?'

'Davina, what are you doing down here?'

She laughed with delight and relief. 'Thank goodness. For a moment I though you were a dead highlander!'

'That's exactly what I'm meant to be.'

With her hands on her hips she swaggered towards him in her killer heels. Her flimsy dress clinging to her slim body and leaving nothing to the imagination.

It was so cold down there that her nipples ached.

She moved forward and thrust herself against him. 'And I'm ghost hunting,' she growled with whisky infused breath.

'Christ Davina, you'll catch your death down here. It's freezing.'

'Then why don't you keep me warm....'

She was standing so close to him that she could feel his heart beating. It was beating so fast that she thought she must have stirred him. She wound her arms around his neck and playfully fingering the buttons on his shirt. Forcing him to inhale her expensive perfume.

He started to say something, but she silenced him by pressed a polished black nail to his lips. 'Shhh. It's okay. I forgive you.'

Innes sighed. 'I'm glad. Does it mean we can finally move on?'

Davina ran a sharp fingernail down the side of his face which left a line through his face paint. 'I like your outfit,' she said. 'You look exactly like him....'

Innes made a little joke. 'But taller I hope. I hear Mel Gibson's just a little guy.'

And before he could do anything to stop her, she was kissing him.

Orley made her way carefully down from her tower room, holding onto the banister rail while she tried not to wobble in the stiletto-heeled black boots. With her free hand, she gathered her cloak against the blast of cold air from the open door below, where she could see Lady Buchanan welcoming guests and telling everyone to call her 'Morticia' whilst at the same time linking arms with someone who was dressed as Uncle Fester.

The lower floor of the house was bustling with witches, demons, vampires, and other unearthly entities. Music pulsed from the sound system and people squealed in horror at the fake blood, the giant spiders, the cobwebs, and the flapping bats that decorated the rooms. A blood oozing zombie, she noticed, was busy pouring a whole bottle of vodka into her bloody punch.

She looked around for Innes.

'Excuse me but are there any non alcoholic drinks?' said a woman dressed as a black cat. 'Only I'm driving later.'

Orley glanced over to the bar. No Fergus.

She turned to the cat woman. 'Yes. I'll go and get it.'

She looked round again for Innes. Lady Buchanan jabbed a finger towards the cellar door. 'Innes is in the cellar getting more wine. The rest of the punch is down there too, keeping cool,' she shouted over the rising hullabaloo.

Orley resigned herself to going down into the cellar. It was a place she had explored only once and once had been enough. It was cold and gloomy as she descended the short flight of stairs. Thankfully, tonight, with all the fires going and the central heating blasting away, the rest of the house was comfortably warm. Just as she reached the bottom stair she stopped. She thought she might have heard a man's voice. The hairs on the back of her neck rose and fear suddenly gripped her.

Maybe she was about to encounter a ghost?

She was just about to call out when she heard a woman's voice too. Orley held her breath and listened. Again she heard the voice. It was definitely a woman's. It sounded familiar but she couldn't be sure so she dived into a rail of coats while she tried to establish whether they were mortal, or spiritual, beings.

'I forgive you,' the woman's voice declared.

The man sighed and said something Orley couldn't make out.

'I like your outfit. You look just like him...'

The distinct clipped tone of the woman's voice was unmistakably Davina's.

She peered out from her hiding place to see Davina, who was dressed as a witch in a dress that looked like a cobweb, and Innes, who was standing with his back to her in his bloodied kilt and ripped shirt. He was laughing. He was obviously enjoying himself. 'But taller I hope,' she heard him said. 'I hear Mel Gibson's just a little guy.'

The laugh, the tone, the voice, the realisation - all hit Orley like a brick. Clearly, Fergus wasn't getting anywhere with Davina, because she was still after Innes!

Orley had to press her hand over her mouth to stop herself from crying out when in the very next moment, the two of them were locked in a passionate embrace. Her stomach contracted as if she had been punched. She fought not to throw up. Her heart, beating erratically and frantically, felt as if it had been stabbed through with a knife.

Innes had been lying to her about his feelings for Davina.

Just friends? She didn't think so. Not from what she had just seen. He had deceived her. He had lied. The way that men do and some women seem happy to go along with.

What had made her think he was going to be any different..?

She stumbled back upstairs, to find the party in full swing. Everyone was dancing, including Lady Buchanan and Uncle Fester. Orley headed for the drinks table. She poured herself a large whisky and drank it down in one gulp.

'Orley, are you alright?'

Innes was suddenly standing behind her.

She turned and glared at him. In his outfit, he looked exactly like the tyrant he really was. A man with no conscience at all. 'No. I'm not alright. I need another drink.'

'Take it easy,' he warned. 'You're still on medication.'

She took a large gulp of whisky in defiance and started coughing, sending her cloak flying. Innes retrieved the cloak and replaced it across her shoulders.

'Okay. Now let me guess?' he said staring into her cleavage. 'I'd say, you're Queen of the Damned.'

'A damned fool is what I am!' she sobbed and pulling herself together, she pushed him away.

Innes grabbed her arm. His eyes blazed. He actually looked hurt. 'What's got into you?' he demanded.

'Let go of me. You're a liar and a cheat. I saw you together in the cellar – you and your so-called ex-fiancée!'

Innes let go.

Orley disappeared into the roomful of throbbing music and hot bodies in bulky outfits. She pushed her way towards the door. Everyone was laughing. Probably at her. And why not - what an idiot she had been. She had let him seduce her body. She had allowed him access to her heart. She thought she could trust him. She had been wrong – again.

Then someone started up the 'Conga' and she could see that every other girl in the line up was dressed as a witch.

Her eyes searched for the tardiest.

She wanted to slap Davina's face.

'Come on, Orley. Let's join in!' Fergus yelled, appearing from nowhere and dragging her into the line.

Orley gasped. He was dressed exactly like Innes. They looked identical. Her heart leapt. She had been mistaken. It had been Fergus down in the cellar with Davina not Innes.

Tears brimmed in her eyes as she looked around her. In a heartbeat everything had changed. The party was riotous, the music was loud, and everyone was having a good time.

She took a deep breath and turned to find Innes and explain. What must he think of her?

He was stood in a daze by the bar with an empty glass in his hand. She went over to apologise. 'I'm so sorry Innes. I thought it was you in the cellar with Davina. I was so chewed up about you two having been engaged that I jumped to the wrong conclusions.'

He looked at her incredulously. His face white behind the fake blood.

Fergus and Davina joined them, panting and laughing from the Conga line. 'Here you both are!' yelled Fergus. 'Where have you been?'

'What happened to your Batman outfit, Fergus?' Orley asked.

'Didn't arrive.'

'You know it's impossible to tell you two apart now? I mistakenly thought it was Innes kissing Davina in the cellar just now. Funny eh?' She waited for him them all to laugh but Innes's face turned even paler.

She looked at Davina who suddenly demanded to Fergus, 'why are we not dancing like everyone else?'

'Cos we don't want to dance like them - they're all crap!' Fergus retorted while giving his brother a look that would kill.

Orley felt her body freeze. She began to shake.

Davina dragged Fergus onto what had become the dance floor. Had she not, Orley might just have just throttled her.

Someone nearby was smoking a cigarette. She caught a whiff of a pungent smouldering sort of smell in her nostrils. She turned around and then together with a strong acrid smell, there was a bright flash. To her horror, the wayward cigarette had set alight to the synthetic fabric of her cloak and it was disintegrating around her, the fabric flaming, melting, and singeing. Orley began to panic.

In just seconds she was left standing in nothing but a plunging body stocking, a pair of long black boots, and a cloak that now resembled a neck scarf. What had seemed a clever idea earlier, now seemed in incredibly bad taste, and she desperately wished she still had her long hair to hide behind. Men still able to see through their drunken haze wolf-whistled at her. The ones dressed as werewolves were howling. Women gasped in embarrassment and covered their husband eyes from the unveiling.

To make matters worse, Innes The Betrayer was standing in front of her with his eyes popping out of his head.

She fled the room. Skidding on her heeled boots across the hallway and stumbling up the staircase to her tower room. Only when she was safely inside with the door slammed shut, did she discard her vampire fangs and allow herself to burst into tears.

Bang bang bang.... Innes hammered on the door. 'Orley, open up!'

'Go away. Leave me alone!' she sobbed.

'You caught fire. There was a big flash!'

'Yeah. It was me – the flasher!'

There was a moments silence from the other side of the door. Orley held her breath and prayed he would go away.

'Are you hurt, Orley?' His voice was low and full of concern. 'Open the door. I need to see you.'

She opened it. 'I'm not injured if that's what you mean....'

She now had a bath robe around her, pulled tightly to her chin. Black smears smudged her eyes and grubby wet streaks ran down her face.

Innes, in his tattered highland garb and grease-paint, looked large and daunting as he stood in her doorway. He opened his sporran and took out a cotton handkerchief. Gently, he dabbed her eyes with it. His eyes shone down on her like bright stars in a pitch black sky.

She frowned and bit her lower lip. A sob escaped. When she allowed herself fall in love with him, she might as well have been handing him a loaded gun.

It took all of her courage to challenge him. She had to tap into all the anger and disappointment in her heart in order to find the fortitude.

'I suggest,' she said with her voice cracking, 'that in the morning while I'm packing, you come back up here and explain to me about you and Davina!'

Then catching him off guard she pushed him out of the door and slammed it shut. It was over between them.

A tear rolled down her face as she leaned back against the locked door. She wiped her eyes and blew her nose on the cotton handkerchief. It smelt of heather and damp moorlands. She asked herself again what had made her believe he was going to be any different?

A little while later, still in her dressing gown, Orley made her way carefully down the tower room steps. She ran quietly down the corridor to the study which was in a far flung corner of the house. At the computer, she logged on with her password and emailed her sister Tanya.

Tanya. I intend leaving here in the morning. Things haven't worked out the way I thought they would. I will get a flight out of Glasgow to Paris tomorrow. Will you please meet me? I will let you know the times. Love from your sister, Orley.

Tanya emailed back immediately with assurances and questions and Orley proceeded to pour her heart out. She told Tanya all about Innes and how she had stupidly let herself fall in love all over again.

She explained about Billy Mitchell, the man she had been about to marry in San Angelo and who she had caught cheating on her with another girl.

'It's happening all over again!' she told Tanya.

There was so much to say and to explain about: from how she had pulled a gun on Billy and held it against his head. To how she had pulled the trigger and escaped from jail. To how she had found herself here in Scotland, with a broken heart, contemplating murder all over again.

Chapter Twenty

Innes had been tempted to hammer on the door again but instead, he decided Orley was right and it would be better left until morning. He didn't want to make excuses. He wanted to offer her explanations. So he walked away feeling remorseful, knowing that he should have told her all about his annulled engagement to Davina long before now.

It had crossed his mind to tell her earlier but somehow the subject hadn't seemed relevant nor the situation pertinent. He had been busy. Then Orley had been in hospital. They just hadn't talked about their past relationships. It was an awkward subject. Orley had her secrets too, of course, the silver cowboy for one.

Nevertheless, Orley finding out about him and his very short engagement to Davina from some other means was going to make it all seem far worse to her.

He returned to his bedroom to put the light on and discover that Davina was in his bed. He didn't know how she had got there and was wondered what to say to get rid of her when there was a gentle knock on his door.

His blood ran cold. His heart seemed to stop beating.

The knock on the door was repeated. He opened it.

It was Orley, just as he feared.

'I just wanted to tell you that I'll definitely be leaving tomorrow,' she said stiffly through the narrow gap of the door. 'I've been in touch with my sister and arranged to stay with her in Paris. I just thought you should know.'

He looked at her in anguish. His face deathly pale. He opened the door just enough to slide out into the hallway and beg her not to leave, when Orley heard Davina's voice calling out his name from inside the room.

Innes's face dropped like a stone.

Orley gazed at him in disbelief. 'Well congratulations, you really had me fooled!'

'I didn't lie to you Orley. This isn't what you think!'

In desperation, he pushing the bedroom door open and grabbing Orley's arm, he pulled her right into the middle of the room. 'Ask her.' He said. 'She'll tell you herself that this is a mistake.'

'Stop. You're hurting me!' Orley yelled. His big hand crushing her arm.

Innes let her go and Orley could see Davina sitting up in Innes's bed, his bedcovers only partly covering her naked body. She looked at Orley in feign surprise. Her bare breasts full and high. Her nipples dark and hard. Her black witches' hat cast aside on top of the lampshade, to shed an ambient light across the room and project stars and moons on the ceiling. She was smiling like a cat that had got the cream.

Innes looked away.

'Don't be long darling,' she purred at Innes. 'Do come back to bed soon won't you?'

Orley ran from the room.

As this wasn't the first time she'd been lied to, you'd think she would have learned a thing or two, maybe she had. Maybe that's why there were no tears this time as she climbed the stairs to her tower room. No sobbing as she went inside and bolted the door. Her heart breaking in dignity and silence as she sat waiting for the sun to rise.

The first rays of morning crept across Orley's curled up body like long fingers checking for a pulse. She was awake but not sure she felt alive. She had not slept, not even a wink, and by the light of the moon she had surreptitiously packed her belongings into her suitcase while shivering with cold, because the central heating had long switched off.

She had been waiting for the cold light of day.

The full force of the previous nights events weighed heavily on her heart as she climbed out of bed. Grabbing her jacket, she crept out of the house. She didn't want to leave without saying goodbye to Hamish and 'her ladies' besides, they would be hungry and looking for their breakfast.

From the barn she pushed a quad bike with a trailer of hay attached to it into the fields without starting the engine. Breath from her mouth and nostrils came out in billows of mist as she pushed the heavy bike across the hard icy-furrows. She complained to herself that if she'd had a horse to ride all this would have been less bother on such a freezing cold morning.

Once out of earshot, she rode across the fields slowly searching for the fold. Hamish would have led the ladies to the sheltered fields under the hill where there might still be a little grass for grazing. She made slow progress across the snow fields and before long she could hardly feel her fingers. She was angry with herself for forgetting her gloves. Soon she spied the cattle. A bright russet patch in the white landscape amongst a swirling mist of vaporous air.

As she approached, each raised their massive upturned horns and moved slowly towards her with their big squat shaggy bodies and dishevelled heads of hair.

They came with hungry and expectant eyes. Orley moved quickly. Stiff with cold and shivering violently, she freed the hay and deposited it in piles. She fed Hamish his bucket of sweet molasses and whilst he ate, she stroked his hairy head and for warmth and rubbed her hands on his warm horns, cuddling up to him and burying her fingers into his long shaggy coat. His hair had a soft layer beneath the top coarse waterproof one. He seem to welcome the attention and grunted his thanks into the bucket while he finished the meal.

She looked around her at the incredibly beautiful scenery around her. Her eyes wide with wonder. Last night's settle of snow was only an inch deep but had enhanced the beauty of the already stunning landscape to unparalleled proportions. Scotland was all and more than she had ever dreamed of. The same, unfortunately, had not applied to Innes. She had fallen in love with a simple piper on a beach not a Laird with secrets: one of which happened to be a fiancé.

She thought back to the time when they had met and she remembered how his black eyes had promised so much love. But those eyes had lied to her. Inadvertently, she had lied to herself.

The ground beneath her was so frozen that it crunched beneath her feet. Her toes were tingling and numb with cold.

'This is too beautiful and cruel a place,' she told herself with a sob, as icy tears coursed down a face burning with frost.

She sat astride the quad bike and blew her breath onto her frozen fingers. They were anaesthetised. She pressed the ignition button. The bike coughed and spluttered in response but it did not start. She tried again and again but now the bike was not even spluttering. She tried to start it by pushing it forward a little. At least the effort warmed her. Soon, the silence around her was eerie.

I'm not going to die out here she told herself.

She could get in amongst the fold and keep warm. She also still had two chocolate bars in her pockets so she wouldn't starve. But soon, the cattle had finished their hay and were starting to move off and it began to snow again, heavily. She was all alone.

When Innes climbed the tower room stairs to find Orley's bedroom door ajar and her luggage still on her bed, he realised she must have gone out to check the cattle. It was with some concern that he went out after her. It was still well below zero and the previous nights snow fall, although not deep, was slippery and dangerous to travel across.

From Hilltop he spotted the fold, Orley, and the quad bike. He also noted the colour of the sky, which was so white and featureless, it promised to engulf them all in new snowfall.

Orley heard the low drone of the quad bike before he came into view. She prayed it was Fergus that had come to rescue her because, given the choice of freezing to death or facing Innes, the numbing death seemed suddenly preferable.

But it wasn't Fergus that climbed off the bike and approached her.

They eyed each other across the frozen space between them.

He could see that her lips were tinged blue and her face pale. Her eyes red and frightened. 'Can we talk Orley?'

She turned away from him to collect up Hamish's feed bucket. 'Not here. I'm too cold. Let's get back to the house.'

He saw she wasn't wearing gloves and removed his own. He passed them to her. She accepted without question.

'I think my bike's frozen,' she told him glumly. 'And my mobile phone wouldn't work.'

Innes tapped her fuel gauge and frowned. 'There is no mobile signal here. You just can't ride off into the hills without first checking you have enough fuel!'

He was angry with her. What a nerve!

She retaliated. 'Well, that's probably because I'm more used to riding something that doesn't have a fuel gauge and that I can trust to get me home safely!'

Innes decided against transferring fuel because the snow which had started to fall slowly, was being whipped up by an icy gale and the temperature had plummeted. 'Come on, get aboard, we'll need to take shelter.'

Half-grudgingly, Orley climbed onto the back of Innes bike. She was even reluctant to wrap her arms around his chest to secure herself for the journey. Yet, it was impossible not to do so, as the bike slid and bumped across the frozen ice beneath the fresh snow.

Innes seemed to know exactly where he was headed, although she doubted this was the way back to Glencorrie.

When they came to a halt a short time later, they were outside a small stone hut. The old door latch opened easily and with the full force of blizzard behind them, they burst through it. It was dark inside and very bare except for two long wooden benches and a fireplace. An alcove next to the fire place was stacked high with dry wood. Innes immediately set to work lighting it.

'This is our Bothy,' he explained. 'From September on we make sure it is equipped for conditions such as these. It's proved to be a lifeline many times over believe me.' He offered more wood to the flames and heat began to radiate from the fire and cast a crimson light across the room. 'The fire will soon warm you,' he told her.

Orley watched as he opened a cupboard at the other side of the fireplace and took out blankets, a pan, a tin opener and tins of soup. He seemed to struggle with the tin opener for a moment and she felt quite useless, unable to do anything because she was too numb with cold.

Eventually, he managed to get the soup into the pan and the pan over the fire. 'Come here,' he instructed, unzipping his waxed jacket.

Even though she still had no feeling in her legs and feet, Orley did as she was told. Innes wrapped her in his arms and a blanket around them both. He held her tightly, so that he could transfer his own heat to her. She did neither object or complain as he moved his hands quickly up and down her body to warm her.

Orley had never experienced cold like this and she never wanted to again and, although she was quite sure that he had saved her from a certain kind of death, she still felt herself dying in his embrace.

As his heat seeped slowly into her and sensations started to rush back, she began to shiver violently and could not help but to cry out in pain.

'It's going to be okay. You need to take your boots off so I can rub your feet. Let me help you.'

He was gentle. He left her thick woollen socks in place and tenderly rubbed her toes. She was clearly in agony as the rush of warm blood pumping through veins and capillaries caused her feet to cramp.

'I'm glad you came out after me,' she suddenly blurted. 'I don't know what I would have done, stuck out here, with no way of getting back...'

'Sshh, he murmured. 'It's going to be okay.'

The soup was beginning to simmer in the pan. Innes fed it to her as her hands were shaking too uncontrollably to hold the spoon.

But soon, with the fire taking hold, they both began to relax. The wind continued to howl outside but inside, wrapped in cosy blankets and with the fire established, they were warm and safe and, as it was clear they were going to be here for some time, Orley, exhausted by her ordeal, drifted off to sleep.

When she awoke she was holding tightly onto him. Her body moulded to his and her head resting on his chest. She was aware of the strong and steady sound of his beating heart before she opened her eyes. In this moment, it felt good and comfortable to be so close to him but once he knew she was awake, he might defend his reasons for deceiving her with more lies and excuses. She was so dreading listening to it that she almost wished herself numb again. Steeling herself to open her eyes, she found him looking down at her.

His face full of tenderness. She wondered if it was possible to hate such a face.

To preserve her fragile sanity, she decided to confront him. After all, he could not walk away or choose not to answer. Not here.

When all alone in the first snow of the winter, she had rehearsed the angry conversation she wanted to have with him. Believing she was certain to freeze to death, she wanted more than anything else a chance to vent her feelings. Then, during the excruciating agony of being warmed, she had wanted to scream at him in frustration.

Again, in despair, she fought her pathetic compulsion to burst into tears and tell him how he had broken her heart and that would never recover.

But Innes spoke first. His voice was even and quiet.

'I did not invite Davina into the cellar last night to kiss me or ask her into my bed. You have to believe me. I was as surprised as you. I have never had those sort of feelings for her and I have never ....'

'Oh Innes. Stop lying to me. You two were engaged to be married!'

'I'm not lying. I've never lied.'

Orley looked into his eyes. *Liars avoided eye contact, didn't they?*

'Innes sighed. 'I'm sorry that I didn't tell you before, but somehow didn't seem relevant to us. I know now that was a mistake.'

'Then why were you marrying her? Was it you who broke it off?'

'Yes, and I thought I'd made myself clear to her.'

'But Innes, I saw you both in the cellar. I saw you kiss her!'

'No. She was kissing me. There's a difference…!'

'But, I saw...'

He silenced her protest with one finger pressed lightly onto her lips. He repeated. 'She followed me into the cellar. She was drunk. She kissed me. It was not the other way round. You have to believe me Orley. I'm in love with you.'

'And what about Davina, didn't you love her once too?'

'No. We have only ever been friends. I was only marrying her for money.'

Orley gasped.

'I know, I know. That almost sounds worse than anything.'

'Poor Davina. You never loved her...?'

Innes shook his head.

'But Fergus does.' Orley told him.

Innes sighed. 'Did he tell you that?'

'Sort of – but it's obvious isn't it?'

Innes groaned. 'No, it wasn't obvious to me. Once I found out though, I couldn't marry her. Not for money. Not for anything. So I called it off and went to Texas to study cattle.' His eyes reflected the firelight flickering on the stone walls. 'Please believe me? he begged.'

'I'm getting there' Orley had to admit. 'It has occurred to me that I may have been too quick to think the worst of you. I didn't trust you. But if you remember, back in Baytown, I warned you that I am a deeply suspicious and untrusting person and I have a foul temper.'

'You also said that you never forgive ever but I'm asking you to forgive me?'

'I want to. See how you have changed me? I'm making exceptions to my own rules!'

'Rules that only came about because some idiot cowboy broke your heart.'

Her head jerked up. She glared at him.

Innes continued. 'A relationship you also choose not to talk about.'

Orley gulped. It was true. She had accused him of not being open with her when she was guilty of the same crime.

Innes held out his arms. 'Let it go Orley. Let *him* go and love *me* instead?'

She fell into them and clung to him with an intensity born of relief.

His words repeated in her head as his mouth came down persuasively on hers and her body shivered its response. Not from cold this time but from a burning ache. She had rediscovered her faith in him and was ready to say those special words and maybe for the first time in her life, they would really mean something.

I love you, Innes....

But then the door of the bothy burst open and a swirling howling blizzard seemed to throw someone in a snowsuit straight into the middle of the room. As the door burst open for a second time, Fergus blew in.

The intruders stood as if rooted to the spot. Their mouths ajar and their expressions aghast, like two long-frozen mountaineers complete with frosted eyebrows and icicle-clad noses.

Innes spoke first. 'Bloody hell, have you never heard of knocking?'

'The rescue team has arrived!' Fergus announced.

Davina removed her gloves and fur-trimmed hood while directing a tempestuous gaze on the cosy sight in front of the fire. 'We have brought some horses to get you back,' she told them.

Innes looked at Orley. 'Are you okay about riding?'

'Yes, of course. How many horses?' Orley asked.

'Two. I'll ride with Fergus. Orley, you can ride with Innes.'

Fergus's eyes were shining with excitement and fear.

The rescuers warmed themselves by the fire and Orley made some hot chocolate from the store cupboard and boiling water from the kettle on the fire.

'Here, this will warm you,' Orley said, handing the drink it over to a woman she had been shocked to discover was an adversary. Innes's explanation had made her feel only pity towards her. A glance of sorts passed between them as Davina accepted the steaming mug.

The ride back was slow and although the horses were sturdy, strong, and sure-footed, they picked their way carefully across the snow fields.

Orley pointed out to Innes where the fold were taking shelter. It was too far away to do a head count but this kind of weather would do them no harm.

Eventually, they could see Glencorrie ahead. Looming up out of the mist. It's snow capped turrets piercing the low cloud. It's ominous presence a curious comfort.

Chapter Twenty-One

It was the strangest thing. It was just a couple of days after the snowstorm but the temperatures had risen again and there was not a flake of snow to be seen anywhere. Instead it rained lightly and steadily, transforming the landscape.

At Glencorrie, the air both inside and outside was damp and rank as misty cloud cover descended.

All of the chimneys had lost their up-draft and smoke and fumes billowed back into the rooms. So, rather than endure coughing and spluttering at best or suffocation at worst, the fires had to be dowsed with water and even the huge new boiler had to be switched off. They were all reduced to walking around indoors in hats and coats.

Orley particularly, felt miserable and cold. She also felt troubled. The joy of knowing that Innes truly loved her was being marred by Davina's and Fergus's unhappiness. In many ways she could understand Davina's hang up on Innes and she could empathise with her jealously. It was such a destructive and all consuming emotion. She liked to think of jealousy as a sickness of the heart rather than a sin of the soul. So she resolved to take a walk over to Castle McKenzie and square things, if only for Fergus's sake.

Poor Fergus, who was as lovesick as ever.

She took the long route via the tarmacadam road, a preferable option on such a grey and foggy day when everything around seemed oppressive and murky.

Fields were left waterlogged by the thaw and the skeletal remains of plants, like the tall rosebay willow herb, that had lined the hedgerows so abundantly were now decimated.

Orley was reminded of the damage caused in Texas by hurricanes. Where whole fields of grain, tall and blowing in the breeze one day, lay flattened and broken in its aftermath the next.

Davina was outside the stable block grooming her horse.

'I do envy you with your horses,' Orley told her as she approached.

She turned and looked uncomfortable. 'Oh it's you,' she said dismissively.

'I just wanted to thank you for coming out for us in the storm.'

'You have already thanked me. There is nothing more to be said.'

'I believe there is. We have to talk.'

'Fergus said the snow was to get worse and we had to get you out,' she snapped. 'It just goes to prove they can never get the weather right.'

'I don't think we can blame Fergus for the weather,' said Orley, missing the point. *What was it with British people and the weather?*

Davina led the horse back into the stable.

'It was very brave of you.' Orley insisted, leaning on the stable half-door and peering into the semi-darkness, 'and awkward under the circumstances.' Davina was out of sight inside the loose box but against the whitewashed walls Orley could see her motionless shadow. She held her breath and waited. This was going to be much harder than she thought. 'Innes told me about your engagement. He couldn't marry you when he found out how Fergus felt about you....'

Waiting for Davina to come out of the stable was agony.

Would she run out with a pitch fork and spear her through the heart with it?

To her relief she came out quietly, but her face was like granite. 'Innes talked to you about me? I bet he didn't tell you everything. I bet he didn't tell you the only reason he brought you over here was to be his big excuse for not going ahead with a wedding planned down to the very last bloody detail!'

Orley looked rocked.

'Well it's true,' Davina told her.

Orley nodded. 'I can see it might have started out like that. I was in the right place in the right time.'

'No Orley, I don't think you do understand. You think Innes is in love with you and he isn't. He never was. He used you. Don't you see that?'

Orley was shaking her head. 'No. You are wrong. He needed a cattle manager.'

Davina laughed cruelly. 'And do you really think he couldn't have got one, if not a dozen, down at the local pub?'

'He had other reasons. We had fallen in love. Though neither of us realised it at the time.' Orley was yelling now. 'He could not be so calculating.'

'You don't think?'

The two women stared at each other. It was like a duel at sundown. Davina dealt the fatal blow with: 'then remember this, Orley MacKenna of the Clan MacKenna, he was marrying me for my money.'

This woman was brutal. She had only pretended to befriend her for the purpose of getting back at Innes or with Innes. One or the other. Maybe she was now trying to drive her away by playing on her insecurities? Orley was damned if she would let that happen. Innes did love her and she loved him. No matter what this bitch said to the contrary.

'I came here to talk to you about Fergus,' Orley told her brusquely. 'But I shouldn't have bothered. I don't know what he sees in you. You string him along. You use him and you drop him. We have a word for girls like you in Texas....'

'And we have words for girls like you in Scotland!' Davina retaliated.

'As we have nothing else in common then I'll be off.'

Orley walked tall back down the driveway of Castle McKenzie with her head held high. She wouldn't put it past a girl like Davina to try and get revenge, so she must make sure she was on guard at all times.

Now she thought about it, revenge that is, she questioned the soup Davina had brought her when she had the 'flu. It had made her much worse. And the haircut because Shona was Davina's hairdresser. And the accident? No.

Impossible. Now her imagination was running away with her.

Later that same afternoon, while Innes was away, Orley planned to ride out over the fields on a quad bike to the fold.

'Don't worry. I'll check my fuel and wear my survival gear,' she assured Innes, whom had pinned a checklist up in the barn to remind her to check her equipment and no doubt to also rub salt into her chilblains.

'I won't worry,' he informed her, 'because Fergus is going with you.'

Something told her not to argue. Which meant she had successfully taught him a thing or two about being formidable. So she and Fergus rode out together across the fields and Orley decided that it might be a good opportunity to talk to him about Davina.

It was slow going uphill, dangerous downhill and difficult not to get stuck in the boggy glens.

'This is what we call Scotch mist,' Fergus explained to Orley as a dense fog descended upon them.

Orley was not impressed. 'And how long will it stay?'

He shrugged. 'It's impossible to say but until you know these hills as we do, only then will you be safe out here.'

'Oh for goodness sake, Fergus. I've learned my lesson.'

He smiled apologetically and insisted on doing all the heavy work with the bales of hay and sacks of grain. Hamish and the ladies had seen them approaching and had made an enthusiastic stampede across the glen to meet with them. Orley filled Hamish's bucket with grain and went over to feed him. 'Here you are my darling.'

Fergus laughed. 'Innes is right. You are crazy!'

'I beg your pardon?' Orley laughed. 'Crazy?'

'Well, his exact words were 'a contradiction.'

Orley gasped. I do hope that's a compliment!'

They stood for a moment and watched the cattle eat. The only sound was the munching and grunting of enthusiastic diners. Orley braced herself to ask Fergus a few pertinent questions.

'So what's the story with you and Davina now?'

Fergus's face dropped. 'There isn't one.'

'Do you still feel strongly about her?'

He shrugged and nodded at the same time which conveyed his confusion.

'Only, if I were you I wouldn't push it. You know. What is meant to be is meant to be....' Orley tried to say but Hamish kicked his bucket over. Meal over. Conversation over.

They drove back to Glencorrie in convoy. Orley riding in Fergus's tracks, carefully following the back lights of his bike through the heavy mist. He was sensibly keeping to the paths carved out of the hillside by the sheep. As even they preferred to walk in straight lines. Not unlike haggis apparently, which according to Innes had three legs, one each longer than the other so that they could run across the Scottish landscape without falling over. *Yeah right.*

It was after four o'clock when they pulled into the yard at Glencorrie. It had already got quite dark. To their surprise there was a smartly dressed man waiting for them in the kitchen porch. 'Can I help you?' Orley asked while wondering why Lady Buchanan hadn't invited this person in.

'I'm looking for Fergus Buchanan.' The man had an English accent.

Orley looked him over and tried to hazard a guess as to what he would want with Fergus. He could hardly be a friend or an estate labourer. Not with that accent or those clothes. He looked like a banker – or a lawyer.

'He's just here,' she said. 'This is Fergus Buchanan.'

Fergus approached and the man stretched out his hand. 'How do you do Mr Buchanan. I'm Lance Henderson from the firm of Henderson and Kirkpatrick.

'Oh.' said Fergus. 'You must be looking for my brother. He deals with all matters concerning the Estate.'

'Erm no. It's definitely you I need to speak to.'

Fergus, visibly taken aback, invited Lance Henderson inside and offered him a drink.

And he doesn't mean tea, thought Orley.

'Thank you. That would be very nice,' said the unsuspecting Mr Henderson.

Orley didn't join them.

'If you gentlemen will excuse me,' she said. 'I'll just finish up a few jobs outside.'

Meanwhile at Castle McKenzie, Davina had the *Great Scot* broadsheet newspaper spread out across the floor of the sitting room and could hardly contain her excitement or believe her unblinking eyes.

Lost Baron Found In Dumfries and Galloway: the headline shouted. She read on:

The lost heir to a multi-million pound fortune kept in trust by the Scottish Chancery for almost three generations has been found. Fergus Douglas Buchanan, 22, the second son of the recently late Hamish Douglas Buchanan of the Buchanan Clan, and brother of the recent successor to the Buchanan seat, Innes Thane Buchanan, 25, is by default, the only rightful claimant to the controversial title in almost two hundred years, etc etc....

'My Goodness.' Davina gasped. 'Then it must be true. Fergus does have a title after all!'

At Glencorrie, Fergus was in a state of disarray at the news imparted by Lance Henderson, who was indeed a lawyer. 'I specialise in genealogy,' he told him.

'I'm afraid I don't understand. Can you run that by me again please?' Fergus asked.

'We have sent you several letters about this, Mr Buchanan. Are you telling me you didn't get any of them?'

Fergus poured them both another large drink. His hands were shaking. 'I though they were some kind of spoof. A joke. You know, the kind you can order off the internet:- "Be the Laird to your own Scottish Kingdom for ten quid." That kind of thing.'

'Oh. I see.' said Mr Henderson. 'But I do assure you, Mr Buchanan that the papers are authentic.'

Fergus remembered what Davina had said about the first letter he had received. 'Surely any such title would fall to Innes?' Fergus asked the question.

'Not in this case, you see hundreds of years ago, there was a clan uprising and the Buchanan chief and his eldest son were killed. The title naturally fell to the second son, who happened to also be called Fergus, and who was away in France. On hearing the news, he returned home to Scotland, but having renounced his Catholic faith, his extended family disinherited him. So, as a leader of the newly established Protestant movement, he split the clan and set about building up the Scottish Kirk.

Fergus of Galloway was a legend after his death in 1161 and from that day on, it was written that only a second son could inherit from his line.'

Fergus's eyes were on stalks. 'A legend…!' he repeated.

'Your father, your grandfather, and his father before him had no siblings. You, Fergus, are the only second son in your family for generations!' Mr Henderson reiterated.

'So you are saying that this is not something Innes can claim?'

'He is still the Laird of Buchanan, the original clan chieftain on the Catholic side is his birthright, but from the Protestant side, as direct descendent and second son, only you can claim The Kingdom of Galloway.'

Fergus's hand was shaking so much that he dropped his glass. It shattered into thousands of pieces. He stepped over it and grabbed the whisky bottle. He held it high. 'To Catholics and Protestants!' he shouted as Innes walked into the room.

'What's going on?' his brother demanded, noting the shattered glass and the infusion of whisky in the air.

'Innes!' yelled Fergus, 'come and celebrate!'

It seemed to Innes that Fergus was nothing short of delirious. His hair was raked up on end. It was vertical. He was excited or drunk or both.

'What is the difference between a Laird and a Baron?' Fergus asked.

Innes plunged his hands deeply into his pockets and contemplated for a while, thinking this was some sort of joke. 'I don't know,' he said. 'What is the difference between a Laird and a Baron?'

'I don't know either,' confessed Fergus with a burst of hysterical laughter, 'but I know someone who does. Mr Henderson will tell us. So how about it Mr Henderson?'

Innes looked to the stranger in the suit who, from his glazed smile, he supposed was even more drunk that his brother.

'Well. Let me see now,' raised Mr Henderson ponderously. 'How is it best put? I believe that if I said every Baron who holds the Caput of his Barony is also a Laird, but not every Laird is a Baron, that would be quite correct.'

'That is very interesting.' Innes said.

Again he looked to Fergus, who now looked quite mad.

'I'll be off,' said Mr Henderson, taking papers from his briefcase and placing them on a side table. 'I'll leave these documents in your safekeeping and next time we meet, you must call me Lance.'

Fergus shook his outstretched hand and once Mr Henderson had left, he turned to Innes saying, 'and next time we meet brother, you must call me Baron....'

Chapter Twenty-Two

Davina folded up the newspaper and went over to her computer. She searched the internet news sites and found all the major newspapers were running the story about Fergus, the new Baron of Galloway.

In the middle ages, said The Telegraph, *Galloway lay outside of Scotland and was much bigger than it is today. In 1124 b.c. Fergus of Galloway married the daughter of Henry I of England and was know as 'Rex Galwitensium' - The King of Galloway.*

On reading this Davina gasped so hard she practically choked herself. She dressed quickly and warmly, intent on congratulating Fergus. The silly squabbles between them were of no consequence after the news of such a fabulous inheritance.

She happily quoted from Macbeth. *If chance will have me king, why chance may crown me..*

They would all be celebrating. So, driving her Range Rover faster than she had ever driven it before and causing the crate of champagne she was carrying to rattle violently when she hit all the potholes in Glencorrie driveway, she sped up to the house and parked abruptly outside the front porch only to find the place in almost total darkness. She rang the bell anyway and to her relief, Lady Buchanan answered.

'Come in Davina,' how lovely to see you.'

Davina waved a bottle of Krug. 'I've just heard the good news.'

'So has the whole world or so it seems.' Lady Buchanan told her. 'The phone hasn't stopped ringing. The newspapers have made such a big deal of it. Oh and they have gone off to the pub. The three of them. To buy everyone drinks I don't doubt. I just hope we don't wake up in the morning to find it's all been a very sick joke.'

'Either way, why don't we open this. It's not everyday your son inherits a kingdom, is it?'

Lady Buchanan scoffed at the idea. 'Kingdom? He inherited what is left of the Galloway Forest, not the whole of Galloway, I don't know what all the fuss is about. Innes has a bigger forest than that at the other side of our river.'

Davina almost hesitated in pouring the champagne but it was too late to put the cork back in. 'But Fergus has the title does he not, the Baron of Galloway?'

'Apparently so.' Lady Buchanan said as she sucked the fizzy froth off the top of her glass. 'But what good will it do us, I ask you?'

'Oh, I'm sure some good will come of it.' Davina replied with the sparkle returning to her eyes. 'I'm sure it will help make all of Fergus's dreams come true.'

Then the phone rang. Lady Buchanan cursed it. 'Excuse me dear, I'll have to answer it. It's probably another nuisance call but I'm waiting for someone to ring me.'

Davina used the opportunity to pay a little visit to the bathroom. As she walked along the hallway she could hear Lady Buchanan's telephone voice in the background. A door almost opposite the bathroom was open. This was the study. She could see the massive oak desk piled high with Innes's papers and his new computer. On the edge of the desk, sat a smaller pile of quite ancient looking documents which had to be the title papers. Almost wetting herself with excitement, she first dashed to the loo and back out again as quickly as she could. Lady Buchanan's voice could still just be heard saying something about how tiresome it was to be the subject of newspaper headlines. Davina tiptoed back into the study and browsed the documents. They only seemed to mention a lot of boring bits of history. One page had a red wax seal and contained lots of signatures. One space remained however, and beneath it was typed in a modern style print, 'Signed This Day', and 'By Fergus Douglas Buchanan, Baron of Galloway'.

'I'm going to be a Baroness!' Davina squealed, 'And perhaps even a Queen!'

She rearranged the pile to make it look undisturbed and then she glanced around the room. It was a dirty, musty looking study. Not a patch on her own, or rather her father's study, whose valuable first editions lined the book wall and grand paintings competed for attention against the valuable highly polished furniture. She traced a line in the dust in the desk in front of her and then tried to rub out the evidence of her finger marks with her handkerchief, which only made matters worse, because now there was a big blatant clean patch.

Her eyes then fell upon the computer screen which happened to be switched on. Davina homed in to see that there were three picture squares on the screen, named Innes, Fergus, and Orley. Innes's picture was of a Highland cow. Fergus's was a sheep and Orley's picture was of a horse. Davina's hand wavered for a moment over the computer mouse and grasping it, she clicked twice on Orley's horse.

'Lets see what the cow gets up to.' Davina whispered to herself. A box appeared on screen asking for a password.

Davina made a little tutting sound and looked round for inspiration and tapped her fingers on the keyboard. *Texas* she typed. Bingo. The words on the screen said, Hello Orley, what do you want to do today?

Davina smiled smugly. Computers were obviously her thing. She imagined how with her skills, she could easily be employed by top banks or by the government to outsmart hackers. It was a shame that her current and future lifestyle plans didn't allow the time for it.

She clicked straight into Orley's inbox and outbox and was fascinated to find several emails to and from someone called Tanya. Orley, it seemed, has a sister with a name as equally tacky as hers.

Although, from reading on it appeared that they were not actually related. 'Oh, I see, through the recent marriage of their respective parents. Ah, that's nice, and Orley says she thinks of Tanya as a proper sister as has always wanted one. How sweet. Tanya sounds like a dog.'

Davina was engrossed. Then, in the next email there was a lot of whining about Innes and horses and sheep and, wow, a viciously stinging comment about Lady Buchanan and another about Davina herself.

Davina read on and on. Her eyes getting larger and larger until they looked like saucers reflected in the monitor screen.

'My Goodness, who would have thought that Miss Texas-Goody-Two-Shoes would be capable of such a terrible thing as murder....'

Then there was a noise outside. A vehicle drawing up and then voices. They must be back from the pub already.

Davina closed Orley's files, logged out of the computer and made her way out of the study and back down the hallway. She met Orley on the way back to the sitting room.

She was rushing for the bathroom. She glared and said. 'Davina, what a surprise. I do believe you are trespassing.'

Davina simply smiled. Orley couldn't have seen her come out of the study. 'There are no law of trespass in Scotland. Anyway, I'm so glad you are all back early as her Ladyship and I thought we might have to drink all the champagne I brought over on our own.'

In contrast. Fergus was overjoyed to see her. He was drunk, of course, but welcoming nevertheless. So Davina had him carry the crate of Krug from her Range Rover.

Orley, she noticed, was spying on them from the sitting room window. Davina laughed loudly and was overtly flirtatious to make it worth her while. The nosy cow-bitch.

Once they were all together and glasses were charged and raised, Innes proposed the toast. 'To his Lairdship the Baron of Galloway!'

They all cheered and shouted Pip-Pip before singing, '*For he's a joy good fellow and so say all of us*'.

Then Innes got out his bagpipes and Orley settled into a comfortable chair to sip her champagne which she was loath to admit, even to herself, that it was the best she had ever tasted and to loose herself in his music.

'Do you do requests?' she asked.

'Of course,' replied Innes. 'What would like me to play?'

'*Mhari's wedding*' she replied. The last time she heard it he had played it on the beach at Baytown.

'Arh,' he said, 'I believe we renamed it Martha's Wedding.' He smiled at her and she smiled back. They were

200

both remembering the same thing. Then both Fergus and Davina leapt to their feet to dance. They danced a traditional Scottish Reel. Linking arms then twirling and clapping their hands. Innes played on jauntily. The music was much faster than he had piped on the beach in Baytown. This was obviously the dance remix version. Lady Buchanan whooped and clapped as Fergus and Davina danced and Innes played. Orley watched in amazement as they swung each other from one side of the room to the other and skipped about. This was just like Texas line dancing except there was no line. 'Come on Orley!' yelled Fergus. 'I can handle the both of you!'

Orley was blushing as she got to her feet but she soon got the hang of things and when Innes played *Comin' Thro' The Rye*, she reeled and clapped and jigged and skipped until she could no more.

While Davina breathlessly popped another cork, Innes slowed the place and piped a haunting lament called *Ae Fond Kiss*, which Davina had requested.

After he played the first few bars, she began to sing.

Davina had a lovely voice. It was shrill and sweet and perfectly in tune. Her normally clipped tone was replaced with a lilt that emphasised the beautiful Gallic lyrics. *Had we never loved sae kindly, Had we never loved so blindly, Never met, or never parted, We had ne'er been broken-hearted,* she sang.

They all applauded once the song was done.

'That was beautiful Davina!' Orley told her. Despite their differences she was impressed.

And Fergus, Orley noticed, who was sweating profusely and still red in the face from all the dancing and drinking, was almost in tears.

Innes stopped and took a few sips of his drink and then began searching through a cupboard in the corner of the room. He pulled out an accordion and a small fiddle case. He then passed the fiddle case to his mother and the accordion to Fergus. Lady Buchanan tucked the fiddle under her small chin and struck off with the first tune.

Again the room was filled with music and Innes, holding out his arm and bowing like a gentleman, asked Orley to dance. At that moment, Davina popped the cork of yet another bottle and the party went on and on.

The next morning of course, the events of the night before were all a bit hazy. Orley lay in her bed trying to remember it all. What a talented lot they were. Davina with the voice of an angel even if she was a bit of a devil. Fergus a skilled accordion player. Lady Buchanan was amazing on the fiddle. And Innes on the pipes. Perfect.

She drifted back to thinking about Davina, who had been all over Fergus. She was winding him around her little finger in front of everyone and when she left for home, she had unashamedly kissed him on the lips. To Orley's certain knowledge, which was based on Fergus's tales of his unrequited love, she had never done that before.

Lucky Fergus. Or was he?

Orley surprised herself by being quite bright at breakfast time. Lady Buchanan wasn't up and about early but then she never was, preferring to arise sometime around ten o'clock. Fergus and Innes were already in the kitchen and had the kettle on. Orley served the porridge, which had been put in the warming oven over night to cook.

'I must be growing a second liver,' she proclaimed as she spooned out the hot porridge. 'I can't believe that after all that champagne last night I haven't got a hangover.'

'I believe you danced it off.' Fergus told her with a warm smile.

'It was a wonderful night, wasn't it?' she replied.

'It was fabulous!' Fergus sighed wistfully.

Innes looked at Orley. He raised his eyes heavenward and grinned. Orley grinned back. She was glad Davina's attentions had been averted away from Innes at long last but wasn't quite sure that was fair on Fergus.

Today's workload was going to be a team effort organised and put into place by Orley. Having heard about the delays over the re-roofing of the estate cottages, and the dilemma over the delivery of the welsh slate, she had swung into action. 'Lets get these folks back into their homes for Christmas,' she had suggested and with Innes's approval, she had liaised with the suppliers and arranged immediate deliveries. 'We can do all this work ourselves.'

Innes and Fergus had risen to the challenge and had managed to sub-contacting a few willing local men to help with all the work. They needed carpenters, joiners, stonemasons and labourers, but because the weather was horrendous, with driving rain and bitterly cold winds, they had to practically bribe any men they could get to help with top money. Innes who doubted they would turn up if the weather got worse, prayed it would not snow.

Orley, who in her past life had re-roofed whole barns in Texas, gave the labourers their instructions. 'We don't use slates in Texas, we use wooden shingles but it's all the same process to put them on,' she told them.

'First you knock holes in the slate like this...'

And at this point she demonstrated the 'two hit' action of the slate hammer. 'And then you nail them on the roof. Simple.'

Innes could see that the men were all slightly intimidated by a woman who could make it look simple and got down to work.

Thankfully the snow held off and the work was finished in time for Christmas. Even then, Orley came up trumps by moving the last remaining families into their cottages on Christmas Eve. She carried boxes, hung curtains, and provided each and every family with a fresh Christmas tree and a brace of pheasant. 'It'll make for a really happy Christmas for them,' she told Innes.

Not to feel outdone, even though they were his trees and his pheasants, and knowing his bank account had been cleaned out, Innes gave each overjoyed tenant a bottle of malt whisky and wished them a happy Christmas.

Chapter Twenty-Three

On Christmas Eve, Innes and Fergus came home from the forest dragging a twelve foot Christmas tree and potted it up in the sitting room. It was a spectacular tree and Orley was so excited with it that she decided not to complain about it being a very prickly Scots Pine. Its needles were so sharp that her fingers were raw and stinging by the time she had it fully decorated.

Lady Buchanan had helped by finding a box of tree decorations, baubles, and tinsel. She sat on a chair while Orley stood on a ladder and she handed each decoration to her one by one. She took great pleasure in telling the story behind each, especially the decorations made by Innes and Fergus when they were children. Orley thought they were charming and Lady Buchanan could be quite charming too, when she wanted to be.

There was a little paper Santa, some glitter stars, and some painted wooden figures of the nativity that Innes had made in school when he was just ten years old.

She thought back to Christmases in Texas with her father. As a girl, she had spent every single Christmas in a different place but always with the wonderful rancher's families and their children. They would decorate the barn and set up an enormous table for dinner. The animals would be in the barn too, watching over the proceedings, and it seemed right and proper to Orley that they did so. It had always been fun and she had always had lots of presents to open.

Last year, she and her father had exchanged gifts at midnight in front of their little plastic tree in their cottage in Baytown and later, they had attended a midnight torch parade on the beach. She closed her eyes and imagined the warm breezes on her face and the salt air in her lungs and opened them again to feel the warmth from the fire and the smell of pine in her nostrils.

Once they had finished decorating, they stood back to admire their work and Lady Buchanan switched on the fairy lights. They both gazed upward at the splendour of the magnificent twinkling tree with it's tiny coloured lights reflecting against the window panes of the sitting room and the darkness outside.

'Lets have a little drink,' said Lady Buchanan.

Then Innes entering the room with Fergus. 'Wow, you've made it look wonderful!'

Orley smiled as he put his arm around her and kissed her cheek. If the truth was known, given the choice of a barn, or beach, or here at Glencorrie, she really wouldn't want to be anywhere else this Christmas.

Fergus handed her a glass of mulled wine.

'I'd like to say something if I may?' said Orley in ponderous tone. She had noticed how fond they all were of making toasts and until now, she had always been the one raising her glass and not doing the toasting.

Lady Buchanan stopped stuffing presents under the tree and sat back down on her chair. Innes and Fergus, who were warming themselves by the fire, looked at her expectantly.

'On the occasion of my first Christmas in Scotland, I'll like to toast you all,' she said.

On her prompt, they each raised their glass.

'To the Buchanan's!' said Orley. 'Thank you for making me so welcome in your home and I'd like to wish you each a very merry Christmas.'

'Merry Christmas one and all,' Fergus responded.

'God bless us every one,' added Lady Buchanan.

Innes walked over to Orley and gave her a kiss on the lips. 'Thank you for that and a happy Christmas to you.'

They were all giving this impromptu togetherness some thought when suddenly, there was an almighty bang on the front door, and a bold but shrill voice shouted out - 'hello, hello, is anyone home?'

With drinks still in hand, they rushed out of the sitting room and into the hallway to greet the unexpected stranger, who was wearing a pink ski-suit, a big white fur hat, and squealing. 'Merry Christmas everyone!'

'Merry Christmas!' Fergus replied in a way that made it quite clear he was actually wishing it to himself.

'Howdy folks, I believe y'all bin expectin' me...!'

'Are you Santa?' asked Fergus in a trembling voice.

'No, silly, I'm Tanya!'

Tanya, with a wide white smile across full pink glossed lips and huge blue eyes which were like bottomless lagoons, removed her hat and let loose her wild long blonde hair. She regarded them all excitedly and giggled.

Orley gasped. So much had happened in the run up to Christmas, with the cattle to tend to and all the cottage renovations, that she had completely forgotten to mention that Tanya might stop by. With a measure of guilt, delight, and euphoria, she threw herself forward to embrace her sister.

Tanya began to scream. The high-pitched sound must have had salmon turning in the burn and birds dropping dead from the sky. Avalanches had been started by less. At the same time, she waved her arms in the air like a cheerleader and grabbing Orley, spun her round while yelling 'Merry Christmas!' at the top of her voice.

Innes laughed, possibly with embarrassment.

Lady Buchanan screwed up her face and jammed her fingers into her ears.

Fergus, stood wide-eyed and open-mouthed, as Tanya bounced up and down like Dolly Parton on a trampoline.

Once in the sitting room and in front of the fire, Tanya chatted at a hundred miles an hour about delayed flights out of Charles De Gaulle and the nightmare of having to transfer through Gatwick to Glasgow and while she did this she removed her snowsuit. She seemed to step out of it in slow motion. Beneath it she wore a tight pink cat-suit which some might have just called a leotard. White leather cowgirl boots and a matching belt slung over non-existent hips, completed the ensemble.

Orley stared in disbelief. Where had this girl, with the most amazing figure and big blonde hair come from? Where was the overweight, fuzzy haired, buck-toothed teenager, in a dress that resembled a pumpkin...?

From the expression on Innes's face, he didn't quite know what to make of this larger than life figure that professed to be Orley's sister either, so he busied himself pouring drinks, large ones.

Lady Buchanan was clearly horrified that she now had, not one but two American girls to contend with and she didn't seem to like the way Fergus was looking at this latest one.

Innes offered around the drinks.

'Oh dear,' said Tanya. 'I do believe this is alcohol.'

'It's whisky actually,' said Innes.

'Single malt,' qualified Fergus. 'Only the best as it's Christmas.'

'No thank you,' said Tanya. 'I do not drink alcohol. It's my choice and I'm not saying that you shouldn't drink it, but…'

'That's all right then,' said Innes abruptly.

'Of course it is,' Orley insisted, 'because we have juice to offer Tanya, don't we, Innes?'

Innes nodded.

Tanya smiled.

Orley rushed out to the kitchen.

She looked in the fridge and the larder but there was nothing remotely non-alcoholic. In desperation, she grabbed a few ice-cubes and put them into a glass of tap water with a quickly chopped apple and a slice of lemon.

Back in the sitting room, Tanya was hauling presents out of a giant Gucci bag and absolutely insisting on everyone unwrapped them immediately.

'No, no,' disagreed Lady Buchanan. 'We always wait until Christmas morning after breakfast. That is when we will open all our gifts. It's a tradition!'

Tanya's glossy lips trembled. 'But back home we always open our presents at the stroke of Midnight on Christmas Eve and this is my very first Christmas away from home!'

They each looked at each other in panic. It was eleven-fifty-eight. Orley gave Innes a pleading look as Tanya's tears threatened to roll.

Lady Buchanan lifted a china sheep ornament off the mantle and hastily parcelled it up in a sheet of newspaper and slid it under the tree for Tanya. When the clock struck twelve everyone moved at once towards the tree in a frenzy of grasping and grabbing. They passed presents around the room and then with sighs and gasps they all opened them.

Fergus received a pocket knife with a horn handle from Innes. A small telescope from Orley, a new Scotland shirt from his mother and the very latest hand-held game console from Tanya. He was very pleased indeed.

Innes got a new golf bag from Fergus, a pen set from his mother and a nice blue sweater, which he suspected might be Cashmere, from Orley. Tanya, to his surprise gave him a very classy Swiss watch.

Lady Buchanan was delighted to receive as a joint present from her two sons, a jewelled necklace and bracelet that exactly matched her favourite old brooch. She thanked them and smiled with equal delight when she opened Orley's present of French perfume. 'Thank you, my dear. I'm sure it will smell divine.'

Orley blushed and said something about being glad she liked it.

'Open mine next, Lady Buchanan,' Tanya insisted, pushing her gift into Lady Buchanan's slender fingers.

Orley watched with interest as another bottle of Parisian perfume, only larger and certainly more expensive, appeared from its elegant wrappings.

Orley opened her own presents next. She had been given a cute barn owl figurine by Fergus. A very nice toiletry set from Lady Buchanan and, from Tanya, a very decent bottle of perfume. From Innes, she had been given a beautifully wrapped box that she had been curious about since he had slid it under the tree. Long and narrow - what could it possibly be?

She unwrapped it slowly and carefully. Too slowly for Innes's liking, because he began to help her with the wrapping. As a brown wooden case appeared, she still could not guess what it was. She opened the clasp and all was soon revealed. Inside was a double-barrelled shotgun. Orley was so shocked that it slipped from her lap and hit the floor.

'Hell's bells - be careful with that!' Fergus said jumping back.

'I do hope it isn't loaded!' said Lady Buchanan.

'Of course it isn't.' Innes assured her and retrieved the weapon. 'I'm going to teach Orley how to shoot.'

'Shoot what exactly,' Tanya asked, getting her perfectly manicured fingers covered in newsprint. 'Peasants..?'

'You mean Pheasants' replied Fergus, laughing like a drain.

Tanya shrugged.

Innes passed the gun back to Orley, whose hands were still shaking. 'No need to be scared. It won't bite you,' he said.

She smiled tensely and thought how rude he must think her not to thank him for what had to have been a very expensive gift. *If he had only known, that the last time she had held a shotgun it had been to a man's head, he might not have been quite so encouraging of her....*

Further moments of anxiety over the gun were avoided by the distraction of someone's mobile phone ringing to the tune of *Jingle Bells*.

Orley put the gun back in its case.

'Who can be calling at this hour?' asked Lady Buchanan.

It was Fergus's phone. He took it out of his pocket and answered it. 'And Happy Christmas to you too, Davina,' he said into it. Then he said, 'yes, we are having a few drinks, in fact it's turned out to be a bit of a party as Orley's sister Tanya has arrived from Paris, and we were....'

Then his covered the mouthpiece and said to everyone, 'is it okay if I invite Davina over to join us, only she says she's dying to meet Tanya?'

The all shrugged and nodded.

'Should I ask Gregor and Daphne too?'

Lady Buchanan glanced at Tanya and went white.

'Oh, what a pity,' said Fergus down the phone. 'Davina says her parents can't come over because are out at midnight service.'

'Why don't we go too!' shrieked Tanya. 'It would be so Christmassy going out in the darkness and the snow to sing carols and....'

'No, it's too late now,' interrupted Lady Buchanan. 'Besides, we go to the Christmas morning service. It's tradition!'

Before Tanya could pout and enter into a battle of wills that Orley doubted she could win again, she suggested that Tanya help her in the kitchen to prepare some food.

'Lets put on some supper. If Davina's coming over it could be a late night and you must be famished after all your travelling.'

'Yes, I could eat a little something. Nothing stodgy though, I've got my figure to consider.'

Tanya's figure was certainly something to consider. Orley couldn't help but compare it with the photo Martha had shown her, when Tanya had looked very different indeed. She was now incredibly slender in all the right places but, my goodness, she defied all of the laws of nature with the size of her breasts. They were huge. She was tempted to ask her if they were real once they were in the kitchen but didn't have the chance because Tanya immediately had a lot to say about Orley's own personal appearance. 'Look at this…' she said, taking a photograph out of her purse and handing it to her.

Orley took it and smiled. It had been taken on her father's and Tanya's mother's wedding day. Orley was standing between them in her bridesmaid dress. They looked so happy.

'What happened to you?' Tanya demanded.

'Happened? What do you mean.'

'You must know what I mean – I mean look at you?'

Orley glanced down again at the photograph and blushed. She knew exactly what Tanya meant. She looked entirely different from her picture too - only not in a good way.

'I hardly recognised you!' Tanya told her, tapped the photograph with a polished fingernail.

Orley stuttered something about getting sick, having a horse riding accident, and how Scotland was a very different from Texas. 'I don't get the same kind of exercise here,' she said meekly in her defence.

'Is that how you got so fat?'

Orley was so shocked that she burst into tears.

'No good crying about it,' continued Tanya, 'cos that ain't gonna make you thin again. Plain speaking is my way - and plain speaking is what you need sister.'

Orley nodded and blew her nose into a tissue.

'And why we are on the subject, what the hell happened to your hair?'

By the time Davina arrived, Orley had recovered herself and she and Tanya had prepared supper for everyone. Bread rolls, dressed potatoes, sliced meats, nut loaf, and a smoked trout. 'Only a slice of meat for me,' insisted Tanya.

'So you're not a vegetarian like Orley, then?' Fergus noted.

'Heavens no. I eat only protein. It keeps my weight down.'

'That's your secret is it?' Orley whispered.

'Yes,' Tanya replied, 'and while I'm here I'm going to let you in on a few more.'

The rest of the evening went well. Tanya and Davina were introduced and Davina pointedly asked Tanya how long she planned staying. When Tanya told her that she had a flight booked for the second of January to take her back to Paris, Davina lightened up considerably.

Orley then managed to dash upstairs with the present she had originally bought for Davina and re-labelled it for Tanya. She searched her jewellery bag and picked out a necklace that had a pretty amber coloured stone in it. It was only costume jewellery but she had never worn it. Wrapping it quickly, she returned to the sitting room just as Davina was handing round her gifts. Perfect timing.

The fire was burning brightly in the grate. The lights of the tree twinkled and everyone was laughing, particularly Davina, Orley noticed, who was sitting so close to Fergus that they looked like they were joined at the hip.

Tanya opened her present from Orley. 'What a beautiful journal! She exclaimed. 'I love it. Thank you.'

Davina gave Orley a book on *Mustangs*, wild horses of the American Plains, which made Orley feel terribly guilty about only giving her a tacky necklace. Tanya was given a huge box of chocolates and after explaining that she never ate chocolate, she passed them round and Fergus finished them off, while Innes played *'Hark the Herald Angels Sing'* on his bagpipes and everyone sang at the top of their voices.

When it was time for Davina to leave, she went round the room kissing everyone and saying 'Happy Christmas'. She saved Fergus until last and dragged him outside to the porch for what might possibly be more than words.

Orley gasped when she looked at the clock and realised it was three-thirty in the morning. Lady Buchanan had already said goodnight at about two a.m.

'Where will Tanya sleep?' she asked Innes under her breath so that Tanya would not hear and realise that they hadn't actually been expecting her after all. 'We haven't got a room ready for her.'

'Give her your bed tonight and you can share mine,' he whispered.

Orley's eyes shot up under her brows. 'And what might your mother say?'

He smiled. 'It's just for tonight. She'll never know.'

Suddenly Orley couldn't wait to get Tanya up to her room at the top of the tower and leave her there. 'I'll help you with your bag,' she told her hastily, tugging at what felt like a tonne weight.

'It's a shame.' Tanya sighed wistfully.

'What is?'

'I had thought Fergus might take my bag up for me. He's so cute'. Tanya fired what could only be described as a smouldering look towards the front porch, where Fergus and Davina were saying goodnight. 'But I see he's got a girlfriend.'

'I wouldn't let her stop you,' said Orley mischievously. 'They haven't been together for all that long.'

'Really?' said Tanya, taking another look.

It was a wonder Fergus hadn't burst into flames.

'Goodnight Tanya,' said Orley, once they were at the top of the stairs.

They hugged and Orley said, 'I'm so glad you are here. I have dreamed of having a sister for my whole life and now I have you. This is going to be a wonderful Christmas.'

Chapter Twenty-Four

Orley woke at first light on Christmas morning and gave out a little sigh of pleasure. She was warm and comfortable, sleepy but satisfied and lying in bed beside Innes.

She watched his face, it looked so relaxed and so handsome. His eyelids and his beautiful dark lashes were closed and flickering with sleep. They had made love again and again, energetically and lazily, and then slept in each others arms. It had indeed been a perfect Christmas morning.

But now she had to get up. She would have done anything to stay in bed with him for just five more minutes, but it was getting late, and it simply wasn't fair on the cattle to make them wait any longer for their breakfast. She tried to wriggle free and not wake him.

'Where do you think you're going?' he said, grabbing her arm. She suspected he had been awake all along.

'It's almost nine. We have slept in and the animals need feeding.'

Innes pulled her close. Her naked body slid back against his. He pulled the warm duvet and blankets back over them both and kissed her. 'It's Fergus's turn. We will do it tomorrow. At Christmas time that's the way it works.'

'Well, if I'd known that, I'd have stayed asleep for longer.' She closed her eyes and made snoring sounds. The next thing she was being tickled and kissed and found herself giggling until they were making love again.

At ten o'clock they had to get up, if only to make sure that Lady Buchanan didn't see them coming out of the same bedroom together. His mother had made it quite clear from the start that it was unacceptable. Innes didn't seem bothered about crossing her but Orley felt differently.

'I am a guest in this house Innes and we must respect your mother's wishes.' Now of course, she should have felt like a terrible hypocrite but being with Innes all night long had offset any guilt and so now, like him, she was prepared to chance her luck on not getting caught.

They crept down the stairs and after putting on their outdoor clothes, they went outside on the pretence of having been up for hours, and with the sole intention of going straight back in again for breakfast, but it had turned out to be such a beautiful morning that Orley begged they take a walk.

'Come on. Its gorgeous out here!' The air was dry and cold and the sun was already at its highest point of the day. 'There is barely four hours of daylight left and it's Christmas Day!'

In Texas, there was twelve hours of light and twelve hour of darkness all year round and she hadn't realised how daylight hours in the northern hemisphere could be so short – or so spectacular - as it was reflected off the cold crisp white snow fields, which beckoned to be walked upon and appreciated. So they called old Piper to join them and headed out across the fields.

They walked arm in arm. Soon, they could see Fergus and Tanya coming towards them on the quad-bike. Tanya was again wearing her pink snowsuit and sitting behind Fergus, holding onto him quite tightly as they laughed and shouted to each other over the sound of the bike's engine.

'Oh look,' said Orley, noting that Fergus was carrying the small telescope that she had given him as a present in his utility belt. 'They must have been out star-gazing together. How romantic….'

Innes frowned and when they met up he hardly offered them a Good Morning never mind a Merry Christmas.

'It's not just a good morning - it's a fabulous morning!' Tanya enthused in reply to Orley's greeting. She jumped off the back of the bike and gave both Orley and Innes a kiss on each cheek, the way French people do. 'We could see every constellation in the sky and, just before dawn, we saw a comet - didn't we, Fergy!'

'Yes, a comet.' 'Fergy' agreed, grinning.

Tanya and Fergus seemed to have hit it off. Only, for some reason, Innes didn't approve of her sister's interest in his brother. 'I do hope you two weren't too busy star gazing to feed the animals?' he snapped.

'All done,' Fergus said brightly, refusing to take any notice.

'We are just off for a walk before church,' Orley told them. 'We won't be long.'

They walked for a while but Innes seemed sulky and untalkative. 'Is there a problem with my sister?' She asked him cautiously.

'It depends on what her intentions are towards my brother.'

'Her intentions? She's just being friendly and so is Fergus, in case you hadn't noticed.'

'My concern is that she will spoil things between Fergus and Davina.'

'But there *was* nothing between Fergus and Davina until he became a Baron. Isn't it obvious that she is after just one thing?'

'You've got it wrong. Davina *is* the one thing Fergus wants!'

'Look. I've known for a while how crazy he is about her - but she's not the one for him.'

'And your sister is?'

'Maybe – and what's wrong with that?'

Now they were shouting at each other now. They were having a big augment and on Christmas morning too. Worse than that, they were arguing about Tanya, who had been at Glencorrie for less that twelve hours.

Once back in the kitchen, they all breakfasted together and civility was restored. Innes gave Orley an apologetic, slightly sheepish smile from over the top of his coffee cup. She reckoned he must have realised that aside from it being Christmas he had behaved rather childishly.

While Orley was clearing the breakfast table and Tanya was setting it again for Christmas lunch, Lady Buchanan was forcing a huge turkey into the roasting oven and complaining about it not feeling much like Christmas.

'It's all because we opened our presents last night instead of this morning,' she grumbled.

'Don't worry,' said Innes. 'I'm quite sure that once we've all been to church and returned to the delicious smell of roast turkey, it will all feel wonderfully festive again.'

Just to be sure, he poured everyone a generous measure of Christmas spirit, everyone that was except for Tanya, who drank milk as there was nothing else on offer. Tanya's objection to alcohol made Orley feel guilty about drinking so early in the morning, although, it was hardly a rare occurrence in this house. So she only pretended to drink hers and tipped it into Innes's glass while he wasn't looking.

'I presume you girls will be accompanying us to the Kirk this morning'?' asked Lady Buchanan. 'We welcome all creeds.'

'Being American isn't a different creed.' Fergus told his mother.

'I just love singing those old Christmas songs.' Tanya said with a wistful sigh, and then to everyone's surprise, she belted out a totally tuneless and crude version of '*We Three Kings*.'

Lady Buchanan was clearly shocked.

Innes was truly amazed.

Fergus, who knew all the rude words, joined in.

Orley, blushing like a beacon with embarrassment, switched on the radio and turned it up so loud that the Choir of The Holy Trinity drowned them both out.

Thornfield's ancient Parish Kirk was draped in a blanket of snow and looked for every purpose like a Victorian Christmas card as they arrived for the noon service.

Parishioners dressed warmly in all of their finery were each wishing each other a happy Christmas.

Orley linked arms with Innes as the path to the church was slippery and her new boots had a high heel and not much grip. He held her steadily and, in a long dark wool coat and red scarf, he looked very handsome indeed.

Tanya, in a full length real arctic-fox fur coat and matching hat, was linked with Fergus and teetered along on heels that made Orley's look dreary. Orley just hoped the anti-fur supporters weren't out in force.

Lady Buchanan, who would normally have enjoyed the festive pre-service banter with friends and neighbours outside the Kirk, hurried inside, in order to take up quiet residence in the family pew. It appeared that the presence of these two vulgar American girls draping themselves over her two sons in public, was too much for her and she needed to pray.

Orley waved as the McKenzie family appeared.

Davina, wearing a long tartan wool coat in the most beautifully muted colours of heather and mauve, waved back with a gloved hand from the door of her Range Rover, where she remained even when her parents went to mingle.

She was clearly waiting to be escorted to the Kirk. Orley bit her lip and wondered what would happen next, because Fergus, she noted, was still firmly attached to Tanya.

A few seconds passed and Fergus's mobile phone rang.

Orley could see that Davina was holding her phone to her ear and glaring at Fergus with a look that could have started the next ice-age.

Fergus was laughing at one of Tanya's jokes when he answered the call. His face dropped, he nodded, glanced over toward Davina and then they both hung up.

'Come on,' he said to Tanya. 'Let's go over and say hello to Davina. She's feeling left out.'

After listening to an uplifting Christmas sermon, watching a traditional nativity production by the Sunday School children, and singing lots of carols, they all headed back to Glencorrie in a fine mood.

'I'm famished,' said Innes.

'I need a drink,' said Fergus.

Orley, whose toes were frozen in the silly thin-soled boots she was wearing, was anticipating the roaring fire.

'Do you mind if we stop off in Thornfield on the way back?' she asked Innes. 'We should get some soft drinks. The Co-op is open until two-thirty today.'

'What in heaven's name are soft drinks?' Lady Buchanan enquired.

They did their detour through Thornfield, bought lots of orange juice and lemonade, and eventually pulled up at

Glencorrie. The house and the trees around it looked so pretty in it's winter stole.

Orley climbed out knowing that the Christmas lunch would be cooking in the Aga, the house would be warm, the sitting room fire banked up in the grate, the tree would be sparkling, and ribbon-wrapped parcels containing chocolates and shortbreads, would be waiting beside each place settings. She had even made the holly and ivy centrepiece herself.

This day was going to be perfect. It was going to be a Christmas to remember. Her first Christmas in Scotland and her very first with Innes and with her sister. She thought she might burst with happiness.

As they reached the front porch Fergus and Innes began a snow ball fight in the yard. Lady Buchanan, understandably, made her excuses to check on the turkey but Orley and Tanya, who were both squealing with excitement, enthusiastically joined in.

Innes's first missile hit the side of Orley's face. It stung as it clipped her ear and was icy cold as it slid down her neck. She yelled and lopped one straight back at him. She missed. He moved too quickly for her, so she ran after him instead, catching up and pushing snow down the back of his neck.

Laughing merrily, Tanya let a snowball loose at Fergus, who ducked. Unfortunately, Tanya's snowball, together with the rock she had managed to scoop up with it, smashed straight through the sitting room window. She gasped in horror.

'Time for a drink, I think,' Innes said dryly.

'Don't worry about it,' Fergus said to her sympathetically. 'I did exactly the same thing last year. Knocked the Christmas tree right over too.'

Unfortunately, Tanya took this as a signal to carry on.

She aimed again at Fergus and missed, hitting Lady Buchanan, who was running out of the house enraged, squarely in the face.

If it doesn't stop bleeding soon we'll have to think about going to casualty,' Orley suggested.

'Do you think it might be broken?' Fergus enquired.

'It could be.' Orley sighed, thinking that Christmas, along with Lady Buchanan's nose, could now be spoiled.

'I think we've all had too much to drink to drive to the hospital,' said Innes glumly. 'It's a sixty mile round trip and in this weather it could take all day.'

Orley was just about to explain that she had hardly drank anything at all when Tanya appeared with a pack of frozen peas to help with the swelling. Unfortunately, in her rush, she tripped over a frayed rug and crashed down straight on top of Lady Buchanan. The screams were unearthly and, if the nose hadn't been broken before, it certainly was now.

Despite Orley's protests to the contrary, Innes insisted on telephoning Davina and asking her if she minded driving them to casualty. 'I'm sorry to have spoiled your Christmas day,' he could be heard saying while from the sound Davina's response, she was insisting that he hadn't.

'You have actually brightened my day,' she told everyone when she arrived at Glencorrie. 'Charades and Bingo bore me to tears!' Then realising a lack of tact, she said. 'Sorry, Lady Buchanan.'

'We'll take our Landrover. It has a full tank of fuel.' Innes insisted.

Davina agreed this was a good idea, saying that she only had half a tank of fuel herself and there might not be any service stations open. 'This is lovely. Is it top of the range?' she asked, admiring the new Landrover.

'Yes it is,' Lady Buchanan intoned nasally as she sat in the back seat clutching a bloodstained packet of frozen peas. 'We have won the lottery twice over. Haven't you heard?'

As Fergus climbed aboard, he popped a kiss onto Davina's cheek and wished her Merry Christmas. Davina blushed and smiled at him sweetly.

Orley received a swift dig in the ribs from Tanya. 'Is she the one you told me about in the emails?' she whispered. 'The bitch that was engaged to Innes?'

'Shhh. Yes.'

By the time they reached casualty, Lady Buchanan's nose had stopped bleeding but they had to wait while she was checked out. The X-Rays showed that her nose had a fracture but was not misplaced and so, with two black eyes and a small plaster, she was eventually discharged.

Unfortunately, on arriving back to Glencorrie, and after Innes had insisted Davina stayed for a late lunch, they discovered that the turkey was still raw in the oven and the Aga was stone cold.

They had all become used to the house being warm and cosy since the installation of central heating but now that the boiler had mysteriously stopped working, they were thrown back into the frozen reality of a winter.

'I can't understand it,' Fergus exclaimed. 'I've pressed the reset button and that usually brings it back on.'

'It might be the thermostat,' suggested Innes, 'I'll try overriding it.'

'We had better get some logs in,' grumped Lady Buchanan, who was dammed if she was going to admit to missing the central heating.

'I'll get some logs and a bucket of coal,' said Orley.

But she found there was no coal because none had been ordered.

Fergus managed to get a fire going with sticks and, after about an hour, finally restoring heat to the sitting room.

'The oil storage tank is empty,' he told them after investigating.

'But it was only filled a few weeks ago. We can't have used it all.' Innes insisted.

'Perhaps it's been stolen. Siphoned out?'

'Not likely. No one could get into this yard without either us or the dogs knowing. There must be a leak.'

Orley suspected that it must have indeed been all used up. The house was so draughty and so big that the central heating never switched off because it never reached the temperature set on the thermostat. 'Don't worry,' she said reassuringly. 'We can joint the turkey and cook it in the microwave. It won't take long. We still have electric.'

There was a sigh of relief.

'Good job we just bought that microwave, I say,' said Fergus. Davina settled Lady Buchanan in her favourite chair with a stiff drink and a couple of paracetamol, while Fergus and Innes built up the fires. Tanya and Orley set to work in the kitchen. 'Sorry about the old lady. I feel so darn bad about it,' Tanya confessed.

'I'm sure it'll be okay. Only I wouldn't call her the old lady if I were you.' An hour later, they were all sitting at the Christmas table eating turkey sandwiches, or in Orley's case, nut roast sandwiches.

Tanya didn't stop talking for a minute. She entertained them all evening with tales of her tour of Europe and in particular, her time spent in Switzerland and Paris, where as a housekeeper and nanny for the family of a top cosmetic surgeon, she had been paid in surgery rather than cash.

'I had my boob implants first then the butt lift,' she explained with one hand under a breast and another under a butt cheek.

Orley tried to appear interested rather than shocked.

Innes, she could tell, was appalled.

Fergus, who found all this fascinating, was getting glares from Davina, who said, 'surely Tanya, you must regret putting yourself through all that pain?'

'Nah,' Tanya shrugged in reply. 'I have a high threshold.'

She then went on to tell how she had been spotted in the lift of the Eiffel Tower by a movie scout. 'That's how I ended up playing a French girl in The Da Vinci Code. I met Tom Hanks. He's so sweet.'

'And do you speak French fluently?' asked Davina

'None,' Tanya answered, quite fluently, with a French accent.

'Terrific!' Fergus was even more impressed.

Eventually Tanya drew breath and rushed off to the loo.

Davina got up to leave. 'Thank you for the sandwiches. I do hope you will be feeling better in the morning Lady Buchanan. Don't worry about the Bullshot tomorrow. I'll be happy to bring it along. And, of course it's our turn to provide the Boxing Day lunch.

Lady Buchanan did not protest. 'Thank you, my dear, as I fear feeding a shooting party would be nigh-on impossible to achieve in a microwave.'

'Shoot? Bullshot? What's this?' Orley queried.

'The traditional Boxing day shoot between the Buchanan's and the McKenzies. Bullshot, by the way, is a drink - so Hamish is safe.' Fergus clarified.

'I will see you all tomorrow.' Davina said.

'Aye, looking forward to it.' Fergus replied.

'Me too.' Innes added. 'Orley can try out her new gun in good company.'

Tanya interrupted from nowhere. 'Shoot? Tomorrow. Fantastic. Do you have a gun I can borrow, Innes?'

'Can you shoot. Tanya?'

Tanya howled like a coyote. 'I'm from Texas, we all shoot. Sometimes we even shoot each other. Ain't that right, Orley?'

Orley went distinctly pale.

Tanya broke into a verse of *Red-Neck Woman* and shook her bottom.

Innes rose to the challenge. 'Then it's Scots against Texans. We have our teams.'

'And the winner will take on the McKenzie's,' declared Davina.

Innes kissed her cheek and walked her out to her vehicle.

Orley did the same and wished her a happy Christmas.

Davina had hesitated before driving away. It was obvious that she was waiting to say goodbye to Fergus but he was still sitting on the sofa deep in conversation with Tanya, on the merits of various shotguns and their cartridges, and hadn't even noticed her leaving.

'Could I have a word, Orley?' Davina asked.

'Sure.' Orley wondered if, because Davina was still glaring at Fergus through the none-boarded-up side of the sitting room window, that she was stalling for time.

Innes was still standing politely in the porch, waiting to wave her off.

'This is girl stuff,' Davina shouted to him and waved her wrist limply in his direction as if to dismiss him.

Innes scowled and went back inside.

Orley leaned closer to the open window of the Range Rover and waited with bated breath to hear this so-called girl-stuff.

'I just wanted to make it clear that I am no longer interested in Innes. I was for a time, it is true, but I was more upset about him bringing you back from America. I hope you will both be very happy together.'

Orley stared at her with wide-eyed astonishment. 'Well, that's very generous of you, Davina, and quite a climb-down since you went to such extreme lengths both in the cellar and in his bed, to get him back!'

'We are both grown women and as such, we understand that sometimes a girl has to do whatever it takes.'

'And that's how you explain the time you drugged me with magic mushroom soup? Not to mention the rumours you spread all over the village that I was pregnant when I certainly was not!'

'Well, I apologise, and I hope you will accept that in the Christmas spirit it is given.'

Orley shrugged. 'I am not normally the forgiving kind, but as I seemed to have had a change of heart - and so it seems have you then yes, sure, I will accept your apology.'

'Good. That's all settled. Now you can tell me what your sister thinks she's doing with Fergus, who is, by the way, the very reason for my change of heart....'

Orley held back on the laughter because this wasn't funny. Not only was Davina mentally unhinged, she was also under-estimating everyone's common-sense, if she thought no one would see through her plans to snare Fergus, The Baron of Galloway.

'I don't know what she is 'doing' because I haven't asked her but Tanya is a lovely person. She is very friendly. A bit over the top, I have to admit, but that's just because she's trying hard to fit in.'

'Fitting in is one thing but trespassing is another,' insisted Davina.

'And yet there is no trespass law in Scotland, is there, Davina?'

Truce or no truce, both women glared at each other before Davina put the Range Rover into gear. She took one last glance through the sitting room window, only to see Fergus roaring with laughter and Tanya practically sitting on his knee.

'Goodnight Orley,' she said before driving off into the night with a forced smile on her face and her fingernails imbedded into the Range Rover's plush leather steering wheel cover.

She was trembling with anger. She had relinquished her ambitions toward Innes because it appeared that her prospects could be improved upon. After all, a Baron was undoubtedly superior to a Laird, and a kingdom better than a borough, but she was dammed if she was going to sit back and have Fergus snatched away from her by a foreign floozy.

Chapter Twenty-Five

The following morning, Orley hadn't needed the alarm clock to wake her because she had been tossing and turning all night with worry over the shoot. How could she tell Innes that she had vowed never to pick up a gun again without having to explain why?

Tanya tapped tentatively on her bedroom door at six o'clock. 'I'm awake but I'm not getting up. I'm sick!' Orley told her. 'You go ahead without me.'

Tanya opened the door and popped her head round. 'What do you mean sick? You were all right last night.'

Lying to her sister through the door was one thing but face to face was another, so Orley confessed. 'I'm not really sick. I just can't face the shoot.'

Tanya laughed. 'No. I'm sure. Not with your track record!'

Orley looked hurt. 'I wished I hadn't told you about that now. I thought I could trust you.'

Tanya came inside the room and sat on the bed. Her expression that of warmth and friendship. 'You can trust me and you were right to tell me about what happened with Billy. Being able to speak about it means that you have moved on and gotton over it.'

'I haven't gotton over it!' Orley wailed. 'I could never pick up a gun again without seeing his face. What am I to do?

'Maybe it's time you faced your demons and told Innes?'

'I couldn't. He's a man. He wouldn't understand, besides I don't want him to know what I did. It's excruciating enough for me to think about it!'

'You told me. And I understood. So will he.' said Tanya.

'I needed to tell someone. I was going crazy. Innes wouldn't talk about his relationship with Davina unless I told him about Billy. Don't you see this is the second chance I never thought I'd get? I love Innes. I don't want him knowing what I did. How could he love me if he knew?'

'If he knew the circumstances, he would understand. Tell him what you told me. Now get dressed and come out with us. You don't have to shoot, if you decide you just can't do it, just pretend you hurt your shoulder or something.'

'I'm not very good at lying.'

'It's not lying, it's acting. There is a difference. Believe me.'

'I also think it's morally wrong to kill for sport.'

'Oh come on! We both know the birds will end up as food for the table. They meet their end quickly after enjoying a free and decent life - isn't that exactly how you justify raising cattle for the beef trade?'

Orley gulped. Tanya was right. The shoot was an important part of traditional Scottish life and it was important to the Buchanan's. Raising game birds not only provided jobs for the keepers but also brought winter income for the estate. She was out of excuses.

'Okay, I'll come, but I will not pick up a gun!'

There had been a fresh sprinkling of snow overnight and as the sun inched over hills, casting a dazzling white radiance on a frozen landscape. The day promised to be clear and bright.

According to Innes, it was a perfect day for shooting. They sat down to breakfast together and Orley, with her face as red as a beetroot with embarrassment, tried to explain why she couldn't shoot that day. 'I have a sore shoulder,' she explained. 'So I'll have to sit this one out.'

'It's called frozen shoulder,' Tanya added, 'when you just wake up with it like that. I helped Orley check and feed the cattle this morning because she could hardly lift anything. Could you Orley?"

'No.' She replied feebly.

Lady Buchanan said she had at one time suffered the same discomfort herself and declared great sympathy.

Innes looked terribly disappointed. 'But what about our team?'

'I'm really sorry.' Orley repeated. She felt terrible either way.

'It cannot be helped.' Lady Buchanan declared. 'You can share my rug in the Landrover, Orley, and we will adjudicate proceedings together.'

Orley felt better with Lady Buchanan on her side.

'Aye, past years have produced some rather heated exchanges,' Fergus told them.

'Of particular merit was the year that my late husband Hamish, shot a bird clean out of the sky and it fell kamikaze-like, straight onto Gregor McKenzie's head, knocking him out cold for twenty minutes!' Lady Buchanan added with a smile that knocked twenty years off her face.

'And later, out of respect, father had the bird stuffed and presented to Gregor McKenzie with a bandanna around its head,' laughed Innes.

'Oh happy days,' Lady Buchanan sighed wistfully.

Soon the yard was bustling with people, conversation, and dogs. Two gamekeepers, four pickers-up, and twelve beaters, all arrived bang on time for the first of eight drives.

When Innes said the Landrovers were leaving at eight-thirty he meant it but to Orley's dismay, Tanya was nowhere to be seen. 'We won't wait,' warned Innes. 'You better go and find her.'

In the nick of time Tanya appeared. She had gone to get changed again. She was now dressed all in black. High-heeled black boots, a wool skirt that looked more like a belt around her hips and a roll-neck jumper that was so strained across her breasts that they looked even larger than they already were.

'Thank goodness she has a long coat with her,' said Innes under his breath as they both climbed aboard the Landrover.

'Fergus told me to wear dark colours so not to frighten off the quarry,' Tanya explained to them while oblivious to that fact that she was in full make-up.

Orley wondered if it was waterproof as it was almost certain to rain. She shifted along the bench seat and squeezed in next to two beaters, who sat with their spaniels and stared at Tanya's breasts in disbelief. Orley prayed that her moleskin trousers and tweed jacket, which were excruciatingly tight due to all the weight she had put on since Innes had bought them for her, would not split.

They moved off. Innes was driving. The gamekeeper rode shotgun. They ambled out across the snowfields. They going was slow and bumpy. Orley felt nauseous and couldn't decide if she was motion sick or just overdosing on Tanya's perfume. She suspected it might be the latter.

'What's that awful smell?' one of the beaters asked the other.

Tanya answered, sniffing the air and opening the window, 'I think it's your dog,'

'Essence of rich bitch more like,' said the other beater.

'Excuse me?' said Orley. 'What did you just say?'

'Nothing.' The beater replied.

His friend sniggered.

'Really, because I thought you said something to my sister or maybe to me?'

'No. I didn't. I was just saying to Davy here about my bitch being worth so much money that she'd make me rich if I sold her, which I wouldn't.'

Orley let her glare subside but that was only to lure them into a false sense of security. While the beaters sat quietly she directed her conversation toward Tanya. 'My arm feels a little better now,' she said. 'I think I'll shoot today after all. I do believe we get to shoot the beaters if we don't see any pheasant. It's allowed in Scotland.'

'Only if you shoot them in the testicles,' Tanya replied loudly. 'That way you don't actually kill them. Unless, of course, you can be sure of hitting the appendix or a single kidney because that's also allowed.

'I'm glad to hear your arm and your shoulder are feeling better Orley.' Innes said to her with a grin.

Orley watched his expression in the rear view mirror and nudged Tanya saying. 'I do wish I'd remembered to bring my new gun along after all.'

'It's okay.' Innes chipped in. 'I put your gun in the Landy at the last minute, just in case....'

Orley face went from red to pale.

'Isn't it incredible here,' said Tanya, changing the subject,' have you ever seen anything quite as beautiful as Scotland in the snow?'

As they crossed a shallow river, the other Landrover, the one that Fergus was driving, drew parallel with them. Tanya waved and shouted to him out of the window, her high pitched screeches setting off the howls and yelps of every dog travelling in both Landrovers.

Innes looked to Orley and winced. 'And you expect me to issue *her* with live ammo..? he said darkly.

They eventually came to a halt on the crest of a gently sloping hill and all climbed out. The McKenzies were yet to arrive. The beaters all moved off to take their places in the thicket of trees in the distance.

On the hill, Orley could see that the shooters positions were marked out with pegs. 'What's all this for?'

She had not seen anything like this. In Texas everyone spread out and just took their own line. It certainly was not as organised as this.

'All the pegs are set out in lines,' Innes explained, 'so that after a drive everyone can move forward to the next peg, always in line, ensuring the safety of the group.'

'It's very cold,' replied Orley with a shiver. 'I'll just stay here in the Landrover for now, if you don't mind.'

'What do you think will happen with the teams if Orley isn't shooting?' Tanya asked Fergus, noting that Orley was back in the Landrover.

'We'll split up and shoot individually against the McKenzies. That what we normally do anyway.'

'Are you sure you can't shoot, Orley?' Innes asked.

She nodded her head and rubbed her shoulder.

'Then do you think you might load for me, instead?'

Orley said she would do her best.

'Good. Then we'll take the next peg.'

She tried to look willing as they all stood around for what seemed like ages. The McKenzies were fashionably late. All the dogs, including Innes's old gundog Piper, waited obediently. Orley crunched ice under her boots and fidgeted to keep warm while Innes checked his cartridges. Silently she counted them with him. One. Two. Click.

Innes snapped the barrel back into position. The sound of it transported Orley straight back to the barn on the day she loaded her gun and shot Billy Mitchell. She suddenly felt terribly dizzy and had to close her eyes to steady herself.

A vision of Billy and the girl writhing naked beneath him filled her head.

Innes was too busy pulling on his gun belt and looking through his field glasses at the distant thicket to see that Orley had tears coursing down her cheeks from tightly closed eyes. 'They are here at last!' he shouted, noting the line of four wheel drive vehicles approaching fast from across the glen.

Orley opened her eyes and quickly wiped away her tears.

She could see the Landrovers in convoy making their way across the glen. They all had flags flying in the wind. The blue and white cross of St Andrew. It was like a medieval jousting competition. A primitive flexing of muscles. The McKenzie's disembarked to their side of the hill. The entire party of keepers, beaters and landed gentry, kitted out in the McKenzie tartan of red, green and black.

As Davina and her party prepared themselves and their equipment. Innes placed his shotgun down on top of its wooden box and put his thick gloves back on.

Orley could see that this was a very fine gun. A twelve gauge with two side by side barrels, it had a beautifully engraved stock. The engraving was that of a mustang. The wild horse of Texas. She recognised that the gun he had given her matched his. It had the same engraving. Maybe that meant something. That they too were a matching pair. A smile played upon her lips.

'This is so Madonna and Guy, don't you think!' Tanya shouted to Orley from several yards away in a voice shrill with excitement.

Fergus was trying to instruct Tanya in the ways of shooting etiquette but she doubted that her sister, who looked more like Cathy of the Catwalk than Madonna Of The Moor was actually listening to him.

'If you want to bag the bird you must aim a little above it,' she heard Fergus say.

'I'd rather bang it than bag it wouldn't you, Fergus?' came Tanya's reply.

Innes was trying to see if the beaters were in their positions in the trees and waiting for the signal from the keepers. He clearly resented all the noise and yelling coming from Tanya and being carried around on the morning mist.

Orley found herself cringing as Tanya continued to laugh loudly and wave her gun around dangerously.

'I thought you said she could shoot.' Innes said irritably.

'*She* said she could shoot!' Orley corrected.

'And what about you, Orley. Do you think you can shoot?'

'Depends what I'm aiming at,' she told him truthfully.

'I meant, how's the shoulder?'

'A bit stiff.' She answered.

'That's where the birds will come from,' he explained, pointing. 'The beaters will drive them forward and over the hill.'

Orley noticed their positions were set back slightly, so that the poor birds wouldn't see the guns until it was too late for them.

Innes picked up his gun and lifted it to his shoulder. He practiced his aim by pointing it at the sky and looking intently through the sight with his right eye while his left was scrunched tightly closed. His finger hovered over the trigger.

Her own trigger finger twitched in her gloves. She thrust her hands into the deep pocket of her wax jacket and tightly scrunched her eyes closed again. The dizziness had returned. She wondered if she might throw up.

She was back in the barn again and the cold tension of the steel trigger felt as real to her today as it did that fateful day when Billy had been too busy screwing to notice a gun pointing at his head.

The girl beneath him certainly saw her as she moaned Billy's name and rolled open her eyes. She had screamed. It was a scream of Hollywood proportions that had Billy jumping up and off of her like a cat off a hot tin roof. He turned to see what the girl was screaming at and he immediately held up his hands. Panicked and shaking. 'Put the gun down you stupid bitch!' he had yelled, glaring at her with his eyes bulging and his face purple with fear.

Orley remembered how the veins were standing right out of his neck. She could see his pulse. It was beating like a fast drum. She could have sworn she could hear it banging in her ears. 'I may be a bitch Billy!' she had yelled. 'But I sure ain't stupid!' He looked so ugly to her, standing there, butt naked. His body wet with sweat and from screwing Anna Rae Williams.

The green mist swam once again in front of her eyes and an incredible feeling of anger, like she had never felt before, took over. The banging in her ears continued. Bang. Bang. BANG.

'Are you alright Orley? Only you have gone very pale?' said Innes's voice. Orley opened her eyes. 'Yes. I'm fine.'

'No you're not, you're shaking!'

'I'm cold that's all.'

'Then I think you should go back to the Landrover and sit under the blanket with mother, she has a hip flask with her.'

Not containing coffee or tea or soup, thought Orley, like normal people might carry into the snowy wilderness. 'No. Really, I'm okay. Now that the McKenzies are here we can all get started.'

Davina had reached them. She was wearing a modern version of the traditional McKenzie tartan with colours so gauche she could have frightened off the wildlife. She strolled up to Orley and Innes with her gun cocked over her arm and a spaniel panting at her feet. 'What a lovely day it's turned out to be,' she gushed. 'You know, I do think we might get to resolve last years draw.'

Innes smiled challengingly rather than charmingly and explained to Orley that the last year's shoot had ended in a draw, despite that they had gone on shooting in a snow storm and a howling gale until the last light had faded.

'Lets hope we don't have to go to such measure this year,' he added.

'I doubt it. We have our transatlantic team here. You do know that Orley has a reputation as being a bit of a killer in Texas don't you, Innes?'

'Really?' Innes raised his eyebrows with interest.

'Oh yes. A real hot shot. Isn't that right Orley?'

Orley was horrified. 'I've hurt my s-s-shoulder,' she stuttered. I'm afraid I won't be shooting today after all.'

Davina raised her severely plucked eye-brows. 'What a shame. I was looking forward to seeing you in action.'

'Please do excuse me, ladies,' Innes said suddenly, as his attention was distracted by Fergus who was signalling on behalf of the beaters.

'No need to be so defensive Orley, I'm only going by what I've read.' Davina said menacingly.

They glared at each other again while Davina laughed triumphantly.

'Heads or tails?' Innes returned to them tossing a coin in the air.

'Heads, of course.' Davina said as the coin landed.

'McKenzie's shoot first!' Innes yelled.

Davina was still laughing as she made her way towards her designated peg. Leaving Orley feeling stunned.

Davina knew something and she meant to use it against her. But how? Had she somehow intercepted her emails to Tanya and read them. She wouldn't put it past her but didn't see how it was possible?

The sound of a high pitched whistle ripped through the air from the wooded area where the beaters were ready to drive forward the birds.

'Ready!' shouted Gregor McKenzie, ' – and fire!'

A frenzied beating of wings sounded in the frozen air, together with the disgruntled cries of those pheasants caught napping on the roost only to find themselves catapulted by their own instincts skyward and to certain death.

Gregor McKenzie blasted and reloaded so quickly that anyone would think he was firing a machine gun. Lady McKenzie shot with a more leisurely attitude but did not miss, not even once. Davina took aim and followed the flight path of the frantic birds precisely and when she took her shot, like her mother, she was brutal.

The sky rained down birds. Orley watched in dismay, willing them to get away. Some did but not very many.

Eventually, the whistle was blown and the dogs sent out from the McKenzie camp to dispatch and retrieve.

'Bloody hell!' swore Innes. 'We have got our work cut out for us today.'

'Lock and load!' Fergus told Tanya.

'I'm not used to shotguns,' Tanya confessed at the last minute. 'I've only ever handled a rifle.'

'It's a bit late now,' Fergus told her. 'Still, if you've been paying attention to all I've told you, you'll be fine.'

Tanya was a rubbish shot. She didn't hit a thing.

Orley was glad. It was wonderful to see the birds she missed flying onto safety and hiding at the other side of the glen.

'I'm glad we're not competing as a team. Our averages would have been shot!' said Innes.

They stopped for Bullshot, a concoction that blended tomato juice with whisky and something else that Orley couldn't identify. Innes asked her again to consider taking up her gun. 'I can't. Like Tanya, I'm not familiar with a shotgun. We shoot rifles in Texas.'

'There's no reason to be afraid,' he said. 'I can teach you.'

'What makes you think I'm afraid?' she asked, tapping her foot anxiously.

'What else can it be. There is clearly nothing wrong with your shoulder.'

She objected but Innes took no notice. He was already retrieving her gun box from the Landrover. Orley looked over to Tanya in desperation.

Her sister shrugged and smiled encouragingly.

'Here.' Innes said offering her the gun. 'Take it.'

Her hands were shaking uncontrollably as she lifted it up and trained her eye down its barrels.

'How am I best to aim?'

'You don't aim as you would a rifle. The cartridge is packed with powder and pellets so you have to think of it as firing a three-dimensional cloud, which has a certain length, width and height. The idea is to anticipate the flight of the bird and fire ahead of them, so the bird flies into the cloud. Let me show you.'

Innes positioned himself behind her. His long strong arms came around her and guided her arms upwards and forwards. Through her Moleskins she could feel his body heat and the power of the muscles in his arms.

'Like this, you mean?'

'Aye, you've got it.'

His chin was hard against the side of her face. He was smoothly shaven and smelling faintly of lemony cologne. 'It is not a precise science but it is something of an art. You only have a split second to work out distance and speed.'

A wave of nausea rose in the pit of her stomach as she fingered the trigger. Her aim wavered.

'The whole point is to kill a bird for the table.' Innes continued. 'For that you have to hit it from the correct range, about 30 yards. If you shoot too close, you will render it unfit.'

'What if I only injure the bird?'

'Then you must send a dog to bring it back and ensure it is dispatched.'

'Dispatched?'

'Killed.'

Suddenly, there was a loud bang and Innes swore loudly.

Orley swung round almost giving herself whiplash in the process.

Tanya had her hands high in the air as if surrendering.

Innes marched towards her angrily. There was blood on his face. 'You shot me!' he yelled.

He was indeed shot. A single shot-gun pellet had passed cleanly through his earlobe, piercing it, and splattering his face with blood.

Davina screamed 'Innes has been shot!'

Tanya's face was stricken with horror. Her gun lay discarded and smoking in the snow.

Davina stormed towards her. 'First you attack Lady Buchanan, you flirt with my boyfriend and then you try to blow Innes's brains out – you stupid bitch!'

'It's okay!' Innes yelled, doing his best to get between the two women. 'It's only a scratch. It was an accident!'

Suddenly Orley appeared. She was holding her gun at Davina's head.

'Oh my gosh!' screamed Tanya. 'Please Orley, don't do it!'

Davina pleaded with her eyes but was too scared to speak.

'Do as your sister says,' begged Innes. 'You don't want to shoot Davina!'

'Oh, but I do,' said Orley quietly. 'She insulted my sister.'

'Then I apologise! I'm sorry. I didn't mean it.'

She jerked the gun forward. The barrel nudged Davina's head and she whimpered with pain. 'She's full of apologies lately. Only last night she apologised for poisoning me and slandering my name. How do I know she means it? She even arranged for all my hair to be cut off, didn't you, Davina. Tell Innes what you did.'

Innes looked truly horrified.

But Davina had decided this was the time to play her hand. 'Why don't you tell Innes what you did instead, back in Texas, how you shot your boyfriend. That was a real crime, wasn't it Orley. One that put you in prison. How did you get out? No don't tell us. Let us guess? I know: you escaped to Scotland!'

Orley thought she was going to faint. Her legs felt like jelly. Her arms heavy. She first looked at Innes, who was staring at her in horror, then she looked back down the barrel of her gun. More than anything she wanted to shut Davina up for good.

Innes just stared. Firstly at Davina and then at Orley.

'Is this true, Orley?'

Her secret was out and there was no putting it back.

It was over.

'Yes, it's true that she poisoned me and slandered my name and cut my hair. It's also true that I shot my fiancé and went to prison.'

'Then put the gun down, Orley,' Innes said firmly.

She did so. Laying it down in the snow beside Tanya's.

Tanya grabbed her immediately and wrapped her arms around her. 'I'm so sorry. This was all my fault.'

'No. It was not your fault! Like Innes said, it was an accident.'

Innes by this time had reached his Landrover. He got into the driver's seat and Orley fully expected him to start the engine and drive away. But he didn't. He simply sat there with his head in his hands.

Davina threatened Orley with the police once more before she scuttled back to her vehicle on the arm of her father.

'And you'll be hearing from our lawyer!' Gregor McKenzie told her, as he comforted his distraught wife and disgruntled daughter. As his parting shot he said to Orley, 'we don't hold guns to people's heads and threaten to shoot them in this country without consequences, young lady.'

'If you'll excuse me a moment,' said Fergus tentatively. 'I'll go and see if Innes is all right.'

'I could have killed him!' Tanya wailed in Fergus's wake.

'Well, you didn't.' Orley assured her. 'You missed. It was just a scratch.'

'Like when you shot Billy?'

'Yes. Exactly.'

They walked back over to the Landrover where Fergus had the first aid kit out and was treating Innes's 'scratch'.

Innes looked up at them and grinned sheepishly.

Orley could hardly believe it. He was not angry at all. Maybe he was concussed and didn't understand what had happened.

'Are you o-o-okay? Tanya stammered nervously. 'I s-s-sure am s-s-sorry I shot you.'

'You didn't. You missed.' Innes corrected. 'Like Orley missed that cheating son of a gun Billy Mitchell.'

Orley's mouth dropped wide open in astonishment. 'You knew? All this time you knew about him?'

'I knew. Your Uncle Jack told me all about you and your broken heart over a few beer's at his place.'

'Oh my gosh. I can't believe it. Why didn't you say something?'

'Because I knew you'd tell me about it one day. Beats me how Davina knew though.'

'She'd been snooping in your study the day we went out celebrating Fergus's good news. I saw her coming out. She must have hacked into the computer and read my emails.'

'But your emails are password protected!' Innes said.

Orley looked further aghast. 'So you tried too?'

He looked terribly guilty.

'She could have guessed the password.' Orley decided.

'Come on lets get back to Glencorrie. I need a drink.' said Innes.

'Here, take this,' came a voice from the back seat.

It was Lady Buchanan offering her hipflask.

'Thanks,' said Innes gratefully only to find it was already empty.

Fergus was strangely quiet during this time.

'If you don't mind, I'll go back with Davina and find out how she is,' he told them. 'She has had a terrible shock after all.'

Chapter Twenty-Six

Fergus pulled up at Castle McKenzie in his Landrover just after Davina and her family arrived home. She was crying as she climbed out of her father's vehicle and her mother was offering comfort. He walked over to her and offered his arms outstretched. She fell into them.

'Can we take a walk?' he asked.

'Yes. Let's.' She dried her eyes and they walked together towards the stables. 'I have to check the horses,' she said to him.

'Of course. I'll come with you. Are you okay?'

She nodded and then immediately burst into tears again.

He rocked her in his arms and then when she took a deep breath and pulled free, he stroked her hair, and looked deeply into her eyes.

'Oh Fergus!' she said. 'I think the whole horrible incident has only just hit me. I almost had my head blown off today by a deranged woman. Look at me – I'm shaking like a leaf!' She held out her quivering hands and Fergus took them in his.

'I feel responsible for all of this,' he told her. 'I told you things that weren't true to make you despise Innes – but instead you hated Orley. I made a terrible mistake.'

'What do you mean – a mistake. Did you lie to me?'

'I really thought Orley might be pregnant. I also thought he was only using her to call off the wedding to you.'

'But why would he want to do that?'

'Because once Innes found out that I was in love with you - he couldn't marry you - no matter what his feelings for you where. Don't you see that this is all my fault?'

Davina's face was a picture of realisation. Orley had been telling the truth after all. She reached out to touch his face tenderly. 'Oh Fergus. I have been a fool. Please don't blame yourself. I love you too.'

'You do?' Fergus's expression was incredulous.

They kissed. It was a kiss that would have gone on and on if not for him being butted painfully in the back from the loose box they were standing next to. It was his old friend Charles.

'I'll just see to the horses and then we'll go inside for a drink,' she said.

'Oh yes please. That would be lovely.' Fergus replied.

It began to rain, so he took shelter inside the tack room. He could hear the horses moving about in the stables and Davina talking to them.

The tack room was as impeccably tidy, as was everything else in Davina's life. Saddles were on saddle stands. Bridles on pegs up on the wall. The smell of saddle soap and leather filled the air. The horses names were beneath each piece of tack. *Misty, Heather, Camilla* and *Charles.*

Rosettes were pinned to a board. There were hundreds. All of them red for first place. There were photographs too. Some of them from when they were all children together. There were lots of Innes, he noticed. Then he noticed something else. A bin with a 'For Repair' label on it.

At the top of the repair pile was a girth strap. Fergus noticed it because it was splattered with blood. It had to be Orley's blood from the day of her accident and it had to be Camilla's girth. He lifted it up. The blood was dried and mixed with mud. He wondered why it hadn't been cleaned but then the other pieces of tack in this bin were dirty too. He decided that the repairer must clean them as part of the service. He fingered the girth and remembered that terrible day. His brother's anxious and stricken face. The love Innes felt for Orley confirmed by his devotion to her bedside and his refusal to leave her until she was out of danger. Orley had been so happy to be riding again and, from what Innes had said, and more recently Tanya, she was an expert rider.

I don't understand how someone like Orley, who has ridden all her life, could have just fallen off her horse? Tanya had said.

Then he noticed something suspicious. The buckle straps on the girth were split. Not stretched or perished from worn stitching, but a split part way along, in fact, they looked as though they had been cut. He looked more closely. Yes, the cut was two thirds across. The strain on the rest of the girth would have been enough, after hard riding, to do the rest.

He went cold with realisation.

He thought back to today, when they were all on the hill, and Orley had pointed the gun at Davina. She had said that Davina had poisoned her with soup. Hadn't he himself been terribly ill with stomach cramps, just after eating soup that Davina left for Orley? Then she had accused Davina of conspiring with her hairdresser to cut off all of her lovely hair. What a wicked thing that would have been to do to a woman. Was there any truth in it?

He, of course, had been totally to blame over Davina thinking Orley was pregnant and - if because of it - she had done what he suspected she had done, then he too was responsible for Orley almost being killed!

He dropped the girth back into the repair bin and walked out of the tack room just as Davina came out of the stable.

She turned to him and smiled. He did not smile back. His feelings for her had evaporated. She suddenly looked ugly to him. So ugly that he wanted to throw up.

He thought about Orley and all she had endured. He felt crushed by his own feelings of guilt. Although he hadn't been to blame for her terrible bout of 'flu not long after she had arrived, pretty much everything else that had gone wrong for Orley had been partly down to him.

He was going to have to make it up to her and he was going to get Tanya to help him. Then he considered his beloved brother and the pain he had seen etched across his worried face when Orley was taken into that air ambulance, knowing that he couldn't go with her. Fergus felt terrible. Innes had so much on his plate with all the stresses to do with the estate and it's spiralling costs. Suddenly, he knew how to try and make things right for him too.

'The horses are bedded down for the night. Lets go inside and get a drink,' Davina suggested saucily with a look that suggested she might be willing to bed down Fergus. She rushed towards him and wrapped her arms around his neck.

'Actually, I can't stay any longer. We are planning to watch a movie tonight and they are all waiting. So I'd better not come in for a drink.'

'Oh dear,' said Davina, disappointedly. 'I think I've been jilted again.'

Fergus took a great gulp of air and unwound her arms from around his shoulders. They were now unwanted binds. 'Yes. I'm sorry Davina. I've actually come over here to tell you that I can't accept your offer of marriage after all. I don't think we are entirely suited.'

'That's not what you said before. It's Orley and her sister, isn't it, they have turned your head against me?'

'No. It's entirely down to me. You see, I'm one of those fellows that enjoys the chase and then quickly looses interest in the catch.'

'What do you mean looses interest? I am not a catch. I'm not one of your lowlife floozies. I am your queen! Then she quoted, somewhat manically: *Hail King! for so thou art, behold where stands, Hail King of Scotland...!'*

'I'm sorry Davina, but I'm afraid we Buchanan's are much the same as those chaps in your favourite play: absolute bastards.' Fergus walked away. He didn't look back.

He couldn't bear to look at her knowing what she was capable of. Then thinking on this, he increased his step until he reached his Landrover, just in case she was thinking of doing a *Lady Macbeth* and knifing him in the back or something.

The next morning at first light, Tanya was up before anyone and had loaded the quad bikes with feed for the cattle. When Orley came down she was impressed with her sister's eagerness. 'My goodness, Tanya. You're keen.'

'Yes. I thought I'd help out. Everyone is always so busy around here and I wouldn't feel right if I didn't do my fair share.'

'But you are a guest. You should still be in bed or at the very least drinking tea in the kitchen next to the Aga.'

'No way. Being busy keeps me fit. By the way, I think you should get changed out of those jeans and put some stretch trousers on.'

'Why?'

'For when we do our exercises.'

'Exercises?'

'Yes. Don't worry. No one will see us. We'll do them while we are out on the fields feeding the cattle. They won't laugh at us. Go on. Go get changed!'

Orley did as she was told. She certainly could do with some physical exercise and if this was Tanya's morning routine, she couldn't expect her not to keep to it could she?'

She came back wearing jogging trousers and had her trainers with her in a bag to swap with her rubber boots.

'Will I do?'

'Sure. Come on, lets get going!' enthused Tanya, while revving up the throttle of her quad-bike loudly.

They raced across the fields. The ground had dried up and the going was firm. 'This sort of day would be perfect for horse riding,' Orley told Tanya when they arrived at the fold. 'I do wish we had horses here. Especially as I'm not likely to ride Davina's horses again. I liked Camilla. She was a bit of a handful but I really liked her long strides and her eagerness.'

'Rather you than me,' said Tanya. 'I have never liked horses much.'

Orley laughed. 'Fergus feels the same way. You two have a lot in common!'

Tanya looked pleased.

They reached the fold and spread out the hay into separate piles. Orley gave Hamish his bucket of molasses. 'He's going to be a champion bull,' she explained to Tanya, 'and in a couple of years, he will be Big Daddy to the new Buchanan herd of composite cattle. He's going to be famous.'

'Not exactly George Clooney though is he,' Tanya laughed.

While the cattle were eating, she showed Orley how to do stretching exercises. 'These will warm your muscles and stretch them so you don't injure yourself exercising.'

'You mean to say this isn't the actual exercise?'

Orley followed Tanya's lead but after a while she complained bitterly as they stretched and jogged and bounced and punched the air because, unlike Tanya, she was short of breath and bright red in the face.

'You are very unfit. It's gonna take quite a bit of effort on your part to get back into shape.' Tanya told her in no uncertain terms.

Orley looked glum and embarrassed. 'When I first arrived here I was both fit and slim. I suppose I got used to not doing anything too physical after I had 'flu. Then the colder weather came in and I hid in my big baggy jumpers.'

'And ate chocolate,' Tanya added.

Orley gasped. 'How did you know. Who told you that?'

Tanya laughed. 'I told me. I've been there, remember.'

Orley did remember. The photo of a fat girl in a pumpkin dress. Tanya had the opposite experience. A photo of a slim girl in a tight silk bridesmaid gown. Orley tool a deep breath.

'Okay, I'll do what you say. I'm in your capable hands.'

She didn't feel quite the same enthusiasm however after their mid-morning run. 'We'll take it easy to start off with.' Tanya had assured her. But she lied, because the only time they stopped, was for Orley to throw up her breakfast.

'Good riddance to full fat milk and heavy stodge!' Tanya had said patting her back just to make sure she had regurgitated every last drop.

After that, Orley had to admit, the going was easier and after four days she found she had lost four pounds and she was determined to keep it up.

It was now the mid-way point between Christmas and New Year when no one knew for certain what day it was.

'Is it a bank holiday today?' asked Orley.

'Not sure,' answered Tanya. 'Although, I know Scotland gets more of them than anywhere else to allow for whisky consumption - or something.'

The answer was no. According to Innes, it was a normal working day and that was why she and Tanya were booked on the ten o'clock train to Glasgow, in order to meet with their one o'clock appointments at a prestigious Glasgow hairdresser.

At this news they could hardly contain their excitement.

Innes gave them a lift to the station in Thornfield.

'We can do a bit of shopping, have lunch, get our hair done, and still make the four o'clock train back, just before it gets dark!' Tanya squealed.

Orley could hardly believe that Innes had done this for them. It was so considerate of him. He knew now that she had been upset about her hair even though she had pretended not to be, and also the truth about how it got to be so short. He also knew that she couldn't face going back to see Shona, who happened to be Thornfield's only hairdresser. He really was a gentleman.

'It's grown over an inch since it was cut. I hope the Glasgow hairdresser can do something with it.' Orley wailed to Tanya in despair once they were on the train.

'I'm sure they can and hopefully, they'll do something with the colour too.' Tanya said, looking over Orley's dark dull hair in disgust.

They arrived in Glasgow and toured the shops on Sauchiehall Street, spending a lot more than they could afford on clothes and shoes, and then went along to have their hair done by Angus and Gillian, at a very stylish hairdressers that offered herbal teas and *Vogue*, rather than whisky and *Trash*, and who coiffured them both into the realms of fabulousness.

'I won't take anything of the length of your hair, Orley,' explained Gillian. 'But I will work with the texture and bring back your natural colour.'

The results were amazing.

Tanya's already glossy blonde locks had been revitalised but Orley's had been transformed.

Gone was the blunt and harsh cut and matt-black colouring and in it's place was a lighter, layered, and curled shape that suited her face and flattered her colouring. She was back to being a subtle red-head again.

'Hot-diggerdy dawg - you look amazing!' exclaimed Tanya.

When they arrived back at Thornfield station, with bags galore, Innes was there to collect them. His expression as he set eyes on Orley was a picture.

He was eager to pull her into his arms. Once there, he whispered how lovely she looked, how beautiful, and how much he'd missed her since that morning. She was so happy she could have wept.

They arrived back at Glencorrie after dusk. As they climbed out of the Landrover, Innes urged them to leave their parcels for a moment because he had something to show them.

'Come with me. There's something I want you to see.'

Curiously they followed Innes and his broad torch beam around the side of Glencorrie outbuildings and into the old stable yard.

In an instant, the area was suddenly floodlit by bright lights they had obviously been installing all day. Now they could see Fergus standing next to the block of stables that he and Orley had renovated together. He was grinning in excitement and his finger was still on the light switch. 'Surprise!' he yelled.

It was then that Orley noticed the two heads and four pairs of eyes that were blinking at her in as equal astonishment as she was at them. It was Charles and Camilla.

They were looking over their half-doors in disbelief at these strange humans who insisted on complete darkness one minute followed by blazing light the next.

'What are they doing here?' Orley asked in confusion.

Innes explained. 'Fergus went over to see Davina and made her an offer for Charles and Camilla. She didn't want them anymore and we thought you might.'

Tanya whooped and hugged Orley.

'I'm overwhelmed!' she gasped. 'Thank you. Thank you both very much.'

She wanted to say that she felt terribly guilty. That she felt like a spoilt child receiving gifts her parents could ill-afford, but that would have sounded ungrateful and spoil the magic of the moment. So instead, she burst into tears and thanked them all over again. 'Although, obviously, I'm still concerned about the Scottish Disease,' she explained. 'Do you think they will be safe here?'

'Innes spoke to the vet while you were away. He said the risk of the horses of getting sick would be the same here or on McKenzie land. So you were right, Orley. There is no real reason for concern at Glencorrie.'

After fussing over the horses and making sure they had every comfort they could possibly wish for, they retrieved their shopping bags and parcels and went inside the house. Innes opened a bottle of champagne.

'Are you sure you won't have a glass with us, Tanya?'

Orley noticed how Tanya had glanced longingly at the champagne for a fraction of a second before refusing it.

'Tanya, my dearest sister,' she told her with a long sigh. 'We have stretched and jogged and done every other exercise know to woman together this week. I have followed your lead in everything – but now it is time for you to follow mine - I want you to have a small glass of champagne to toast these two wonderful men of ours. Innes and Fergus Buchanan.'

Tanya, with her blonde hair puffed up like candyfloss and her face beaming through multiple layers of *Max Factor*, nodded her head and said that she would be honoured.

'To Innes and Fergus Buchanan.'

Lady Buchanan entered the room having been prompted to join them by Innes. She looked, in Orley's opinion, a little off-colour. 'Are you all right Lady Buchanan. Only you look a little peaky. Is your nose still hurting?'

Lady Buchanan insisted she was feeling fine. 'I had a headache earlier and I have not long woken from my nap, that's all, dear.'

They all raised their glasses again.

'It's my turn to propose the toast,' said Innes.

He looked round at their expectant faces. 'To Transatlantic relations!'

They all laughed, clashed glasses and then drained them.

Orley didn't know whether she was over-tired, over-excited, or both, but she detected that the atmosphere back at the house had changed since that morning. Lady Buchanan was certainly not her usual self. Even Innes was behaving strangely, by toasting to 'Transatlantic relations' in the plural. He now seemed incredibly amicable towards Tanya, when even up to yesterday, he had been anti-Tanya and counting down the days until she went home.

She couldn't help but wonder what had gone on in their absence....

Unbeknown to Orley or Tanya, as soon as Innes had returned to the house that morning from seeing them safely onto the train, he could see that Fergus and his mother were waiting for him at the kitchen table.

'Still celebrating?' he asked, as ten-thirty was a little early even for him.

'Waiting for you actually. Family meeting.'

'Business?'

'No. Personal. You had better sit down.'

Fergus poured him a drink. 'You are going to need this.'

He went on to tell them both about Davina's campaign of hate against Orley. He spared no detail and took no pleasure in implicating himself by explaining how he had fed Davina's obsession with information he had fabricated, in order to turn her attention to himself.

'Except that my plan backfired and she blamed everything on Orley.'

Innes insisted that his brother was not solely to blame.

'No, this is the plan we both agreed upon. I don't understand why you feel responsible for what happened?'

'What plan – what agreement – what has happened?' their mother asked with some confusion.

'We decided to make Davina hate me so she might marry Fergus instead.'

'Why on earth would you…?' Lady Buchanan looked at both her sons in horror and took in their angst expressions.

'He did it for me, mother.' Fergus admitted. 'Innes was going to marry Davina, just like you wanted him to, until I begged him not to. I had been in love with Davina for a long time - for years - and Innes hadn't realised. Once he did, he agreed to back out of the engagement.'

Lady Buchanan looked stunned.

'So you see it really is all my fault that Orley was almost murdered.'

Innes, who was still taking all of this in, was totally taken aback by this last statement and almost choked.

'I took it too far, you see?' Fergus explained further. 'By telling Davina that Orley was pregnant.'

'What?'

'After I told her that she must have planned the riding accident and sabotaged the horse's tack, by cutting part-way through the girth strap, so it would break.'

'Hang on Fergus!' Innes was standing bolt upright now, his chair upturned behind him. His voice was raised and his face was purple with anger. 'Has Davina confessed to you - because these are pretty serious accusations?'

'No. She hasn't and I'm sure she would deny absolutely everything, but I saw the girth with my own eyes in her tack room. It still had Orley's blood on it. It was clear to me what she had done.'

'Sit down, Innes,' his mother said, 'I know I haven't been the most supportive person towards Orley but I was upset that you hadn't married Davina and I too thought Orley might be pregnant. I couldn't think why else you had brought her here.'

Innes sat down. His fists closed. His expression was that of someone himself capable of murder. 'I brought her here because I fell in love with her the first moment I saw her and I couldn't bear to leave her behind.' Then he turned to his brother. 'You should have taken the girth and brought it back here as evidence.'

'I could go back and get it before it is taken for repair?'

'Yes. Otherwise we won't have any proof.'

'And what, if the evidence does point to Davina trying to murder Orley, do you intend to do about it?' Lady Buchanan asked.

'Report it to the police, of course!' Innes said firmly. 'At the very least she should be arrested. I will never ever forgive her for what she has done to Orley!'

'I think having Davina arrested might just cause her to counter-prosecute Orley for raising a gun to her head.'

They all considered this quietly for a moment and then Fergus spoke again. 'There is one other thing I must tell you,' he said anxiously.

'Oh, for heaven's sake, Fergus!' Innes yelled, rolling his eyes and throwing his hands in the air while expecting another of his brother's excruciating revelations. 'What next?'

'I think I'm in love with Tanya….'

Chapter Twenty-Seven

A cold silvery light slipped through the gaps in the curtains in Innes's room and across the bed where Orley lay awake in his arms. It was still too early to get up.

This was getting to be a delicious habit. Saying goodnight to each other and making moves to separate rooms, only to close doors noisily and wait quietly for the opportunity to creep along the hallway into his room, into his arms and his bed.

She listened to Innes's breathing which was slow and deep. The house creaked and groaned. Outside, in the brightest of moonlight, owls cried and dogs stirred in the kennels below. All was well with the world. Her world.

She reflected on past events as was customary on the last day of the year, or Hogmanay, as it is known in Scotland.

It was a year that had turned her life around and taken her from the depths of despair when she had despised both herself and everyone else because of guilt and jealousy.

Hate had consumed her heart. She had been scared and alone. That is how she had felt on the day she met Innes. He was like that bright moon outside. Offering light in the darkness. He had represented everything her heart desired.

He was dark and handsome, mysterious and alluring, affectionate and loving. And Scottish. A temptation in the extreme. Like a gift from the Gods.

Had she placed a cosmic order for this man?

Yes. She had and her guardian angel had been listening.

He stirred and awoke.

He reached out for her.

She kissed his sleep-filled face.

He opened his eyes and smiled. 'Good morning beautiful and happy Hogmanay,' he murmured.

It was their turn to stay in bed again that morning and they intended to use it. Eventually hunger and the need to disguise their waywardness drove them downstairs to the kitchen, where the Aga was radiating heat and the kettle was still warm. Fergus and Tanya had obviously had breakfast and had gone outside to feed animals. It was mid morning already yet dawn was just breaking. Orley put the kettle back on to boil and eyed a white envelope with their names scrawled across it on the kitchen table.

'What do you think that might be? You open it. It's your brother's writing.'

Innes looked just as puzzled.

'I don't know. Christ, I hope it's not a note to say they have ran off to Gretna Green together!'

Orley smiled. It was a possibility. While sneaking into Innes room last night, she had seen a fleeting image dashing into Fergus's and she had doubted, on this particular occasion, that it had been a ghost.

'My goodness. I don't know how he got these but this is fantastic!' Innes yelled.

Orley slid to his side. 'Tickets?'

'Four tickets for tonight's Edinburgh's Hogmanay street party!'

They looked at each other in amazement and embraced.

Orley emitted an squeal of ecstatic delight. 'Edinburgh, the city of my dreams - how wonderful!'

As the kettle came to a high pitched boil, Tanya and Fergus walked into the kitchen. Innes waved the tickets at him and laughed. Fergus began to laugh too. Orley grabbed her sister who seemed confused at all the excitement and quite obviously didn't know anything about the tickets.

'Tanya, look. We are all going to tonight's Hogmanay street party in Edinburgh, followed by midnight fireworks over the Castle. How exciting is that?'

'How did you get them?' Innes asked his brother. 'These sold out last summer!'

'Ebay.' said Fergus. 'And they were worth every penny.'

Orley noticed a troubled look flash across Innes's brow.

Mention of money troubled him lately. She felt her stomach turn over because she suspected buying Charles and Camilla had wiped him out completely.

Fergus was soon by his brothers side. He must have seen the frown too. He clapped Innes on the back. 'Don't worry about it, bro. Plenty more where that came from.'

Innes lifted his eyebrows. 'You wish, Fergus!'

Fergus was still laughing heartily. 'I'm a Baron remember. I have a Kingdom.'

Innes laughed along with him. 'You own a forest and not a very big one at that,' he scoffed.

'Which I have just sold forty-five percent of to a shooting syndicate in London for over a million quid.'

They all stared at him in silence, aghast.

'I'm a rich Baron now and tonight I'm going to the world's biggest street party with the world's nicest people, and we're gonna party like we've never partied before. Hurrah!'

'Hurrah!' They chorused in agreement.

'So do not worry any more my brother. You shall have your composite cows and your imported embryos. You shall have everything your heart desires!'

'Everything?' Innes was looking directly at Orley. His black eyes shining. He then suggested opening a bottle of whisky so they could all toast Fergus the Baron of Galloway and the very last day of the year but Tanya objected.

'It's too early,' she insisted. 'You really must ask yourselves why you drink so much. It isn't healthy.'

Innes and Fergus looked at her as if she had said something alien.

'I agree with Tanya.' Orley chipped in. 'You do drink too much and I think you should stop. Not altogether of course, but maybe you should confine your drinking to the hours between 6 o'clock and midnight?'

'But we already do that.' Fergus informed her glibly.

'I am talking p.m. not a.m. Fergus!' Orley giggled.

When they arrived in Edinburgh it was well below zero and the city was wrapped in fog. In coats and scarves, they joined the throngs along Princes Street. The air was buzzing with excitement and anticipation. The atmosphere was infectious, although a rumour was going around that if the fog didn't lift, the firework display at twelve might not go ahead. 'Never heed,' Fergus said. 'It's early yet. Let's find a pub.'

It was only seven thirty. They did have lots of time.

Fergus took them all into Rose Street, a narrow ancient small cobbled place directly behind Princes Street. It was busy. People of every nationality had flocked to Edinburgh for the celebrations. Everyone was shouting and laughing, drinking and singing. There was music on every corner. Buskers with bagpipes, groups with guitars, and chorusing choirs all competed with the noise of the lively crowds.

Orley was in awe of it all. Here she was at the biggest street party in the world. The very place to be on New Years Eve. She tried to drink in the moment, the atmosphere, and had to pinch herself for any of it to even feel remotely real.

She looked to Innes. His handsome face smiling at her. She smiled in return and blew him a kiss with her gloved hand. His arm passed over her shoulder and he pulled her close. Above, in the shadows of The Mound, was Edinburgh castle. The instantly recognisable fortress. The majestic landmark that dominated the skyline just as it had dominated the history of Scotland. It was large and looming and steeped in romance. At least it was for Orley.

She gazed up at the ramparts and wondered where exactly her father had proposed to her mother over twenty-two years ago.

At the Auld Ale Hoose, Fergus bought drinks and thrust them into each of their hands. 'Here's to the old and soon to the new!'

After three packed pubs and large whiskies in each, Tanya whispered to her sister that she desperately needed to visit the ladies room before they moved on again.

'I think Fergus has spiked my juice,' she told Orley.

'Surely not - with what?'

'With whisky!' she explained. 'I feel a bit light-headed!'

Orley laughed. 'I'm sure that's just pure excitement, Tanya.'

They soon found themselves back on Princes Street and opposite Waverley station. In front of them, lit up and turning in the air like an enormous Ferris Wheel, was a smaller version of the London-Eye that had been erected especially for the Hogmanay celebrations. Orley tugged at Innes coat like an excited child. 'Please?'

He nodded, grabbed her hand, and they ran together to secure a pod. Fergus and Tanya grabbed the one following on behind. Each held just two people. As their pod swung slowly into the air, Orley sighed with pleasure and gazed out at the ancient city sprawled in front of her. In the darkness, the lights of The Scottish Gallery, New Street Bridge, Princes Street Gardens, the Scottish law courts, could all be clearly seen, while above the castle itself was still shrouded in white mist. As their pod reached its highest point, Innes took his cue to kiss her.

It wasn't a polite kiss.

Orley threw her arms around him.

As the pod reached the ground again they were still locked together but Innes managed to free a hand and press a ten pound note into the glove of the ride attendant. The door immediately slammed shut again and they climbed upwards once more into their blissfully private sanctuary.

They climbed off the Edinburgh Eye once the music had struck up from the huge theatre in the gardens. The famous Scottish group *Texas* were due on stage and Innes was pretending that he had been the one to arrange for them to play in honour of Orley and Tanya. Tanya had them all in hysterics, because she was completely taken in by this and was thanking Innes quite sincerely.

Orley thought when Charleen Spitari burst onto the stage with a zillion decibels of applause that the song she was singing was equally as apt. It was *Black Eyed Boy*.

The music was incredible. The atmosphere was intoxicating. In the surging crowds, Orley hung onto Innes just as he had instructed her to. 'I don't want to loose you,' he had said and she had replied that she didn't want to loose him either.

Texas were followed by *Travis*. All the bands that night were playing live on the huge outdoor stage and being televised live by satellite all over the world. The sound was so loud that Orley doubted it needed any help in reaching Baytown's shores.

Orley's father and Tanya's mother had promised to watch and Orley and Tanya had promised to wave at the cameras. They were five hours behind in Texas. It was still early evening there. Which, to Orley, seemed very strange when they were keeping an eye on the last minutes leading up to the New Year.

'Where are we staying tonight – do you know?' she thought to ask Innes as the last minutes of the year were counted down.

Innes shrugged before leaning towards Fergus to pass on Orley's question. She bit her lip and hoped that Fergus had remembered to book somewhere for them as by the look of things, Edinburgh was full up and it was freezing cold.

Literally. It was at least ten degrees below zero.

Fergus was nodding his head eagerly in response. He said something to Innes and Innes's eyes shot up. He looked impressed. Orley deduced that this had to be good news. Innes came back to her and mouthed 'The Balmoral!'

Orley shrugged her shoulders.

Innes pointed behind her to a magnificent golden-coloured sandstone hotel built on top of the Waverley station. It overlooked the castle, the gardens, and the whole of Princes Street.

'That's our hotel?' she mouthed back.

He nodded and smiled.

At just before midnight the fog and mist hovering in the air just above them cleared. The view was breathtaking. The castle, which was lit from the gardens below, was highlighted and every ancient detail evident. It was a backdrop of epic proportions.

The dull thud of canon fire from the castle walls heralded the arrival of the New Year. It resonated through the air and everyone seemed to hold their breath. A hundred thousand souls looked skyward as explosions began erupting above them and white light illuminated their upturned faces and gaping mouths. One after another the fireworks ripped upward. Plumes of gold shot into the sky. Upward and outward, only to be replaced with sparkling flares of silver and purple, red and blue. An orchestrated performance in the sky.

Tears of excitement and sentiment streamed down Orley's face as firecrackers danced and twirled across the star-filled sky. It was like nothing she had ever seen before.

Smoke filled the air and replaced the mist of earlier. Burning emotions erupted from the very depths of her soul. Never had she felt so happy. So in awe or so overwhelmed.

She looked to Innes and found that he was looking straight at her rather than the final throes of the display. 'Happy New Year, Orley,' he said and lowered his head to kiss her. She clung to him and kissed him back accompanied by the whole of Edinburgh singing *Auld Lang's Syne.*

What they didn't realise was that at that moment, their image was being projected onto a giant screen on the stage and at the same time, being beamed across the world to be watched by millions. Tanya, ceasing the moment with Fergus, also managed to be captured by the all-seeing eye.

In Baytown Texas, watching live and with both of their daughters obviously having the time of their lives in Edinburgh, Bobby Mac and Martha MacKenna were celebrating too.

Closer to home however, Davina McKenzie was only contemplating hers. She was spending the evening as she usually spent Hogmanay, at her castle home where they always held a sumptuous party.

She had taken particular care with her appearance. Her hair extensions had all been redone by Shona and although they had taken practically all day to do, the result was worth it. Back were the long thick glossy red locks that curled down her back and framed her slender figure, which she compensated for by wearing a push up bra and a low cut fitted velvet dress, in the colour of deepest purple. At her neck and wrists she wore sparkling amethysts.

Every pair of eyes were on her as she descended the staircase looking fabulous. She was, however, on the hunt for one particular person that evening. A gentleman recently detached from his lady wife whom she suspected might be lonely: Geoffrey Sinclair.

There he was, standing next to a plant in the corner. He had a whisky in his hand and a sheepish expression on his woolly face. Davina made straight for him and linked her arm through his as if to claim him as her own before her father announced the toast.

Gregor McKenzie was standing on the fourth stair of the magnificent staircase not only to give him height but also to ensure he was looking down on everyone.

'I know you'll all want to raise your glass tonight in wishing for a prosperous New Year, but before the midnight bells, I would like you all to toast our very dear friend Geoffrey, who has just confided in me over a little piece of good news he has received this evening.'

Everyone went silent and turned to look at Geoffrey.

'You'd think old Geoff would have known me well enough by now,' Gregor laughed jauntily, 'to know I'm not exactly known for my discretion!'

Everyone laughed.

'I should have known you couldn't be trusted, my friend!' Geoffrey replied with a crooked smile that betrayed his delight in what was about to be said.

'Friends and family please charge your glasses and raise them to the newly knighted, Sir Geoffrey Sinclair, who has just been recognised in Her Majesty's New Years Honours List for his services to banking.

Everyone applauded.

Davina clung to Sir Geoffrey and kissed his cheek.

Someone took a flash photograph.

'Congratulations Sir Geoffrey!' she gushed.

'Oh, I think that a title can be such a mouthful, don't you, my dear, just call me Sir.'

Davina giggled.

'And aren't you all grown up these days, Davina....'

At three-thirty in the morning, Orley and Innes, Fergus and Tanya, were heading back up Princes Street towards

The Balmoral hotel. A cold wind whipped around them, but they seemed oblivious to it.

Orley had removed her shoes and was carrying them. The heels clicked together in her hands. Tanya, whose heels were at least an inch higher, was still skipping along with her shoes on her feet. Orley said she didn't know how she managed to stay on them.

'Practice,' Tanya explained. 'Ladies in Paris always wear high fashion and high heels!'

'I suppose you'll be looking forward to going back to your glamorous life in Paris tomorrow?' suggested Fergus, whose expression had turned suddenly glum.

'You must be kidding me? Edinburgh is just as stylish as Paris in my opinion,' she told him. 'And the gentlemen are just as handsome.'

They reached The Balmoral and went inside. It was bright with lights from crystal chandeliers reflecting off opulent marble. Orley and Tanya held back as the men checked in. Orley suspected that her make up now looked as smudged and streaked as Tanya's.

'How many rooms do you think they've booked for us?' Tanya giggled.

'No need to come all innocent with me,' Orley told her. 'I've seen you sneaking into Fergus's room late at night.'

Tanya gasped. 'Really, when?'

'When I was sneaking into Innes's of course!'

They were both still giggling when Innes and Fergus returned.

'Night-cap anyone? More champagne?' Fergus asked, hands in his pockets, keys jangling.

They both shook their heads.

'I think we've had plenty, don't you Orley?'

Orley nodded and yawned

'Then I believe it's bedtime.' Innes announced.

Chapter Twenty-Eight

The rooms at The Balmoral were sumptuous. Silken drapes hung from ceiling to floor framing landscape windows that overlooked the castle.

Orley collapsed on the huge bed. 'Thank you for the night of my life,' she sighed happily.

Innes practically jumped on top of her. 'That's a bit presumptuous of you, isn't it. I haven't even begun to give you the night of your life yet!'

Then you'll just have to gird your manly loins until I've had a nice hot bath. A hotel like this must have a heavenly bathroom and endless hot water and for what it's cost you to stay here, I intend to take full advantage.'

'As I do with you in this heavenly bed,' he replied.

'Then don't you dare fall asleep,' she whispered.

In the bathroom, she ran hot water that emptied into the bath like Niagara falls. She sprinkled guest bath-oils into the huge tub and helped herself to shampoo and soap. The toiletries smelt of coconut oil which reminded her of hot sunshine and, in turn, about the first time she ever set eyes on Innes. She knew now it had been love at first sight.

An enormous mirror on the wall opposite her stayed clear. She decided it must be heated. What luxury.

She assessed her reflection. Her hair still looked good from her session with Gillian the hairdresser. It was almost touching her shoulders now and had started to twist and curl in the humidity of the bathroom. In the mirror, her body shone and her face looked flushed with love. She felt good about herself. Sure, there were curves were none had been before, but her skin was soft and smooth.

She slipped into the bathwater and sighed with pleasure. There was a tap on the door. She hadn't locked it.

'Room service,' said Innes's voice.

'Room for two in here,' she answered back.

After their languorous bath, they wrapped each other in soft white towels and padded back into the bedroom. Lights from the castle opposite illuminated the room in a warm soft glow. Innes took her hand and led her to the bed.

Her bathrobe slid to the floor.

'You are so very beautiful,' he said, his voice thick with desire.

Her hands reached to his head. She twisted her fingers around his thick dark hair. She pulled his hot mouth against her breast. He ran a finger down the length of her spine, causing her back to arch. 'Oh Innes. I do love you.'

His hands, his torso, his lips, his tongue, all trailed downwards while passion washed over her like hot surf.

'I love you too,' he breathed. 'And I'm going to show you how much…'

She closed her eyes and gave a low moan of joy, as deliciously, he lay her onto the bed and made love to her in the shadow of Edinburgh's stronghold.

Never had she felt so loved or so fulfilled.

In the morning, a shaft of white light sliced through a crack in the curtain and across the bed where they lay, with arms and legs entwined. Orley was awake but had not moved a muscle. She wanted to lie there watching his sleeping face for as long as possible.

She wanted the blissful feeling to last forever.

Eventually he stirred. Black lashes fluttered on his cheekbones like midnight moths. When his eyes opened they were smiling at her. 'Good morning, my love.' He pulled her closer to kiss her hungrily. His body fully aroused. 'Come here,' he said. 'I want you.'

But Orley was already halfway to the bathroom. 'I need a shower and to brush my teeth before you make love to me again.'

'There is no need. I like it when you're dirty. Come back here…'

She was laughing but she wasn't listening.

By ten o'clock they realised how hungry they both were for food. 'You have sapped all my manly strength,' Innes declared to her brashly. 'I'm in need of a full Scottish breakfast. I need haggis.'

'Well, breakfast finishes in about thirty minutes, so we had better get a move on.' she told him. 'I'm off for another shower.'

'Not another one! You'll use all the hot water. Tanya and Fergus will be complaining.'

Tanya and Fergus will have no doubt have finished their breakfast by now and will be wondering where we are.'

'I wonder how Fergus got on. He was going to ask Tanya to stay on for a while.' Innes told her casually.

Orley was both surprised and delighted. 'Although she might loose her job if she did,' she said with concern.

'Plenty of work at Glencorrie.' Innes shrugged.

Orley looked at him curiously. 'What's brought on the change of heart? I thought you had warmed to her over the past few days – but is there something I should know?'

'Fergus likes her.'

'Likes her?'

'Well, okay, he loves her.'

Orley giggled. 'Holy cow! Both the Buchanan Boys are in love with Texan Women. Whatever will your poor mother have to say about that?'

While they were in the breakfast room enjoying a full Scottish breakfast, Fergus and Tanya came over to let them know they were going shopping. 'The sale is on at Jenners!' Tanya told Orley with great excitement.

'Then we'll see you two later. We're off to tour the castle.'

Orley ate her breakfast slowly, although she was tempted to bolt it down in order to get to the castle more quickly but Innes was clearly enjoying his breakfast and had just ordered more coffee.

'What a breathtaking view,' he sighed.

'Isn't it,' Orley agreed, looking out at the ancient rock-face and the castle above it, but when she turned to look back at Innes, he wasn't looking out of the window, he was looking straight at her.

She blushed and then carried on eating her vegetarian haggis.

He checked his watch. 'We don't have to check out until twelve. Do you fancy another shower?' he suggested mischievously.

They finished breakfast and dashed back up to their room.

After checking out with only seconds to spare, they made their way out into the cold Edinburgh sunshine and along the Royal Mile towards the castle. They entered at the Portcullis Gate after which they deviated from the main path and climbed a narrow stone staircase. Innes offered his hand in assistance. 'This is the Lang Staircase, the original way into the castle built in the middle ages.'

The steps were worn and bent with age. They reached the top and found themselves on the battlements on the north side of the castle. 'This is the Argyle Battery named in honour of the Duke of Argyle, who led an army against the Jacobites in 1715.' Innes told her.

Orley looked about her. The ancient stonework. The arch shaped artillery housings. The line of cannons pointing out over the distant Kingdom of Fife and below them, Princes Street, where Tanya and Fergus were shopping.

She was about to say how well he knew his history, when she spotted a small *Castle Visitors Book* sticking out of his back pocket.

'Are you sure it was 1715 Innes, only I thought it was 1718?'

She walked away from him to look over the side of the wall but glanced discreetly back again to see him turning pages, thumbing quickly through the book to check his facts. 'Oh, I'm pretty sure it was 1715,' he told her airily, as he joined her to look out over the panoramic views.

Just then, there was an earth shattering thud. A noise so loud that it almost caused Orley's legs to collapse beneath her. She gasped and clung to Innes for dear life.

He pulled her close. Clearly enjoying having to comfort her. 'It's the one o'clock gun,' he said checking his watch again: 'And it's time for our tour.'

Orley had hardly time to recover herself from what she thought might be a bomb going off, before she found herself in the Great Hall. From there, they were taken around each part of the castle and the guide explained expertly about the history of each room. He also provided amusing anecdotes about famous people of the past, who had either been born, died or killed, in those very rooms.

'What did you like best, Orley?' Innes asked her when the tour came to an end.

'Getting to see The Stone of Destiny, I think,' she told him with her eyes shining. 'Just knowing how old it was. That all those Kings and Queens had been crowned while sitting on it.'

'There is one more place I have to show you. It's very special so I've arranged for us to have a private viewing.'

Orley's eyes were wide with excitement. Her hands trembling with anticipation, as Innes took her across Crown Square and towards a rather rough stone building on the highest crag of castle rock. Outside, as if to guard it, was a truly massive cannon. 'Is that what I heard earlier – the one o'clock gun?' she asked.

Innes shook his head. 'No. This gun is called Mons Meg. She's a very famous gun and we Scots used her to intimidate foreigners.'

'Oh, believe me, it still works.' Orley told him.

At the door of the rough stone building, a uniformed guide was waiting for them. He opened the locked door with a huge iron key and swung it open. He didn't, however, accompany them inside.

'Where are we?' Orley whispered, feeling that it was necessary to lower her voice. 'Is this a church?'

It certainly felt like a church. It was small and had round whitewashed walls. It wouldn't have held many people, perhaps twenty at most, so Orley was glad they had it all to themselves. At the top, the room opened out from a sandstone archway and light from a narrow stained-glass window shone down onto an alter and it's holy chalice.

'It's St Margaret's Chapel,' Innes told her. 'The oldest part of the castle, dating back to the twelfth century. It was built as a private chapel for the Royal Family of the time, by David The First in honour of his mother, Margaret.'

Orley's mouth mouthed 'wow' but no sound came out.

She wandered over to touch the thick stone ancient walls. Her hands trembled as if the emotions of centuries before were passing through time into her fingers. 'You are right, Innes. This place is very special.'

He could see she had tears brimming in her eyes. She walked towards the alter and stopped to look at the multicoloured lights coming through the arched window.

'You know, Margaret was my mother's name and although she wasn't royalty or anyone famous, I feel she is here with me in this chapel. I think it's because my father proposed to her on the battlements just outside here….'

Her voice cracked. Tears were flowing freely now.

Innes took her in his arms.

'Thank you for bringing me here, Innes. You don't know what it means to me.' she sobbed openly into his coat.

Innes passed her his handkerchief and she blew her nose.

It smelt of heather and damp moorlands.

'Are you okay?' he asked her gently.

She nodded and sniffed.

'Orley, I brought you here to ask you something special.'

She looked up and blinked away the remaining tears.

'I though you might like to get married here, in St Margaret's Chapel.'

She looked at him blankly. 'Married here - you mean - to you?'

He rolled his eyes. 'Yes to me!'

Her lip trembled. She bit it to stop the tears flowing. Her teeth chattered together. It seemed to her that simply yes wasn't a big enough word to house her thoughts and feelings, her happiness and her hopes, her love and desire for him.

'Although,' he added, 'you should know that I am a deeply suspicious and untrusting person. I never ever forgive people that do me wrong and I have a terrible temper. Do you think you can handle all of that?'

Orley thought these traits of his sounded vaguely familiar to her.

'Oh, I see,' she said choosing her words carefully. 'Okay, I think we might get along, although I have to warn you that I suspect nothing and no one until it is too late. I trust far too easily for my own good. I am forgiving to a fault and consequentially people think they can walk all over me.'

'We could be good for each other,' he suggested.

Orley looked deeply into his shining black eyes. 'You mean like opposites attracting?'

'That's exactly it.'

'Then the answer is yes…!'

♥

Printed in the United States
209672BV00002B/80/P